APESHIT

Also by Bill Olver

Clones, Fairies & Monsters in the Closet (editor, 2013)
The Kennedy Curse (editor, 2013)

APESHIT

A Gorill-anthology

Edited by
BILL OLVER

Exter Press

Credits

Apeshit

ISBN 978-0-9836449-9-6

Visit us online:
www.bigpulp.com
www.exterpress.com
Facebook (Facebook.com/bigpulp)
Twitter (twitter.com/BigPulp)

Distributed by Ingram Periodicals.

Ebook versions available from Amazon
and other online venues

Exter Press
BILL OLVER Editor/Publisher
BILL BOSLEGO Associate Editor (Editorial)
PHIL GOOD Associate Editor (Art Direction)

Cover illustration by Ken Knudtsen
Interior illustrations by Greg Woronchak

Table of Contents

Illustrations

All interior illustrations
by Gregory Woronchak
(tones by Phil Good)

Superior/ Inferior

by James Frederick William Rowe

I once saw a monkey…
Throw his shit at another

I once saw a monkey…
Masturbate with the throat of a frog

I once saw a monkey…
Piss in its own mouth to quench his thirst

But I never saw a monkey…
Watch *Keeping up with the Kardashians*

Who then is the superior
And the other the inferior?

The Last Winged Monkey

by Michael D. Turner

Gobo flexed his brawny shoulders, spread his magnificent wings and frowned at the sun rising over the Deadly Desert. "Oh, for the days a winged monkey could actually be a winged monkey!"

"What was that, Gobo?" The winged monkey had forgotten he was sitting on top of Elmer, one of the living trees who had, in days long past, served his mistress well. After her melting, they'd both gone west, as far west as you could go in the Land of Oz, though it had taken Elmer years to cross what Gobo had traversed in hours. In the end, they'd both fetched up here, on the edge of the Forest of the Winged Monkeys, where they sat now together on the literal edge of ruin.

"Just grousing about old times," Gobo said. "As usual."

"Starting a bit early in the day, aren't you?" Elmer frowned, which twisted his already warped face into a contorted knot. "Normally, you're asleep until the sun is far out on the desert sands. You moan about how you winged monkeys are no longer allowed to act within your natures until well after breakfast, go on about the faithless Winkies abandoning our mistress and the principles she represented at least until tea-time, and then you grumble about Queen Ozma's phony manumission of your people right through supper and into the night. If you start this early in the day, whatever will you talk about after supper?"

Gobo squatted silently for a long moment, scratching his ass and considering Elmer's question. He also considered pasting the tree in the face with a nice, steaming handful of crap, but decided he just didn't have the heart to. Elmer was just about the last of the old corps he saw any more. Besides which, it would probably violate the prohibition on getting into trouble, even here in the so-called "Forest of the Winged Monkeys." Less likely than elsewhere in Oz, maybe, but still…

"Maybe," Gobo started, with a wistful look at the horizon, "I'll talk about leaving."

"Leaving? Leaving what? To go where?"

"Leaving Oz," said Gobo, "to go where I can be a winged monkey. A real winged monkey."

Elmer considered Gobo's words a moment while his leaves shivered in the gentle morning breeze. "Aren't you real enough, right here? I don't think winged monkeys exist outside fairy countries like Oz."

"I was, once, maybe. A long, long time ago, now. I could fly where I wanted, do what I wanted. A monkey, winged or not, is meant for trouble. We were made curious, crafty, and clever. Winged monkeys a hundred times more so than others."

"That was how you winged monkeys got into trouble in the first place."

Gobo stared out over the Deadly Desert, watching as the breeze blew a few of Elmer's fallen leaves out onto the sand. They dissolved on contact, leaving leaf-shaped images of themselves on the lifeless sand, which blew away almost as fast as the leaves themselves. "It's true, we got in trouble by following our nature. A bunch of us saw a foppish dandy walking down the road near the old capitol and dumped him in the river. It's not as if he drowned. How were we to know he was the Queen's intended, or that he was on his way to their wedding?"

"That little stunt earned my people two-hundred years of servitude to whoever wore the golden cap. All of us, not just the dozen or so who actually dumped that lad in the river. I ask you, where is the justice in that?"

"Well," Elmer replied after a moment, "that was hardly the first prank you winged monkeys ever pulled."

"No, it wasn't." Gobo allowed himself a wistful grin at the memory of those pre-cap days. "I don't dispute that we winged monkeys had made pests of ourselves. Two-hundred years of punishment ought to have made good on all of that, though. Even Ozma said as much, when she had her sorceress Glinda 'free' us from our servitude. Ha!"

"I still think it was Glinda who played you monkeys dirty, and not the queen," Elmer said. "After all, Ozma had no direct experience of your people's pranking."

"Makes no difference." Gobo rose up and stretched his wings wide. "Ozma has the final say, and she's let Glinda's restrictions stand all these years."

"'Stay out of trouble' is hardly an onerous restriction for most folk."

"It is for us!" roared Gobo. "And it's one I've endured for far too long."

"You can hardly go petition the queen for the right to commit mischief in her own realm."

"No," admitted Gobo, "I can hardly do that. But Oz is not the only fairy country in the world."

"It might as well be. It's surrounded by the most destructive lands ever known, fairy realms or no." Elmer shivered his limbs at the thought of the deadly effects of the deserts around Oz. "No one comes or goes across the deserts."

"Some have," Gobo pointed out.

"Not in the last hundred years," the tree replied. "Since Glinda and the queen erected the barrier that prevents outsiders from being able to see Oz, no one has crossed the deserts except by teleportation magic."

"That's because most traffic over the desert has been to Oz. At least the ones you hear about. Sure the Wizard flew over in a balloon and Dorothy—" Gobo's mouth twisted into a scowl at the name, "on a cyclone. But back in those days, lots of birds used to cross over. In both directions.

"They can't find their way here, any more. But that doesn't mean you can't fly out."

"I can't fly out," Elmer replied. "Good or bad, my roots are here. I don't think you can, either. Not all the way across, anyway. You're not an eagle or an albatross, you know."

"I may not be an eagle," Gobo replied, puffing out his chest and curling his ears back, "but I am a strong flier. The strongest of all my people, I think. When our mistress sent us against the Wizard's army, I flew right from this forest, on the edge of Oz, all the way to the lands of Emerald. With a shield on one arm and a spear clutched in my other hand!"

"Huh! That's not half the distance across the desert."

"I fought a battle at the end of that flight!"

"And you lost, as I recall." Elmer smiled a nasty smile at his old comrade. "You ended up pulled back with the rest of our Mistress' army, while we trees held the line and kept the Wizard out of the West."

Gobo shook his head sadly. "For all the good it did us, in the end."

"My point," Elmer continued, "is that it's not enough to just fly the distance across the desert. The deserts around Oz give off poisonous fumes that rise high over the deadly sands. You have to fly very, very high over the desert or those fumes will poison you. You'll get dizzy, and then weak. Then you fall into the sands and—poof!—you're finished."

Gobo grunted. "Maybe. Across the desert, though, Glinda's admonition would have no weight. Across the desert, I could live and act as I please. I could snatch pies from a window sill, crap down a chimney, toss laundry into a lake, and snatch the hats from the heads of every townsman whose path I crossed, with no magic to hold me back and make me behave."

"Seems like a lot of effort, not to mention an awful risk, just to be able to make a pest of yourself."

"Maybe it is." Gobo stared at the sky over the desert. "Maybe, but I wouldn't be making myself a pest. I'd just be being the pest I was made, you see."

Elmer didn't see, but didn't say so, either. If he did not understand his friend after all the long years they'd kept company, he never would. "What if you're wrong?"

Gobo snorted. "Why, then I'll be just another pile of sand."

"No, I mean what if you cross the desert and find out you still must behave yourself?"

The winged monkey didn't hesitate to reply. "I'd have to cross the desert to find that out."

Before his friend could respond, he launched himself from the branch and few off into the forest. Not toward the desert, but down deep under the trees. He knew that Elmer was right. No monkey in the history of Oz had ever flown so high and so far as to cross the Deadly Desert.

The problem was one that had troubled Gobo's people since the beginning of forever—there simply wasn't much space between a winged monkey having an idea and doing it. There never had been, and nearly three-hundred years of punishment and forced good behavior hadn't changed that. Not one little bit.

While Gobo might be impulsive, he wasn't stupid. He knew that to have any chance at all of crossing the desert, he couldn't start in the middle of the day. The sun's rays would only make the desert hotter, and its poisonous fumes rise higher. So Gobo lounged in the shade of the forest where he'd been born so long ago, and ate fruit that ripened year-round in Oz, and drank sweet water that flowed in the streams, and waited until the sun began to wane.

Then, with rested limbs and a full belly, he launched himself skyward. Round and round he flew, higher and higher over the land he'd lived his long, long life in. He flew much higher than he'd ever flown before, so high the forest below was just a smudge of green. He finally flew so high, he passed through the enchantment that shielded Oz from those outside it.

That was his signal to start. He let loose his bladder and voided his bowels one last time from the sky of his homeland, and then pointed his nose at the setting sun, and soared.

Far below at the desert's edge, Elmer watched the sky. He saw a speck he presumed was his friend climb higher and higher in the clear sky of Oz. He saw the speck streak out over the forbidding barrier, saw the last light of the day catch at its wings, still high over the sands as the world plunged into darkness. He wondered if Gobo would make it across the desert, and if he did, would he finally be free.

Elmer knew he'd never know. "Stupid monkey."

THE COALING STATION

by Ian Welke

The morning light realized our worst fears; the smoke we'd seen rising from the island the day before came from the coaling station. As our ship rounded the corner and entered the bay, the destruction became apparent. Chunks of debris were everywhere, floating on the gentle waves and littering the rocks of the peninsula that shielded the bay from the straits. Trees had been leveled around the blast site. The thick black plumes of smoke we'd seen over the forested rocks had gone, leaving smoldering grey wisps rising from the wreckage.

The ship, running on cut steam, coasted in the waters of the bay. At first. Something collided with the hull at the bow just enough to jostle us in our coasting speed. I regained my footing, and looked over the rails expecting to see wreckage from the tower. Instead, I saw the first of the bodies, floating, waterlogged.

I alerted the captain while the crew set about fishing the unfortunate man's corpse from the water.

"Damned nasty business," the captain said as he walked the periphery of the ship. He looked ashore and then out to sea through his spyglass. He brought his lower lip up into his mustache. "Well, Johnson. What do you think?"

"We can make any number of other stations under sail. Continue on. Ahead to Thursday Island. Or we could turn around, Ceylon or even back to the Seychelles. Inform the admiralty." I swatted at an insect buzzing past my ear.

"Quite right. We must inform the admiralty. But I believe it would be better if we knew what we were informing them of. Do you think this was accident or the result of action by Her Majesty's enemies?"

Crew members hauled a corpse out of the water over the starboard side, followed by two more. I stared at the captain. "That would depend upon what we discover."

We made ready to anchor where we were, not approaching the ruined dock with Her Majesty's ship, but with the small boats instead.

Ashore the damage was extensive. What remained of the dock was now submerged, and we had to pull our rowboat onto the beach. I led a shore party consisting of four service men and a naturalist, a member of the Royal Society on board to join a scientific mission operating out of the northern territories of Australia.

The crane was nowhere to be found and the coaling house was shattered into planks and splinters. The smoldering pyres scattered on the beach and the wet jungle appeared to be all that was left of the fuel it once housed.

"Lieutenant!" One of the men called from behind a heap of driftwood.

The man had found another corpse. It smiled up at us, its face froze in an insane grin.

"Why are they all smiling?" The Warrant Officer's voice wavered, like he was on the edge of tears.

"I can't say. Do you see how he was killed? He wasn't shot. There's no sign of damage from shrapnel. Turn the unfortunate man over, if you would."

The ensign did as I asked, and it became apparent. The back of the man's head was matted with blood and hair surrounding a narrow wound.

"Could be shrapnel?"

"I don't believe so," I said. "It's more like a stab wound. A bayonet, perhaps."

Finding two more bodies disproved the shrapnel notion. The first man's throat had been cut with a sharp blade. The next had a similar wound to the first man's, but stabbed in his left side. All of the corpses smiled up at the sky, grinning like lunatics.

I shook my head in confusion. The dead men had their Enfields, they sustained wounds from what appeared to be close range weapons, but there was no sign of casualties from their attackers.

I jumped to my feet, startled by a loud series of shouts, hooting like nothing I've ever heard. The men aimed their rifles.

"Don't shoot," Andrews, our naturalist said. "It's just an ape."

It stood on nearby rock, light brown hair hanging from its lengthy limbs.

"Christ. It scared me." The Warrant Officer lowered his rifle.

The ape gestured in every direction, frantically, hooting at us, seemingly growing annoyed that we couldn't understand its crude language. Eventually it fell silent, looked around, and waved at us as if to follow.

"Jensen," I said, remembering the Warrant Officer's name at last. "Have the men do what they can to salvage any of the unspoilt fuel. I suspect it will take the better part of the day. Report back to the captain that we are going into the jungle to find further evidence of the station's attackers."

◊ ◊ ◊ ◊ ◊

The hairless ones from the flotation understood me no better than the shore dwellers had. I knew that if I didn't make them understand, they would share the same fate. My mission would fail. Finally I convinced them to follow.

There seemed to be a small argument first between their king and his firstservant. The king's wisdom was apparent in the skins he wore. His servants' dress didn't suit the sticky work ahead. The subservants set about other tasks, and the king, his firstservant, and two subservants with bangsticks followed me into the green.

I'd have to go slow. Stubby arms not good for branches. The hairless ones would have to follow as groundlings.

Halfway to the great temple, I stopped to give them rest. The king seemed to understand my motions, holding my chest and pretending to breathe as hard as they were. I hoped that the king didn't feel that I was mocking him or his people. I couldn't understand their mouth sounds any better than they seemed to understand mine, but I sensed that the king was dispersing his wisdom, pointing to the canopy and telling his servants how they might better travel if they had longer arms and greater strength.

I let them recover their breath and take food. Like the shore dwellers, they took food at set times, instead of when they were hungry, and took too long to feed and recover. After much time at this, I led on, but they didn't follow at first. The king's firstservant seemed to disrespect the king. I expected the king to react by dominating the first servant in front of the others, but instead he spoke some of their strange words, and the firstservant complied, commanding the others to obey the king's commands and follow.

The subservants appeared unhappy as the canopy thickened and a water storm broke open overhead. They complained about the dark and the wet. The end-of-day dark came early, brought soon by the water storm. Winged rodents fluttered beneath the branches, and the hairless ones dropped to the forest floor like their legs had been taken off.

Their king seemed suitably embarrassed and scolded the others for their mistake. Fortunately, the first of the flat rocks wasn't far, and we began the climb into our ancient temple.

◊ ◊ ◊ ◊ ◊

The jungle had claimed this stone structure well before Her Majesty's rule over these territories. The stonework began as flat rocks, smoothed into a series of steps that led to walls covered in ivy and branches of trees. Inside, if it would be deemed as being inside when the walls are more hole than stone, there was a faded mural between the cracks on the walls that I could barely discern.

Our hairy guide had taken a clear liking to our naturalist, taking him by the hand towards a great statue at the end of what I suppose was once a great hall or temple. The naturalist reached up to the statue, pulling moss off of its massive face, revealing a stone statue of a large monkey, sitting on a throne like a great king.

"What is this place?" I asked. Frankly it was too much. I, who had been most happy in the toil at sea, longed suddenly for England. I couldn't imagine what the other men felt. Perhaps they pondered jumping ship when we reached at Australia, assigning themselves to a penal colony rather than be ordered into a similar situation again. Put miles of arid land between themselves and such places in the dark jungles of the world.

"I believe this is a statue of Hanuman. This must be the ruins of a Hindu Temple. Probably abandoned after the Muslim conquests." The naturalist looked down at his hairy friend. The ape held something in both hands, offering it to the naturalist. The offering resembled a massive leaf, rolled into a cylinder. The naturalist bowed his head and accepted the object. He unrolled it carefully.

"What is it?" I couldn't contain my excitement nor my confusion.

"It's a scroll. It's written on some sort of reed, not unlike the Egyptian papyrus scrolls. Actually, written is an incorrect choice of words. It's all told in pictures. Here. Hanuman towering over an island. Fighting with some great monster. An octopus perhaps. Much of the island sinking below the waves in the fight. Further down we see the same fight again. Now there are smaller fighters alongside, what look like apes fighting these white shapes." He pointed at the scroll for me to see. It was hard to tell one shape from the next at first, I guessed that the scroll must be as old as the temple, and that's when it struck me.

"That picture. I've seen it elsewhere."

"Where?" He peered at me through his eyeglasses.

"All around us. It's painted in the faded stone of the temple."

◊ ◊ ◊ ◊ ◊

The hairless creatures' laziness made them hard to save. Despite their fear, they began to make camp in the temple ruins. I had to shout to get them back on the path back toward their flotation. We went a short way before they convinced their king to convey their need to sleep to me, him making motions closing his eyes, pretending to rest his head on his hands.

I tried to make him know the danger, mimicking attacks, and pointing at the scroll. He didn't understand. They took their rest on the forest floor, not even taking to the trees even at night when their eyes would be shut and even normal world predators could bite them.

I took to the low branches. I could at least maintain a watch and alert them to attack. I didn't have to wait long. The white flame came, and in force, probably sensing the disturbance of the temple.

I waited, hoping the first glow would pass overhead, looking much like a shooting-night-skyflame. But one of the hairless ones cried out. The flame stopped, emitting a shrieking sound, and darted towards us. I started shouting to wake everyone that wasn't already jumping to their feet and grabbing their bangsticks.

The first bang popped. The servant firing it fell backwards, knocked to the ground by a fast moving flame hurtling along the path. The light-being dimmed, looking much the same as a hairless one, smiling over the prone servant. A crooked grin spread across the servant's face, and he began to hoot, sounding more like a poor impersonation of my tribe than the hairless speech. The monster plunged a blade through the servant's eye hole.

A second bangstick servant dodged a fastlight-being. The fastlight skidded to a stop on the path, tearing up the ground growth. Stopped, it looked exactly the same as the other. It grinned before shining into a bright smear back towards the servant, who fired his bangstick wide, tearing leaves from the tree to my right.

The attacker above us came plummeting through the canopy towards the king's firstservant. The servant shrieked and pulled out a one-hand bangstick. This fired six small bangs, up into the creature, which dissolved into white fleshy bits raining down onto the firstservant.

I leapt to help the servant who nearly hit me by mistake. He was now wielding his bangstick like a club in front of him, which I judged to be a better idea. With the attacker distracted guessing the timing on the club, I jumped onto the monster's back, grabbing its wrist and forcing its own blade into its chest. The light being melted into white light the way they do when they're destroyed, but it was too much for the servant with the bangstick club who started grinning and laughing, his mind destroyed. He fell to his knees.

The last of the light creatures fled, a fast white smear leaving my vision blurred. The king and his first servant seemed as stunned as the laughing man. I had to grab the hand of the king to get them moving again.

◊ ◊ ◊ ◊ ◊

It pains me to recall the encounter in the island's jungle. My mind recoils and does its best to protect me from the memory of our monstrous attackers. On our run through the dark I might have convinced myself that I had dreamt it, were it not for our missing comrade and the terrible laughter and stare on the young seaman we had to help carry back to the ship. And that our guide, the ape, now carried one of the monster's knives in its hand.

This last fact troubled me greatly, until we arrived at the beach in front of the lagoon where the HMS Kestrel was anchored. The reports of rifle fire told me before I could see that our ship was under attack by the same creatures that fell upon us in the forest. The brave beast, our guide, was first into the landing boat to return to the ship and fight off our attackers.

Myself and the naturalist had to do the rowing. True to his function in the jungle, our guide stood at the bow, whereas the poor, mad seaman remained seated in the aft.

By the time we reached the ship the rifle fire had died down to sporadic shots. All hopes that this was due to the attack having been repelled faded as we climbed the ratlines and were met by a sound as unworldly and malevolent as the horrible visage of the monsters themselves. Though I understood none of their foul language, I did discern that it must have been some sort of chant, given the repetition and rhythm of the terrible droning.

We made the deck to find five of the light creatures standing in a ring. Light shone from their gaze, shining up towards the stars. Something moved beneath the water behind the Kestrel. Something vast and huge, displacing greater volume than Her Majesty's ship. The ape pointed towards the water and then pointed back to the chanting creatures of light on the deck. Without speaking, I understood at once, and moved forward with my revolver, firing into the back of the closest star-man demon. It took all six shots, but the fiend fell into pieces on the deck.

The remaining four creatures backed into a line at the aft of the ship. They stood shoulder to shoulder. A hissing sound came over the sounds of their chants and the creatures melded into one vast light, two dimensional, flat. To the sides of the amalgam, it was night. Within, the lagoon was lit as if by the sun. To the left or right, the sea was calm. In the bright center the sea bubbled. Six enormous tentacles, each as large as the trunk of tall oak, leapt from the lagoon, protruding through the vision the light creature amalgam created, as if escaping the canvas of a mad man's painting, and thrashing about on our deck.

I dropped to my knees fumbling with the bullets for my revolver. The creature's enormous head broke the top of the waves from the center of the vision brought to us by the amalgamated light creature.

Ashamed of my own inaction I looked to our naturalist, but he merely dropped to the deck beside me, babbling, crying out for his mother. Only our guide maintained his deportment, moving past me to my left. I caught but a flash of it out of the corner of my eye, through my own tears of fear and lament. The ape reared back and flung the monster's knife into the flat amalgamated creature, ripping open a tear as if a sheet of canvas. What happened next I am unable to say. It was as though two realities existed before me and as the one tore open and destroyed itself, some portion of my memory, or perhaps my imagined memory, was destroyed with it.

I do know that when my memory began anew, I felt numb, like a patient suffering shock. With the help of several survivors we managed to get the ship underway and headed towards Thursday Island.

On the way we dropped anchor once. Our guide pointed at a nearby island. Having grown accustomed to following his directions, we pulled the ship towards the small peninsula at the southern end. Seeing several apes of the same hair color and size as our friend, I guessed his purpose. The naturalist and I took him in the rowboat to the beach. We watched him, reunited with what I assumed to be his family. I wished that I could convey the gratitude I felt towards the beast. I wondered about the horrors he had saved us from. Were we truly safe? It was then that I at last understood our guide's purpose. Saving us was just the first half.

The other was that we would bring the knowledge we'd gained, back to the world of man, that our guide was passing the torch as protector, and that protecting the world from the monsters we'd witnessed would be our responsibility from here on out.

Unabashedly, Eduardo.

by Julie Mark Cohen

Should Dates Be Left in History?

A Terran creature trotted out of the transporter-like pod. "¿Dónde estoy?" He clutched his tin cup and hastily clenched his other hand. "¿Es esto me va a matar? Lea las palmas!"

"Here." Lucinda-Lucretia-Louise dropped a universal translator into his cup and waved her wing, attempting to waft words from his mouth. "Say again, please."

He extended an arm, testing his jacket's seams. "Is this gonna kill me? Read my palms!" He hesitated, then thrust his hand forward, unfurling his fingers, revealing shreds from a Terran newspaper.

Lucinda-Lucretia-Louise quickly scanned them in her multi-function translator. "Brooklyn Daily Eagle. 1898. Valentine's Day? Meaningless, I'm sure." She smirked. "But, *I* did it! I'm *the first one!!*" She peered over his shoulder at a chart of Terran mammals. "Are you a Terran monkey?"

"Terran? Not sure. I'm a white-faced capuchin, species *Cebus capucinus*. My parents named me 'Eduardo,' but the man with the hand organ calls me 'Nico'." Alternating between propping himself against a desk leg to balance on his legs and scratching himself, he said, "Where am I?"

"Well, Eduardo, you're on MoxAT-TAxoM, a planet far away from Earth in a future time." She puffed out her frilly-frock-clad chest. "I brought you here."

"Doesn't make sense. Three years ago, I read H.G. Wells' book, *The Time Machine*. Pure unadulterated fiction. Skimble-skamble!"

"I read it, too. Amusing tale," she said, glancing at the computer hardware she had modified. "You're *my* Time Traveler."

"I can't be." He tentatively tip-toed around her, ogling. "What are you? What's your name?"

"Anthropologists know little about my species, but we're intelligent and uniquely beautiful." She swiveled her six iridescent eyes under the room light and displayed her hard mandibles. "I'm Dr. Lucinda-Lucretia-Louise, laboratory technician in the Saturnalia Laboratory in the Et Alia Research Complex."

"You're an educated woman? I long for such companionship." Eduardo tipped his cap and bowed. "May I call you L-3?"

"Yes." L-3 flitted her half dozen eyelids, flirting, her feathers fluffing.

"I'd guess we're about the same age, seasoned, but not old. Will you be my date, my Valentine? My sweetheart?"

L-3 thought, *What do I do? I don't want to send him back. But, should I?*

Ascent in a Scratch of Time

Eduardo drew a long green feather along his nostrils. *That Lucinda-Lucretia-Louise is gorgeous, intelligent, and smells sooo good.* He stabbed the quill into the blanket draped over a desk chair.

"Ouch!" The blanket pushed aside a small computing device, re-folded itself, settling at the edge of the seat.

"What—Who are you?" He squinted, removed his red and black pillbox cap, and picked two lice off his greying head.

"Felicia Feinseam, sentient blankette and mathematician." She moved away from him, tightening her folds.

"Another educated woman?"

"I assume you've met Lucinda-Lucretia-Louise?"

Eduardo salivated, then wiped the drool with the back of his hand.

"How crude. Who are—What are you?"

"A white-faced capuchin monkey."

"A what?" She fanned four of her mitts in front of her noses. "You stink."

"I'm sorry." Eduardo unbuttoned the brass fasteners on his red jacket, removed his arms from its long sleeves, and tossed it across the room. "Wool. Must've gotten wet travelling here."

Bunched against the back of the chair, reviewing capuchin monkey data on her computer monitor, Felicia said, "From where do you hail?"

"Brooklyn."

She re-engaged her computer and tapped several keys. "I can't find that planet."

"Planet Earth."

"South America?"

"No."

"I found Brooklyn. It's north of New Orleans."

"I guess," he said, flicking several more lice off of his matted chest fur.

"Watch what you're doing," she said, brushing herself off. "Our Dr. Seyfert loves New Orleans. It's our Terran reference point. You still stink." She glanced at his black woolen knickers and yellow suspenders.

"I'm not taking my pants off in front of you."

"Well, go take a shower." She extended herself so that one of her mitts reached the counter and removed a small rectangular prism. "Here, take this. It's sodium hydroxide and vegetable fat."

"Soap?"

"Yes."

"Good. I'll wash while I'm waiting for Lucinda-Lucretia-Louise to fix a problem with that crapper stimulant." As he pointed, half a dozen lice dropped from his forearm.

"Sim-u-la-tion cham-ber," she sharply corrected. "Take the universal translator out of your metal cup, wear it as a necklace, so there's no electromagnetic interference. Why don't you get out of here now while I can still breathe?" she said, furiously digging at her warp and weft with her mitts. "Where's the anti-lousing spray?"

He padded his way out of the Saturnalia Laboratory, the soles of his feet skidding as he tried to stay upright on the highly polished, smooth floor.

Once outside, he soaked up the warmth of the MoxAT-TAxoM afternoon bi-symmetric dual suns and unfastened his suspenders, allowing his pants to fall to the ground. He stretched while the breeze ruffled the white fur on his upper arms. *I wonder where I can find new clothes?*

With the soap in one hand, he used his arms for stability as he ambulated toward a five-point symmetric MoxAT-TAxoM tree at the edge of the large pond.

Blocking the suns' rays from his eyes, he climbed the tree trunk and yanked off a curl-edged leaf larger in diameter than he was tall. *Should make a perfect raft.* He tossed the soap into the hollow of the leaf.

While he hauled his make-shift floating device to the shoreline, he noticed the other four leaves float to the ground. *Strange effect of symmetry.*

After launching the leaf, he hopped onto it, leaned over the edge to wet the bar of soap, and fell into the water. The necklace slipped over his head and sank to the bottom of the pond, his limbs flailing.

"Gevalt! Gevalt! GEVALT!"

"Gevalt? Is that Yiddish? Does someone need help?" Seyfert snapped his nubby-digited hand to his ear. "Where are you?"

"Aquí fuera! Aquí fuera!"

"I don't understand you. Speak Yiddish. Where are you? Keeping talking." Seyfert spun on the longest of his three unequal legs trying to locate the voice.

"No puedo nadir!" Eduardo swallowed a mouthful of water. "Ge-"

Seyfert galloped in cyclic repetitions of long-short-medium strides, the water barely reaching his knees. "I'm coming."

No sooner had Eduardo disappeared from view than Seyfert scooped him up, snagging the universal translator. Cradling the monkey, he carefully strode to the shade of the tree and then laid him on one of the fallen leaves.

A groundskeeper, with a universal cardiopulmonary resuscitation device on his tail, slithered to Eduardo and precisely positioned it above his chest. "No one dies on my watch."

Eduardo vomited water, then looked toward the sky only to see Seyfert leaning over him and placing the translator at his side.

"Thank you," Eduardo said, rubbing his widening eyes. "Oi vey. Either you're particularly ugly and disturbingly asymmetric or I'm in hell."

"And, you're cute, too. I'm Seyfert."

"That talking blanket mentioned your name," Eduardo said, sitting up, leaning against the tree. "I need clothes. I have a date with Lucinda-Lucretia-Louise."

"L-3?" Seyfert's laughed, then stifled himself, ripping off about one-third of a meter of cloth from the bottom of his toga and breaking off a vine for a belt.

"Girly pink?"

"On my planet, SeyTTT, pink is worn by the most virile men."

Eduardo tentatively thumped his fists on his chest.

"So, who are you? Where are you fr—" Seyfert suddenly twitched, then frenziedly scratched his left armpit.

If Only It Were Chicken Feed: Luncinda-Lucretia-Louise Cautiously Recalculates Calories

"Oh, no! I forgot to account for Eduardo's clothes." L-3 paced on top of Felicia Feinseam.

"You're snagging my weft."

"Sorry. I'm upset. I was short 386.03752 grams."

"Unfortunately, you're accurate in your calculations. Five Terran hours have elapsed, leaving the tiniest time window to conserve mass and energy, so Earth's history is left unchanged."

"I did some research." L-3 tossed dozens of kernels into the air and opened her beak. "Tasty."

"You're eating?"

"These were invented in Chicago on Valentine's Day in 1898, exactly when I found Eduardo in Brooklyn. Close enough."

"Excellent!"

L-3 pitched candy corn into her time travel machine.

Suited for Romance

"If you want to win over L-3, you'll need to stop gaping. Your teeth aren't one of your better features." Susannah Svetlana Sebastianne flapped her wings and encircled Eduardo just above his shoulders, occasionally scraping a talon on the floor. "Not bad, not bad at all for a Terran primate."

"*Cebus capucinus.*" Eduardo snarled, then curled his lips into a smile as he fixated on the 3-D virtual image of himself facing him from the open door of a simulation room. "Dashing. The thin vertical white stripes make me look tall. This suit is perfect for wooing." He puffed out his chest and steadied himself by holding onto the back of a chair.

"It's called a 'zoot suit.'" She pointed to a computer monitor. "1940s, Harlem, Jazz Age."

"Jazz Age? I'll read about this later." Eduardo handled a gold watch chain that dangled from his belt to below his knee, then back to a side pants pocket. "What's this?"

"Check your pocket. It's a Terran-style gold watch, but its 'workings' as you call them are a computer plus universal translator."

"I need a boutonnière." Eduardo stuck his thumb through a finished hole in the lapel.

"A what?"

"A flower. One that's fuchsia. Make that two fuchsia flowers."

Annie flew out the window and returned with two flowers in her beak. "Here. These are L-3's favorites."

Eduardo placed one flower in his lapel and the other on the chair seat, re-settled the coat's wide-padded shoulders, and rubbed the back of his fingers on his wide lapel. "Very nice material."

She gently landed on the floor, then pitter-pattered back-and-forth in arcs, while using her beak to press on the keys of her wing-mounted computer.

Eduardo intently watched as stitches moved by millimeters to change the fit. "How did you do this, Susannah Svetlana Sebastianne? We're in the Saturnalia Laboratory, not in your seamstress shop?"

"I asked you to call me Annie. The technology is very simple and transportable, so I can work anyplace. Stay here on MoxAT-TAxoM and I'll teach you how to be a tailor."

"I'd like that, thank you. I need to earn my keep." Trying to stay upright, but rubbing his coat over his stomach, Eduardo said, "I'm hungry. Spätzle with banana sauce, please."

"Yes, of course. I forgot." Annie turned away from Eduardo, then spun back to face him. "Shoes."

"Oy vey. I can't stand up on my own and you're expecting me to wear shoes with these yellow things to cover my instep and ankles?" He rubbed his stomach again. "Where's my food?"

"I thought you requested banana-colored spats. I gave you an Italian pair circa 1910. Aren't you in a hurry to see L-3?"

"No, I'm hungry." As Eduardo picked up the shoes and spats, he caught a glimpse of Toski, a slug-like graduate student who was leaving his cubicle. He tossed the footwear into the time travel machine, nodded when they instantaneously vanished, and noted that the machine was still set for Brooklyn, February 14, 1898. Turning his attention to the slug, he snickered, grabbed several computer styluses from Toski's work station, then smacked his lips. "Skewers."

"Skewers? Did I hear you correctly?" Toski exited the main laboratory room post-haste, leaving a continuous trail of his signature silver slime.

Eduardo laughed uncontrollably and fell to the floor. "Pishen. I have to pishen!" His coat was unbuttoned, but his high-waisted pants were zipped shut. Although he possessed opposable thumbs, he repeatedly fumbled and failed to open the zipper. "It's stuck."

As he rolled around on his back, Annie giggled so hard that she shed several dozen torso feathers and awkwardly hopped trying not to step on them, but attempting to pick them up.

Toski returned dragging a hook on a string. "I don't know who or what you are, but it's intolerable to me if a creature can't void when he needs to do so." He balanced on his chin, twirled his foot, and launched the hook in the direction of Eduardo's pants and successfully opened the zipper.

"Thank you. At least my suit is dry," Eduardo said to Toski who offered a smirk from underneath his Terran-style umbrella.

L-3 entered the room, saw Eduardo kicking his feet in the air, and headed toward him full-tilt on her talons. "Are you all ri—" She slid on the dry floor, lost her balance, and fell, her tush landing in Eduardo's puddle and her ankles slowed to a stop in Toski's slime. Stunned, her half dozen eyes swiveling out-of-sync, she sobbed. "I don't believe this. Look at my favorite frilly frock."

"It was an accident. Let me help you clean up." Annie dropped her jettisoned feathers into the slot marked for recycling and whispered into L-3's ear. "You're lucky. He's quite some fellow."

"Quite some fellow, indeed." L-3 wiped her eyes with a pink cloth that was Eduardo's makeshift toga, then said, "I meticulously equilibrated the mass and energy exchange to the thousandth decimal piece, so that he could stay here without changing Earth's history. But, look at him."

Annie said, "Looks aren't everything. He's unusually smart. You need to give him a chance."

Eduardo grabbed the string, skittering Toski across the floor, pulled on the hook to zip up his pants, and paused. "Conservation of mass and energy? 1898 is too early. Uh oh."

MONKEY HOUSE

by Mike Bogart

Baldy the Chimp was not in his cage. It was well before sunrise and Ian Brixey, the night watchman, stood among his simian charges in mute anguish. He was at that time the sole human occupant of the Monkey House: it was his duty to patrol the place from sundown to sunup; to prevent anyone from coming in, and, though he'd never really thought of it this way, to prevent any*thing* from leaving.

His bony fingers clutched at the iron bars of Baldy's enclosure. Inside were an artificial plaster-cast tree, an old tractor tire worn to fringes, a mirror smeared with fingerprints, a pair of frayed ropes hanging from the ceiling, piles of straw that reeked of chimp urine. Ian peered into the moonlit gloom of the cage, scanning for a patch of fur. A trail of peanut shells. Anything. He knew Baldy to have become increasingly prone to intense bouts of anxiety in recent months, but he'd never just up and disappeared.

Finally Ian spied Susie, Baldy's partner, crouching in a corner, blinking sleepy-eyed at him.

"Susie, come over here," he whispered, curling a finger in the air. She sighed almost imperceptibly and knuckled toward the bars.

Ian dug his hand into his pocket and came out holding a few pieces of lint-covered candy corn which had melted slightly against the heat of his leg. They were Susie's favorite. He held his palm just outside of her reach. "Where's Baldy?" he asked.

Susie glanced up at him knowingly when she heard her friend's name.

"Give it up, girl," he said, kneeling and removing his bifocals to meet Susie face-to-face. Her black eyes stared back at him, each of them motionless for a few seconds, locked in a battle of wills. Susie's palm was still stubbornly outstretched in anticipation of the sweets, so Ian played the only advantage he had: he popped one of the candy corns into his mouth and rubbed his belly. "This is so delicious," he said, chewing loudly and moaning.

Susie furrowed her brow and reached her arm farther outside the cage, her leathery palm open flat against the air. She ooked a little, and stuck her bottom lip out.

"Not unless you show me where he went," Ian said. He popped another piece into his mouth.

The chimp plopped her rear onto the concrete and scratched her head a moment, gazing upward. The stars above pooled in her eyes through the glass ceiling. She appeared, to Ian, to be weighing his ultimatum with great care. Ultimately, tragically powerless against the allure of candy corn, she lowered her head in shame and pointed a single finger at the trap door that led to the chimps' outside enclosure. Of course, Ian thought, relieved. He's just gone out for some fresh air.

Ian dumped the rest of the candy corn into Susie's hand, patted her on the head, and for the first time ever, he abandoned his post in the Monkey House.

The Bronx Zoological Gardens' most prized chimp, Baldy was aptly named: there was a small, circular patch bereft of fur at the crown of his head. It had started to thin in only his tenth year so that, by his fifteenth birthday, he was the world's only officially balding chimp. As the years went on, he'd pick at the spot incessantly, beholding his countenance in the mirror that had been installed in his enclosure with a look of nearly human shame.

Keeper Engelholm had taught Baldy through much unfortunate trial and error to shake people's hands without crushing them ("Baldy is exceptionally strong," the Keeper explained). This ability, combined with his aptitude for stacking and unstacking colored blocks, a task that in his estimation demeaned his intelligence, had made him one of the zoo's most popular attractions.

The attention had also made him, as Ian had come to notice, a nervous wreck. Whenever he wasn't putting on a show for a crowd of hungry gawkers, Baldy was pacing back and forth in front of the mirror, fingering the bald patch atop his head. As he became more popular, he grew more irritable and was easily agitated—he even began to lash out at Susie, baring his canines at her slightest infraction in his presence.

And just as Ian's luck would have it, President William Howard Taft, the very President of the United States himself, was scheduled to shake Baldy's hand at eleven that morning.

Along with Senator Bacon, Major Butt, and a few other political heavyweights, President Taft would be visiting the zoo in a rare attempt at a public appearance. For a man of such imposing stature and genuine geniality of spirit, he skirted the public eye like a bashful field mouse.

He was, respectfully, not natural in front of a crowd the way that Roosevelt had been—a fact of which the President was acutely aware. During his last public appearance, as he was orating determinedly and without regard for either punctuation or his audience, a little girl, a long-haired sprite wearing a dress and a bow in her hair, had broken free from her mother and ran at him, grasping against one of his thick, meaty legs beside the lectern.

Taft, understandably flustered, halted in the middle of a sentence and looked about in panic for a number of agonizing moments. When no one rose immediately to claim the child, and realizing that he'd lost his chance to crack a timely joke, he knelt down to her in an attempt to make the best of the situation.

"Are you a little boy, or a little girl?" was the best he could come up with.

Roosevelt, damn him, would have scooped her up, thrown her onto his shoulders, and given her a ride around the stage. And instead he'd brought the poor little girl's gender into question. The two, Taft and Roosevelt, that is, had once been great friends; Taft had even served in Teddy's Cabinet. Lately, though, differences of opinion over the former's less-than-Progressive policies had made them, in private, bitter adversaries.

But, in Taft's innermost thoughts, his own most egregious deficit as a President was found neither in his policy-making nor in his ideology. It resided instead in the fact that while Teddy had relished the spotlight, Taft himself was taciturn and shy about putting himself on display, which made him awkward and clammy-handed in public.

Despite all this, Taft's appearance was to be the most significant moment in the Zoo's brief ten years. Nothing was more important than presenting to the President of these United States a crisp, clean zoo filled with happy, healthy animals, preferably inside their cages.

Madison Grant, the chair of the New York Zoological Society, had taken great pains to personally belabor this point to each and every employee, even the night watchmen. The handshake between Taft and Baldy was to be the day's crowning moment—the ultimate picture for the papers.

There was to be an election in the following year. Roosevelt was, privately, considering running for a third term. This picture, insignificant as it may have seemed, was what Taft believed he needed most—demonstrable proof of his likable, easygoing nature. Something he could point to and say, "See? I, too, enjoy leisure." Anything else could go wrong, so long as that handshake went right. After all, who wouldn't cast a vote for the affable man who'd shaken the hand of Baldy the Chimp?

As he circled around to the outdoor portion of the chimp habitat, Ian stroked his long, manicured fingernails through his hair. He had broken into such a sweat that his glasses slid right back down the bridge of his nose each time he pushed them up again.

He suffered from a general fear of darkness, which up until this moment he hadn't considered a disqualifier for employment as a night watchman, so long as said night watchman remained at all times indoors, among familiar surroundings.

Thoroughly engulfed in his fear by now, he focused the dim beam of his new Eveready in front of his feet rather than into the enclosure in search of Baldy. Not that he could have seen much even with the flashlight and his glasses—the dark beads of his eyes, sunken a little too deep into his skull, were barely serviceable even in daylight. But, he thought, frightened and nervous as he was, at least the noise of his heels clicking against the pavement granted him some thin veneer of authority.

He had taken the job just after graduating from high school specifically to avoid having to interact with people or deal with anything one might consider difficult. What better place to relax, he'd reasoned, than a completely deserted zoo? Unfortunately for Ian, another aspect of the job that he'd failed to consider completely was the fact that a night watchman is an arm, perhaps in some cases even a fist, of martial authority. There was nothing martial about Ian. He was tall and thin as a twig, with all the inherent physical sturdiness and heroic character implied therein. Not given much to physical activity, he routinely lost his breath just making his rounds. He would sit on a bench to regain it, gazing into the hollowed enclosures, thinking how much easier it must be to be an ape.

Ian was, at best, a pinky finger of authority.

Nevertheless, he had never encountered any trouble, not so much as a single incident during one of his shifts. After a while he figured that he was perfect for this job—a silent observer, a detached wanderer, but never an actor. So he had made his rounds night after night, walking back and forth through the halls of the Monkey House, surrounded by the proto-people.

Meanwhile, across the Zoo, President Taft's tummy rumbled. He was pretending to nap in a recliner in Keeper Engelholm's overnight quarters, snoring loudly so that his Secret Service entourage might relax and grant him some privacy. The President, determined to make the morning's appearance his best performance yet, had arrived at the Zoo earlier that night to acclimate himself with his surroundings. In his experience, foreknowledge, a good night's rest, and a full stomach translated to his best chance at aplomb in front of a crowd.

Thus, the growling in Taft's belly concerned him. It was late, far too late to snack, really, and he'd already eaten quite a hefty plate of lamb chops before bed. But there it was, the rumbling, keeping him awake despite himself. How would he take this tour, shake this monkey's hand, on an empty stomach, without any sleep? He resolved against his better judgment to satisfy his urges. A heavyweight wrestling champion at Yale, Taft summoned the last modicum of litheness and deftness of movement left in his body, smoothed his mustache between thumb and forefinger, and tip-toed out the back door, in search of snacks.

For Ian Brixey, Baldy was nowhere to be found outside, either. He quickly canvassed the immediate area surrounding the habitat and found ripped in the fine wire netting surrounding it a savage, chimp-sized hole. Baldy had evidently busted through the latch on the outside of the trap door and used it to tear the wire. Or so Ian deduced upon finding the latch, now rendered impotent, in the dirt surrounding the hole.

The deep navy of the sky was getting lighter in the East—soon it would be morning. Soon, Ian thought, everyone would know that Baldy, the very same Baldy who later that day was scheduled to shake hands with the President of the United States, had gone missing on *his* watch.

Just then, there was a great crashing of metal on metal. Ian, operating on a pure instinct he'd later recall with incredulity, as if he couldn't be sure that it was really *him* who'd done it, forgot for a moment his fear and his shame and sprinted to the noise, heels clicking behind him.

When he reached the kitchen (he had pinpointed the location of the noise by its successive tremors), he slowed to a walk. There was no cacophony coming from inside any longer—just the dull glow of the electric lights radiating from underneath the door.

Recovered by then from his fit of heroism, Ian found himself once again gripped with paralyzing terror. Motivated simply by a desire not to be the laughing-stock of the entire Zoo, a prospect even more terrifying than the abject, shrouded unknown, he turned the doorknob and poked his head inside, like a turtle testing the air.

At first he saw only pots and pans littering the tile floor. They, no doubt, had been the source of the commotion that had drawn him to the kitchen. Ian ventured a few feet inside, shining his flashlight about despite the bright electric lights above him.

He found, slumped against a cabinet to the left of the door, staring intently at his reflection in a shiny metal pan, Baldy the Chimp. Next to him, lying inert, face-down on the floor, was the body of President Taft.

Ian approached the scene timidly, his hand secured over his mouth to stop him from screaming. He had no training whatsoever with animals—Keeper Engelholm had assured him in no uncertain terms that he was only to walk the halls and never to interact with them. Nevertheless, he had over his short time at the Zoo developed an affinity for the chimps that he could not explain if pressed.

"Baldy?" he asked.

Baldy looked up suddenly, a wild grin smeared across his face.

Just then, from deep within Taft's considerable belly, there issued a monumental groan.

"What on *Earth* has happened to me?" he asked, pushing himself up onto an elbow and clutching at a pronounced lump on his head.

Ian hesitated to respond to the President. Baldy glanced at Taft and returned to the pot, entranced by his own reflection, oblivious again to the affairs of the two men beside him.

"Well, boy, what is the meaning of this?" asked the President. He was seated now, slumped against a cabinet in much the same fashion as Baldy, still clutching his skull.

"Mr. President, sir, I haven't the faintest," said Ian. He set his flashlight down and stepped back from Baldy nervously. "What are you doing in here?"

"Well," Taft looked suddenly embarrassed. His eyes were unfocused, and he didn't look at Ian as he slurred out his words. "I'm ashamed to say that I got hungry. I got hungry, damnit. I couldn't sleep. And the boys couldn't know about it, could they?" he asked.

Ian realized that Taft was waiting for his response. "No, sir," he said.

"I used to be a wrestler you know. Big Lub, they called me. I was a champion."

"I'm impressed, sir."

Taft, groggy, nodded his head. "So I slipped out to the kitchen while they thought I was napping. Next thing I know, I wake up on the floor with a massive pain in my head and you standing here." Taft pointed at Ian, accusing him. "I demand that you tell me what's happened at once." The President gave his most authoritative harrumph.

"Mr. President, sir, the thing is that I've only just arrived here."

Taft arched an eyebrow. "Only just?" he asked. "Then who was it that caused this lump on my head?"

Ian pointed at Baldy, still admiring his reflection. Taft pivoted on one hand and beheld, apparently for the first time, his assailant. As he turned to face Baldy, Ian noticed a sphere of hair missing from the top of the President's head. In its place was a shiny, freckled dome of marbled skin.

"I believe you're missing something, Mr. President," Ian said, reaching to the crown of his own head. The President groped at himself.

"Ah, so I am, so I am. He's stolen it, has he?" Taft stood up, defiant. Ian was befuddled beyond reply. "If we've learned one thing from the reign of Roosevelt, boy, we've learned that a President must, above all else, champion his virility. A balding Commander in Chief simply *would not do.*"

Ian's gaze drifted to Baldy as the chimp continued to hold the pot up to his face. It was no longer the mask of anxiety, of torment, of shame that it once had been. Instead, he seemed content, lazy even, smiling genuinely for the first time in years. For nested at the crown of his head, though it was far too large and the colors hardly matched, was President Taft's secret toupée.

After receiving bandages and several doses of aspirin, the President insisted that the show go on, despite his lingering concussion. It was rather Rooseveltian of him, he thought.

Madison Grant and Keeper Engelholm gave him the grand tour, on which he saw, in the following order: (to his eternal consternation) the stuffed head of a rhinoceros killed by Roosevelt the year prior; an angry and reluctant lioness;

two elephants do headstands in his honor; waltzing mice; singing rattlesnakes; a mongoose devour three blind mice; and a royal python, who dines on a whole pig once every three months.

"How long does it take the snake to digest the pig?" the President wanted to know.

Finally, at the very end of the tour, Baldy and Taft came together for their photo opportunity. The former adversaries had become quick friends in the hours following their encounter. Once everything had been sorted out, Taft saw to it that Baldy be allowed to keep the Presidential toupée, for he recognized in the ape a kindred spirit.

President Taft also saw to it that Ian Brixey be publicly commended for his bravery in halting the dangerous chimp attack. After that he stood with his back a little straighter, his chin held a little higher. Yes, he thought, I was a proper night watchman today. He stuck around even after his shift was over (something he was normally loathe to do) in order to see to it that everything went smoothly for the President during his visit.

That said, Ian was not formally or otherwise invited into the President's entourage, thus having no tangible way to ensure anything of the sort. Instead, he contented himself with pacing around the perimeter of the zoo, ever-vigilant against a second animal escape, until Taft and Baldy finally met.

He watched as cameras swarmed them. Baldy peeled back his lips in a minstrel's grin as Taft approached, returning an effervescent smile. The chimp, his toupée knitted more neatly onto his scalp now, extended a long, leathery palm out to the balding President, who grasped it and shook, Ian thought, with the heft and confidence of a greater man.

THE HOUND DOGS IN THE BOUGAINVILLEA

by Lon Prater

Prof. Renfro,

I came upon several rubber-banded sheaves of paper in an attic chest that belonged to my grandfather, and when I read them, I immediately thought of you. More precisely, your anthropological theory that a hidden line of Neanderthal have been living among us all these years. The papers appear to have been written by my great grandfather Wallace M. You may recall he led something of a dashing life in the twenties as a bootlegger a few rungs down the ladder from Capone. I suspect it won't be Wallace who attracts your scientific interest, but rather the descriptions of his partner Pinky Clade. (A figure even Google holds no record of ever having existed, I might add.)

I couldn't help but wonder, in the light of what you've already uncovered among the Scandinavians—But no! I'll let the scanned pages of this memoir speak for themselves. There are a few more of these bundles tucked away in the chest, I've not read them yet; the handwriting is atrocious. Do let me know when you've read this, and whether it would be worthwhile to scan and send the remainder. It was quite the chore getting these papers to lay flat on the scanner; I'd rather not go through the effort if you aren't as excited by the possibilities as I am.

Yours,

Yvonne Mortimer

◊ ◊ ◊ ◊ ◊

The only smell worse than some squatter's hellhole in Des Ourses Swamp is that same marshy hellhole where there's a working still. If it was enough to make my eyes water as we pulled up, I knew it had to be driving Pinky absolutely off his nuts. As I slammed the door of the hopped up tin lizzy our boss lent us, I looked across the shiny hood at Pinky. He had pulled a hankie out of his back pocket and gave it a vigorous honk before stuffing it back into place. Pinky was a conscientious fella, for all that he looked the big dumb lug with his nose the size of Plymouth Rock and those close-set eyes always darting around beneath the reddish underbrush of his low and prominent eyebrows. The man tended to carry at least four handkerchiefs on him at any given time, always reserving the one in the breast pocket of his light wool jacket for mopping sweat from his brow or wiping smudges of lipstick from any golddigging flapper kind enough to kiss his ugly mug.

He tucked his left hand under his jacket and withdrew Shillelagh, what he called his .45 revolver. "No sense pretending this is a social call, eh, Wally? We ain't exactly here to play cards."

I kind of wished we were. It had been over a week since we left Chicago, and my palms were itching to find a good stud game in a proper speakeasy or even a blind pig somewhere. I got out my own heat. I don't bother to give it a name. Way I see it, names are only good for making conversation. The sort of chats my pistol gets involved in are usually short, one-way affairs.

With the gun snug in my hand, I walked in front of the black T-model and stood beside my associate.

Some might say I stood over him, because at nearly six and a half feet, I had a good two feet on him. But they wouldn't dare say it out loud. Even though I had him in height and I'd kept my muscle from a tour in the Marine Corps in Nicaragua, Pinky was one solid specimen. He had a short torso, but great meaty trunks instead of legs, and long arms that gave him some serious reach. He never talked much about himself, but once over a few drinks while we were still running protection rackets, he had mentioned doing a round or two of prizefighting when he'd first got off the boat. "From Ireland?" I'd asked, thinking about what he called his weapon. But he hadn't responded out loud, just nodded his head and called for another round. It's okay not knowing so much about your partner, so long as you know you can trust him. And Pinky was a stand-up guy, far as hoods go. Besides, there's plenty of things I don't want to talk about, like my tour in the jungle and what happened when I came back. So having a partner who knows how a man sometimes needs to throw up a privacy fence and have others respect it makes Pinky and me a perfect fit.

We looked out across the squatter's little slice of Louisiana paradise. A low shack with hand-cut timber walls patched here and there with mud, and not a single window to be found. There was a pit for a cooking fire that looked like it hadn't been used in some time, and farther off, a ramshackle outhouse with a nice wrought iron handle on the clapboard door. The cabin's own less-well-appointed door hung ajar and gave the little hovel a sort of gaptoothed charm. An old Army tent had been roped into place just behind the cabin. Two sides of the canvas were ripped away and what was left of it had been torn in dozens of places, making the tent more of a shady gazebo than any real shelter. We walked along what passed for a path through the spongy marsh soil toward the cabin's open door.

"Mr. Reardon?" Pinky called. There was no answer.

I glanced left and right, wondering when the old moonshiner would start shooting, and where from. "Come on out, Mr. Reardon. We just want to talk. A mutual acquaintance of ours asked us to check in on you."

No sound greeted us beyond the buzz of a wayward fly lolling about on the stink of soft wind. Pinky gave me the look that meant he'd go in first, and then he did it. I followed, looping around so that by the time he said "Housekeeping" and kicked the shack door in, I'd set up on the corner of the house where I could keep an eye on the outhouse, the car, and the tattered Army tent all at once with just a little swivel of my head.

"It's empty," Pinky called. I let myself relax, but only a little. Until we knew for sure nobody was hiding in that outhouse or tent, it'd be bad business to start heaving sighs of relief.

Pinky came out, his head back, nostrils flaring. He had something in his hand. "Car coming," he said, handing me what turned out to be a picture frame.

By now I'd learned not to doubt Pinky, and not to bother asking whether he smelled it or heard it. So I just nodded and inspected the picture.

They'd had it made for a family get together of some sort. A trio of unsmiling men, clearly brothers, stood to the right of a scowling crabapple of an oldtimer, complete with long whiskers and only one bracer holding up his britches. A pair of gangly boys stood with them, looking like they weren't quite sure whether they qualified to be standing in the back row with the men just yet. A row of women in bonnets and kerchiefs completed the portrait, a couple holding babies on their knee. Someone had scratched the year 1921 into one of the corners. Not so many years ago.

"Anything else in there?"

"Just some shoes. Nobody's been here in a good bit. Let's check out the still." He started toward the tent, which of course proved to contain exactly that.

And it was operating too. A confoundment of curling copper tubes, barrels crusted over with fermenting mash, a ready supply of jugs and jars. I counted seconds as a few dewy drops fell into various collecting jars.

"Probably cooking about a quart or two every day or so," I told Pinky.

"Old Man Reardon's got some explaining to do." He grunted, holding a clean hankie up to his nose. "The boss ain't gonna like it, being held out on. See that?"

He pointed at a track beaten into the marshy scrub. It went on a few yards before curling off out of sight around a clump of swamp myrtle. Before we could go looking farther, an old Packard touring car chuffed up into the front, parking alongside the Ford.

A portly fellow got out, lifted his hat at the pair of us and walked right up like we were old friends he sure was glad to see. If he noticed how me and Pinky both had one hand in our jacket pockets, he hardly seemed to care.

"You boys Prohibition Agents?" the man asked.

I chuckled. "Yeah, we're a regular Izzy and Moe. You got a badge?"

The man grinned a horsey grin and waved both hands in the air, foolin' like we were stickup men.

"No badge here. Make it hard to check up on my uncle's still if I had to worry about arresting myself."

Pinky grinned back at him. It was never a pretty thing when he did that. "Speaking of that still…" he began.

It was about here that the fellow caught on. He took in the cut of our suits and the bulges in our jacket pockets and swallowed. "You from Chicago?"

I nodded. "Where's the old man?"

"Passed on to that great open bar in the sky. Three weeks back, it's been."

"Dead or not," I said, putting on my 'this is how it's gonna be' voice. "He still owes the boss two shipments."

"I don't know anything about that, fellas. But I do know there's a more local boss I do have to worry about. Why don't you take it up with him?"

"Oh, yeah? Who's that?" I asked, keeping the steel in my voice and giving it a smart-alecky edge.

"Old voodoo man who lives out somewhere deep in the swamp. He's the one killed my uncle. And another man a week or two before that. He moved in and anybody who don't pay up a portion of their whiskey for him to sell, he curses them. Next thing you know, come the full moon, a pack of dogs sets upon them and worries them down to bones before anybody can say 'boo' about it. He's set himself up as the new boss in town and he's taking a piece of every working still in five counties."

"That so," Pinky said, pulling Shillelagh out into view.

The man wiped his palms on his trouser legs. "What do you want me to do? Pay him money and give you free shine? I'd sooner just shut it down, and then where would we all be?"

"You'd be in the boneyard snuggled up next to your uncle," I said. "But we're reasonable men. We don't work for an unreasonable man. I'm sure it's all a misunderstanding."

"What's this voodoo man's name and where can we find him?" Pinky asked.

"I don't know his name, boys. Nobody does. And you don't find him, he finds you and tells you what you owe. If you don't pay up, he sics them wild dogs on you."

"Sure, pal," I said, getting in his face. "And the Women's Temperance Union probably keeps this devil-worshipper on the payroll. Who do you think you're fooling?"

"Nobody," the man said. He looked down distracted by the picture frame in my hand. "Which one's you?" I asked.

He pointed with a finger at one of the two boys. I cracked the picture frame on the man's head, crumpling his hat and breaking the glass. He whimpered.

"What's your name?" Pinky demanded.

"Tim. Tim Reardon."

I cracked his skull one more time. His hat fell to the ground. The frame broke into flinders and left glass in the man's hair. "You asking us or telling us?"

"Tim Reardon," he said again.

"See how easy that was," I said. "Now tell us where to find this voodoo man."

"I don't know. I don't know, I swear it."

I glanced over at Pinky. He jerked his head a little. Far as he could tell, Timmy was being straight with us.

I dusted some of the glass from his hair and reached down to pick up the man's hat. I punched it back into a semblance of its former shape and set it back on Timmy's head.

"You got two days to arrange a meeting for us. Here's good. We'll be staying in the Marmont. No need to call us unless you set up a meeting sooner."

I stepped back. Pinky still had the gun on him. "Every bit of this whiskey belongs to the boss. We'll figure out how much more you owe next time. And don't try anything funny, if you know what's good for you."

Timmy made it clear that he did in fact know just what was good for him.

As we stalked toward the Ford, Pinky walked too close to a briar bush and ended up with a good rip in the leg of his trousers.

"You'll want to see Betty for that," the man called out from behind us.

"Oh, yeah? Who's Betty?"

"She does most of the laundry, pressing and sewing needs done in town. She's not three blocks from the Marmont."

Pinky gave him the hairy eyeball. "Regular chamber of commerce, ain't you, Mr. Reardon?"

"Just because we have ourselves a *situation* doesn't mean a fellow can't be neighborly, does it?"

"Maybe it does, maybe it doesn't," Pinky said.

"Well, gentlemen, all due respects to Chicago, but in Louisiana, we're always neighborly."

"We'll remember that," Pinky said. "You just make sure to get your voodoo neighbor out here to meet us."

◊ ◊ ◊ ◊ ◊

Reardon never called to say he'd arranged an earlier meet with the voodoo man turned aspiring bootlegger boss, and I spent most of the next day playing cards in Al Killenen's little speakeasy behind the general store. The sucker got me with a pair of jacks more often than necessary, but otherwise it wasn't a bad joint. The food was good, the whiskey decent, and the dames not so hard on the eyes as some of the places we'd been sent to do business. Pinky took his pants out to be sewn after hearing from one of Al's patrons that this Betty was a looker, but came back disappointed. She hadn't been in; the boy who does her running for her had taken the pants and promised to deliver them within a day or two. Apparently, there's a whole lot of folks in the town of Rowland who could afford to get their washing done despite the depression.

When I asked Al about the voodoo man, he clammed right up, "All I know is I buy from anybody else and things get ugly. Spooky ugly."

I tried to pry a little more out of him, but he wasn't giving. "Spooky like a pack of dogs eating Old Man Reardon?"

His eyelids came down to half-mast for a minute, like he was thinking about calling my bluff, but he folded his hand. "If you know that much about it, you know more than I do, Mister—?"

"Wally, just Wally." I tossed a couple of chips out as ante for the next hand. "But you can call me Wally from Chicago, if you want."

The other men at the table perked up a bit at that like scared little dogs. One by one over the next few hands, they all got up and cashed out, leaving just me and Al.

Before he quit the game, he leveled a cautious look my way. "I could get killed for telling you this," he said. "So I appreciate it if I never told you anything. And appreciate it even more if Chicago looks favorably on my operation without letting the local boys know."

"I'm listening. What am I supposed to not hear?"

"Tim Reardon, the old man's son," he whispered. "He's the voodoo man's messenger and right hand man. Nobody ever sees the V-man, but they know if they get a visit from Tim Reardon, them hexed dogs won't be far behind. Reardon's uncle Renard wasn't the first they got. Not by a long shot. Them dogs have been feeding on shiners who don't play the voodoo man's ball for a couple months now. And speakeasies that don't buy from him. Truth is, right now we're all more afraid of the hexes than we are of Chicago—and we'd all rather be on good terms with Chicago than in fear of some crazy swamp wizard nobody's ever seen."

"Anybody ever go looking for him?"

"A few did. Then their kin had to go lookin' for them. A couple times that happens and you get people's attention. Specially old country folk like live out here in Rowland."

"Thanks, Al," I said. "We'll see if we can get things back the way they need to be."

He looked around nervously. "It might be best if you and me not spend much more time playing heads up poker."

"A shame," I said. "I think I was finally starting to get a read on you."

He gave me a wavering grin, puffed a time or two on his cigar and shuffled toward the bar.

Pinky came back shaking his head with that gentle and reluctant grin he gets whenever he talks to the boss. "We're to put this voodoo man under the boss's thumb or put him down like a dog," he told me later when we were in the hotel room.

I spat out of the window into the muggy Louisiana night. "If he shows." I explained to him what Al had told me.

"That puts a different spin on it right there."

We went back out to Old Man Reardon's cabin at the appointed time and scratched around a bit, but his nephew never showed up and neither did any voodoo man. We walked the path back into the brush we had seen the first time we had been here and discovered it led—after a maze of muck and low bushes and sprawling, stunted trees—to a clearing out in the deeper swamp with an even dozen more army tents, all of these in good repair and each containing two or three bathtub stills operating at full perk.

I whistled low and serious through my front teeth. "Timmy's been holding out on us."

"The boss ain't gonna like this," Pinky said.

"Unless he starts getting a bigger piece of the action."

Pinky nodded. "Guess Old Man Reardon kept the still up by the house for anyone wants to bust him. Not a bad strategy."

We spent another two days in Rowland, scratching our heads and trying not to look like too big of fools when the boss asked why we couldn't find the voodoo man nor Tim Reardon. We got to where we'd spent so much time combing over that swamp and asking questions around town that we were arousing suspicion. The sheriff sent one of his deputies out just to warn us how Prohibition agents tend to disappear around Rowland and so did people who aroused their interest. Pinky wanted to punch the deputy, but I could tell he held himself back. I promised we'd not be drawing any further attention to ourselves. So long as we could help it.

"If you can't help it, we can arrange for somebody to help you help it," the deputy said before he strutted off.

I grabbed Pinky by the shoulder before he could follow and clobber the little prick.

At some point, Pinky's pants came back and he wrinkled his nose up at them. They were sewed up nice, all the mud washed clean and now they sported a pair of crisp straight creases, extra starch like he likes.

"What's wrong?" I asked, smoking by the window out of courtesy. Pinky's okay with cigarette smoke when he has to be, when the job calls for it. But I can tell it bugs him, the way he repeatedly pulls out one of his handkerchiefs or another and pretends to blow on it. With that in mind, I try not to make things hard on him when he's off the clock if I can. It's just being neighborly, as our missing friend Tim Reardon would say.

His furry brow went up just a fraction of an inch. "Nothing," he said. "You need to get any clothes done?"

"Sure," I said. I'd only packed two suits, thinking this would be a shorter trip than it was turning out to be.

We called the front desk and they sent for Betty's boy to come get pick them up.

The next two days were uneventful. Quiet drinks and poker in Al's little pub, increasingly irate chats over the phone with the boss. The biggest thrill was when our suits came back. Pinky, ever the connoisseur, held the pants leg up to his face and breathed in deeply. "Smell yours," he said.

I'm not one to get as big a thrill out of such things as fresh laundry as Pinky is, but I humored him. "Some kind of flower," I said.

"Bougainvillea. They were growing all over the back of that building."

"It's nice. Maybe I'll get some perfume that smells like it for Daisy when we get back to Chicago."

He grunted at me.

Next time we went out to Reardon's, his car was parked in front. It was near to dusk and the man was nowhere to be seen. We went back to the extra stills working in the tents and he wasn't there. But it was obvious someone had been. The collectors were all empty and the racks of jugs and mason jars were significantly diminished.

"Did you hear that?" Pinky said.

"Hear what?"

There was a rumble of an engine starting up and the chunk of Reardon's Packard shifting into gear. Me and Pinky shared an almost telepathic glance and instantly we were sprinting through the swampy maze for Reardon's dilapidated shack.

And we were being followed. When I heard the barking, I looked back at Pinky. He'd already pulled Shillelagh out. I grabbed for my own weapon. When we got back to the shack, it was full-on dark. I couldn't hear Reardon's car anymore, but I could hear that pack of dogs baying behind us. We scrambled for the Model T.

I began cranking it while Pinky got behind the wheel, his gun leveled in the direction of the howling in the darkness.

The tin lizzy turned over just as the beasts, gigantic, slavering, mottled mongrels, every one of them, burst out of the swamp and into the moonlight.

"Go, go, go!" I shouted. There were at least two dozen of them. No way we could put them all down with a couple revolvers and a pocketful of bullets.

But that didn't stop us from trying. I spent all my shells firing at shadows and Pinky did the same. He cocked his head to one side as he began to reload. The gunshots had only held them back, not frightened them off, but now the wild dogs did the strangest thing. As a pack, they all tore off in front of the cabin and past the outhouse into the darkness like their tails were on fire. Baffled, I looked at Pinky. He shrugged at me, but he had that look he gets when his intuition kicks in.

"What do you think?"

"Not sure," he lied.

"Okay, fine. What's our next step?"

He said nothing, but squirmed around in his seat as he began to give the T some gas. He reached one big paw behind him and pulled out a dirty black bag of some kind.

I squinted at it in the darkness. "What's that?"

"A warning." He tossed the thing to me. It felt like it was filled with corn meal and had been sewn with neat stitchwork into the shape of a little man. There were even nice little wooden buttons sewn on for eyes.

"Our voodoo man lets the dogs kill Reardon, but he's just going to try to scare us away?" I said. "Something doesn't smell right about that."

Pinky grinned at me like I'd made a joke. "You got that right. You sure you didn't hear anything, uh, unusual, in all of that?"

"With all the gunfire and barking, I didn't hear much beyond the ringing in my ears."

He pondered that for a second, as if he hadn't considered the noise a gun makes before and it was a whole new concept for him. "Suppose so," he said finally. "So what you want to do?"

"I say we get some food and ammo, ditch the car a ways up the road and wait here for that sonuvabitch Reardon to come back. Him or the voodoo man, either one."

"Works for me," Pinky said. "But there's a couple other things we need to do, too."

"Like what?" I asked.

He told me, and as he did, I figured the smell of that still had got him all screwy, but what he wanted to do wouldn't really hurt anything, so why not?

◇ ◇ ◇ ◇ ◇

Back in Rowland, the boss yelled at Pinky through the phone for a while, then he yelled at me some. We explained we had it under control.

"You better." he said in that gravelly voice of his, then hung up abruptly. We made the arrangements Pinky had outlined, paid our tab at Al's and made a good show of having been scared out of town. We tucked the Model T away into a side road and covered it over with deadfall branches enough to not be easily seen from the road. We were not-so-comfortably camped out in Old Man Reardon's decrepit shack by noon. Pinky took a long walk out with a couple of his arrangements out into the swamp and came back empty-handed.

"No sign of him so far," I said, dealing us out a hand and tugging at my collar. It fit a little tighter than I liked and we were in the middle of a godforsaken swamp, so I took off my tie and unbuttoned the top button. No way I was wearing my jacket out here in the daylight. I left it hanging on a nail over Old Man Reardon's boots and looked at my cards.

"No sign of anything moving in this godforsaken hole, unless you count the swamp critters," Pinky agreed.

Long about five o'clock in the afternoon, Reardon's car skidded to a halt in front of the outhouse and as we watched from the shadows of the cabin a lady jumped out of the passenger seat and ran into the outhouse, slamming the door behind her.

"Honey," he called, stepping carefully out of the Packard. Something glinted on a chain at his neck, but I couldn't make out what it was.

"You all right?" he hollered, a note of concern in his voice.

"Fine," she replied. "Could you have drove here any slower?"

"On this road, I should have. We about wore out the axles on some of those ruts." He started walking toward the cabin, then angled off to our right.

"Be glad I didn't pull over and make you go on the side of the road," he yelled over his shoulder at her as he passed our hiding place just inside the cabin door. Pinky and I hunkered down on either side listening to his footsteps trail away. We kept still as Baptists at a barn dance, but inside we were giddy as their daughters.

"I'd almost have rathered," she yelled back.

He got out of the Packard and lit up a cigarette.

"I'm going back to the stills, Betty" he said. "Join me when you're able."

So Tim and the local laundress were an item, eh? A piece of the scheme clicked into place. Looking at Pinky, I could tell he was way ahead.

"Which one you want?" he whispered.

"The dame."

"Figured. I'll go say hello to our fella."

He rushed out of the cabin, spattering the cuffs of his new pants with mud as he did. I followed him out and gazed over at the outhouse with its fancy wrought iron handle. It gave me an idea. I trotted softly over to the tent and cut a length of rope from it. Hurrying all the way, I approached the outhouse. There was no sound from inside. I tied off one end of the rope to the door's metal hoop handle and ran around the little building, stringing the rope along behind me. I pulled it taut when I got back to the front and looped it through the handle just as Betty was beginning to stir inside.

Sorry, lady, I thought. *But you ain't going anywhere just yet.*

"Tim?" she asked, uncertainly.

"He ain't here," I said. "Why don't you take a load off and sit a spell?" Sometimes, the things I say amuse myself. Especially when they get the person I'm talking to as worked up as they did Betty. The door vibrated as she slammed into it, but the rope held. She slapped her fists against it and wailed. "Let me out of here, you bastard!"

"Nothing doing, sister. You stay put and I'll be back for you after we see to little Timmy."

She shrieked, and the clapboard door hardly muffled it. "Tim! Tim! Get me out of here!"

"Yell all you want. Timmy's busy."

She beat her fists against the door again, screaming for Tim. I slammed the heel of my gun against the door and she stopped suddenly. "That's better."

Once I was sure the outhouse door was good and secure, I ran at full sprint past the cabin and the now lopsided tent. I didn't stop till I practically ran into Pinky and Reardon.

"Am I interrupting?" I said.

Pinky covered Reardon with his gun, but the man hardly looked scared. Reardon had the silver thing stuck half in his mouth like a penny candy he wanted to last a while. He blew into it like jazz man's trumpet, but not a sound emerged except the rush of air.

"Maybe I *am* the voodoo boss," he said. "And maybe you will shoot me. But you ain't going to make it out of these swamps alive. Not this time. Them dogs are hungry and Chicago hoods are on the menu."

Pinky took a step closer and punched Reardon hard. The man staggered back. Pinky gave the man's whistle chain a good yank and it came free. The whistle fell into the dirt and I picked it up. "That ain't a voodoo hex," Pinky said. "It's a dog whistle."

Tim spat. His saliva was thick with blood and a thin line dribbled down his chin unnoticed.

"Why just us?" I said. "Why won't they come after you?"

He looked at me like I was an idiot, so I slammed the butt of my pistol into his cheekbone. "Feel like talking now?"

"No need," Pinky said. "I can tell you why."

Reardon's eyes got big and white as milk saucers. "Your lady-friend the laundress made sure the laundry came back smelling all nice, like flowers. And you've been training the dogs to come running for food when they hear that whistle and smell the bougainvilleas haven't you?"

Timmy gaped. "How did you know that?"

Pinky sniffed. "Lucky guess. You seen the size of my beak?"

The baying dogs could be heard now, fierce and hungry and getting closer.

"But we're wearing brand new clothes that your Betty has never touched," I said, figuring out Pinky's strange arrangements at last. And the bundle he'd taken out into the swamp? All the old clothes that Betty had laundered, plus a couple pounds of ground up beef and butcher's scraps. The dogs weren't coming to get us anytime soon.

Timmy realized he'd been beaten all the way around and his shoulders slumped. "Where's Betty?" he said. "If you hurt her…"

It was an empty threat, considering the situation, and we let it hang there in the air for a minute like a sad balloon before it dropped to the ground, deflated.

"It wasn't her idea," he said. "She just did what I asked. She's the one who talked me into just giving you boys a warning instead of letting the dogs have their way with you."

We could hear the high-pitched yelps and barks of joy and hunger-maddened posturing as the dogs came upon the meat and our old suits off in the distant swampland.

"Please don't hurt Betty," he pleaded. "She hasn't even seen you two. Let her go—Let *us* go, and I'll give Chicago 50% of my output, not to mention 50% of the business I've brought in with the voodoo boss scam. What you say, fellas?"

I looked at Pinky. He still had Shillelagh pointed right at Reardon's nose, but with his other hand he scratched thoughtfully at his chin. He raised an eyebrow at me, questioning.

Reardon's eyes didn't look like they could get any wider or more pitiful and begging as they rolled in their wet orbits toward me. He nodded his head at me as if willing me to agree.

"I'll see your fifty percent of output and collections, and raise the boss's share of collections to seventy-five percent."

Reardon gulped, swallowing air.

"Seventy-five—"

Pinky wagged the gun at him. "That, or maybe we tie you up naked with a bunch of bougainvillea and Wally plays a little ditty on that whistle."

Timmy shook his head violently. "No. No! I'll go along. Please."

"You sure?" I asked him. "I do so love the wind instruments."

"Please," he said again, falling to his knees. "Tell Chicago I'll be their boy from now on. What you say, fellas?"

I gave Pinky a curt little nod that he interpreted as 'kick Timmy in the stomach'. Which he did. Timmy cried out and bent in two.

"We're taking what you got ready, and you're still behind. If there isn't a delivery to our man in Mobile in two weeks to catch you up to the new agreement, more than just a couple of us will be down here, and it won't go so easy on you."

Reardon sobbed. "Thank you. I'll deliver. I promise."

Pinky kicked him again, tossed me the whistle and we each grabbed a wooden milk crate full of whiskey-filled mason jars. Tim Reardon, Voodoo Boss of Des Ourses Swamp, Louisiana, didn't get up to follow us.

At the cabin, Betty had started up again pounding against the outhouse door. She yelled Tim's name and few other choice words. As we passed the cabin, I ducked in for my new jacket. I slipped it on and pulled the hand-sewn voodoo doll from one of the pockets, setting it atop the crate full of whiskey. Once the hooch was stowed under the car's bench seat, I grabbed up the doll and laid it carefully on the hood of Reardon's Packard.

"Nice stitchwork, Betty," I yelled toward the outhouse door. "You should keep your nose out of the bootlegging business. People tend to get dead in it, if they fall in with the wrong gang."

Silence greeted us at that, and Pinky started cranking on the T-Model to turn it over. I slid behind the wheel and waited to push the starter button and adjust the switches.

Finally, the engine sputtered to life and Pinky bounded in beside me.

"You sure do have a way with things," I said to him, backing the car up.

He was quiet.

"How'd you know it was a dog whistle calling them?"

"Heard it," he said. It was the first inkling I had that maybe Pinky was a little more different than just being a big-nosed bruiser who wasn't any more Irish than I was Nicaraguan. Not that it made much nevermind to me. He was a good partner, and you can't just whistle one of those up whenever you want to.

He pulled a handkerchief from his breast pocket and held it up to his oversized nose. He gave a good honk as Tim came around the side of the cabin and rushed to let Betty out of the outhouse. The car bounced down the spongy dirt road out of Des Ourses Swamp, past Rowland and out of Louisiana.

"When we get back to Chicago," Pinky said, about an hour later, "You still going to get that flower perfume for Daisy?"

"Maybe," I fibbed. I'd had my fill of the smell of bougainvillea. "But I *am* going to see if the boss'll spring for some new suits. This one's just not up to my standards."

"Yeah," Pinky chuckled. "He'll probably cover it. Cost of doing business." He reached back under the bench seat and pulled out a jar full of clear, strong-smelling whiskey.

"You thirsty?" he asked.

I smiled and took one hand off the wheel.

◊ ◊ ◊ ◊ ◊

Yvonne,

Long time, no e-mail! How long has it been since your time at Oxford? No, no, don't tell me any damning numbers. I'm trying too hard already to forget my age. Any chance of you coming across the pond and bringing those papers with you?

Yes, my dear, you should consider this old crypto-anthropologist as "on the scent" as any one of those mongrels running amuck in Des Ourses Swamp. And if you can't be convinced to visit, I beg—nay, demand—that you promptly scan the rest of those memoirs and send them post-haste! (It's as polite a demand as you'll ever get. Much more polite than the clamoring voices demanding my retirement, to be sure.)

I urgently await your next installment.

Augustine Renfro

P.S. Demands and jocularity aside, Yvonne, I implore you: Keep these documents safe and tell no one about them! This is no mere gangland diary; Pinky Clade, once researched and verified with more rigor, could well be the sort of find that explodes history as we know it! (Not to mention forming the pinnacle of my academic career.)

CASE OF THE ACCURSED AMULET

by Timothy Sayell

An Adventure of the Phantom Sleuth

The heavy summer night smothered Stockport like a blanket. The oppressive heat of afternoon lingered in the close confines of the city and showed no intent of leaving. Some small relief came in a sea breeze from somewhere out on the ocean, but even this wind seemed reluctant to run through the streets.

Despite the refreshing sea air, the waterfront still suffered from stifling temperatures. Nevertheless, a mysterious figure skulked the docks clad in a dark trench coat and wide-brimmed hat. The coloring of his costume allowed him to blend almost perfectly with the deep shadows, unseen by dockhands, sailors, and other denizens of the nighttime wharfs.

Ignoring these potential distractions, the Sleuth exercised his enviable patience, waiting for the object of his mission. It arrived at eight minutes past midnight, when the *S.S. Gertrude Burrows* pulled into port, ending its long trip from Africa. Through a sweat-soaked mask the Sleuth watched it dock, and knew it was time to learn the validity of his tip-off.

◊ ◊ ◊ ◊ ◊

The *Gertrude Burrows* was a sturdy freighter, finished only a few short months before the invasion of Poland. Thanks to the war contracts won by the Burrows Shipping Line, it was chiefly employed to transport precious supplies to the Allied war machine. As such, the cavernous cargo hold was all but empty on the return voyage, much to the Sleuth's chagrin. According to his information, something was going to be stolen off this boat tonight. Alas, he lacked further details.

Undaunted, the Sleuth turned away from the open hatches and traversed the main deck. He made up his mind to locate the records room, where he expected to find a cargo manifest among the ship's logs.

The Sleuth made it to the shadows beside the mast-house without being spotted by any of the crew. He was casing an opportunity to bolt unseen to the bridge castle when his keen ears detected a muffled moan and a soft thump. The Sleuth peered around the corner of the mast-house and spied a sailor laying prone on the narrow walkway between the two open cargo hatches.

With haste, the Sleuth ran to the victim, dropped to one knee, and pressed two fingers against the man's neck in search of a pulse. He sighed in relief as he felt the rhythmic throb of pumping blood. The sailor moaned and stirred. With a start, the Sleuth reached into his trench coat and pulled out his disguise kit.

The kit was a shiny silver flip-top box, like an oversized cigarette case. He flipped the lid open, plucked out a random mustache and pressed it onto his upper lip. The Sleuth then ripped the mask from his face, and thrust it and the kit back into his coat as the sailor's eyes flickered open.

The Sleuth smiled, reached out to assist the man to his feet. "There now, you'll be all right in a mo…"

The sailor's fist shot out, caught the Sleuth squarely on the chin, knocked him off his feet. "So! Troyin' t'get the jump on me, are ya?"

The Sleuth frowned in astonishment as the sailor jumped up from the deck and balled up his fists for a fight. He was young, not very tall, but blessed with beefy arms that packed a wallop. The Sleuth scrabbled to his feet, held one hand out in a calming gesture as he thrust his other hand into one of his pockets. "Wait! You don't understand…"

The sailor advanced behind a ready pair of fists. "Sure then you'd best be makin' me understand, afore I give ya a damn good thrashin'! Who are you? What's yer business aboard this here ship?"

The Sleuth drew the badge from his coat pocket and held it out before him. "Saunders, War Department!"

The sailor froze in place and stared with wide eyes. Then he unclenched his fists and fidgeted with embarrassment as he stammered, "Beggin' yer pardon, sir! Ya must understand, to awake after bein' kayoed like that, an' seein' a stranger on deck…"

"I understand perfectly," the Sleuth replied with a kind smile. Then the grin vanished, leaving only the usual steely stare. "What's your name, sailor, and what happened here?"

The sailor, still wide-eyed, stood up straight, brought one hand to his temple in salute. "Deck hand Mike Flaherty!" He slumped where he stood, frowned away for a moment. "Sure and the truth is that I'm not rightly certain what happened. One moment I'm openin' the hatches to the cargo hold, next thing I know I wake up with a bump on me noggin and you hoverin' over me."

The Sleuth placed a hand on Flaherty's shoulder. "You didn't see who attacked you?"

"No, sir."

The Sleuth ran his gaze across the ship's deck, spied nothing amiss. "Listen carefully, Flaherty. My people have obtained information that this ship has been targeted for a robbery tonight. My guess is that the guy who clobbered you is my thief. So I need a list of the cargo you're carrying so we can identify his target and nab him!"

"That's impossible!" the deck hand replied, rubbing the lump on his head. "After we drop off our shipment, we always return home empty. There *is* no cargo on board." A thought flashed through his mind and his face turned toward the bridge castle. "Unless…"

"Unless what?"

"Mr. Wilson, he's the mate, he went ashore and brought back a small package which he kept in his cabin," Flaherty told.

"What was it?" the Sleuth pressed him.

The sailor shrugged. "I assumed it was some souvenir for his family."

The Sleuth snorted. "It could be intelligence vital to the war effort!"

"No!" Flaherty gasped. "Mr. Wilson's no spy! He can't be!"

The Sleuth narrowed his eyes. "We'd better make sure of that. Take me to him."

◊ ◊ ◊ ◊ ◊

The sailor guided the Sleuth through the ship to the officers' quarters. "This is it, Mr. Saunders." With a curt thanks, the Sleuth rapped on the door. A few seconds went by with no response, and he knocked again. Flaherty shrugged. "Could be that he's up on the bridge. Come along, I'll take ya straight there," he said as he started down the corridor, waving for the Sleuth to follow.

The Sleuth took a single step before he heard the thump beyond the door. "What was that?" he asked as his hand flew to the handle. He found the portal unlocked, and flung the door wide.

The mate's cabin was a fifteen-by-ten box with modest furnishings and in the middle of it all two men were caught in a dance of death. The victim, blond haired and blue eyed, was dressed in a typical naval uniform: a blue blazer and slacks over a white turtleneck. In manic desperation, he clawed at his throat. The garrote was pulled tight by the strong hands of the Chinaman behind him, who looked like something out of a nightmare in his black cap and changshan. Surprise was in his murderous eyes as they flashed to the open door, and he yanked on his wire with renewed effort.

The Sleuth charged into the cabin, threw one fist into the Chinaman's ribs. The pain raced through the villain and his grip on the garrote loosened until Wilson pulled free, gasping for precious air.

"Mr. Wilson!" Flaherty exclaimed from the doorway.

The Sleuth swung his fist again, but the Chinaman blocked and threw a punch of his own. The Sleuth crashed onto the bunk, and Flaherty ran in to replace him.

One hit to his gut and another to his jaw sent the deckhand crumbling to the cabin floor. The Chinaman snatched a small package wrapped in brown paper from the table below the porthole even as Wilson, still massaging his tender throat with one hand, pulled a gun from his dresser drawer. Almost as though expecting it, the Chinaman grabbed a book from the table and flung it at Wilson as he whipped around.

The book collided with the gun barrel, knocking it aside as it fired. The wild shot hit the lamp, plunging the cabin into darkness with a short rain of glass. Undaunted, the Chinaman bolted for the lighted hallway, slamming the door shut behind him.

"He's getting away!" the Sleuth cried as he jumped over Flaherty and rushed for the door. He burst into the hall, checked both directions and spied the Chinaman's long, braided queue vanish around a corner and charged in pursuit.

The Sleuth chased the clanging footsteps up a stairwell, the two sailors trailing in his wake. The Chinaman, package in hand, bolted across the open deck on course for the aft guard rail and the open ocean beyond. Without pause, the Sleuth ran after him, Flaherty at his heels. Wilson stepped to the side, raised his pistol and croaked out the fair warning, "Halt or I fire!"

Ignoring the alert, the Chinaman leapt for the rail and the gun in Wilson's hand barked a vicious thundercrack. The Chinaman, still clutching the topmost rail, fell over the barrier and dangled above the churning waters below. Breathless, the Sleuth braced himself against the railing and clutched at the assassin with desperate fingers. The killer looked up at him, his mouth trembling as though he struggled to speak. Instead, he released the rail and fell into the water, leaving only the package in the Sleuth's hands.

The Sleuth frowned down at the watery grave, but the killer's body never floated to the surface. There was no smaller craft nearby, no convenient getaway boat in sight. Wilson and Flaherty joined him at the rail as other sailors arrived, ready for trouble, attracted by the gunshot.

"I don't know who you are," Wilson rasped, "but I thank you for showing up when you did. A moment later, and I would've been done for."

Flaherty jabbed one thumb toward the Sleuth and said, "This here's a Mr. Saunders, come down from the war department…"

"That's right," the Sleuth interrupted. "I'll have to ask you what you've got in this package, and who wants it bad enough to kill you for it."

Wilson didn't hesitate. "I don't know, exactly. Some sort of antique, jewelry I think. I was merely bringing it Stateside at the request of Montgomery Fisk."

The Sleuth's eyes widened. "Montgomery Fisk? The industrialist?"

"The same. You see, my father was Mr. Fisk's butler since…before I was born until his death last year. Mr. Fisk liked children, and doted on those of his servants just as much as his own. In fact, I believe he offered me every opportunity that he provided for his own son. So when he asked me to meet up with his man, pick up a package and bring it home, I could hardly refuse. He said it was some valuable antique and that he needed someone he could trust, I assured him he could rely upon me."

"Have you any idea who may be after it?" the Sleuth persisted.

"No, not specifically," Wilson replied. "But if it's some valuable artifact, I expect any number of thieves would be interested in it. I've never even opened the package, so all I know is what I was told when I picked it up. It was implied to be a piece of jewelry, and there was some nonsense about a curse."

The deck hand snorted and poked his elbow into the Sleuth's ribs. "Hardly sounds like war secrets, eh, Mr. Saunders?"

The Sleuth regarded the package with disappointment in his eyes. "No, no, it doesn't." A feeling in his gut told him there was more to the mystery, but that he could not dig deeper in his current identity. Hiding his regret, he held the package out to the first mate. "Well, I guess this is out of my department. Here you go, Mr. Wilson, sorry for the questions."

"Not at all," the mate replied as he took the box in his hands.

"However, there has been one attempt on your life," the Sleuth continued, "if you'd like I could make a few calls, get a man assigned to help you guard that until you get it to Fisk."

Wilson smiled in gratitude. "That shouldn't be necessary. He's expecting me first thing in the morning. Besides, I have a whole boatload of trustworthy men to stand guard for me. All I have to do is ask."

"Sure and that's right!" Flaherty exclaimed, punching the air for emphasis. "In fact, ya don't even have to ask! Oy'll stand watch over ya tonight, Mr. Wilson. Rest assured that nobody will get past me, now that I know to be lookin' for 'em!" He was not the only volunteer.

◇ ◇ ◇ ◇ ◇

Late the following morning found the Sleuth, *sans* mustache or mask, at the wheel of a Ford Sedan. In the seat beside him sat Jane Wayland, seasoned reporter from the *Stockport Globe*, twirling her long blond locks around one finger, an anxious gesture that he found endearing.

"Byron?" It was not his own name, but his twin brother's. Nonetheless, he had long ago learned to answer to it as Brian Twain had been legally dead for years. "Are you sure you can get me in to see Montgomery Fisk? He never sees reporters. Too important for us, I suppose."

Brian smiled. "Don't worry; I'm an important man, too," he said with playful pomp. "Monty is an old family friend. Don't forget, he used to work for my father before he managed to buy his first steel mill, and made his own fortune. I'm sure he'll see us."

Before long the Sedan pulled onto the Fisk estate through a pair of wrought iron gates. The massive house stood surrounded by green hills and colorful flower gardens, flanked by shady trees that rustled in a slight breeze that offered no relief from the summer heat. In a matter of minutes, they were inside the manor speaking with the man himself, in his study overlooking the gardens.

Montgomery Fisk was a short man in his early sixties. His gray hair was thinning, but still covered his head. His eyes were sharp and alert behind thin spectacles that were attached to his jacket lapel by a lanyard. He offered a warm welcome to his visitors, also believing the Sleuth to be Byron Twain. Jane was introduced both as a reporter and the police commissioner's daughter. Fisk played the proper host, bade them to sit, offered them coffee. The obligatory small talk was amicable, but cut short as Jane wasted no time getting down to business.

"Mr. Fisk, I hope I'm not being presumptuous, but I'm most anxious to ask you about this mystery package of yours! From what I've heard, what was meant to be a secret arrival in the middle of the night was spoiled. As soon as the ship docked, a thief attempted to steal it. Shots were fired; they say a man was killed..."

Fisk forced out a good-natured chuckle and held up one hand to stop her. "The account you've heard is greatly exaggerated, which is no surprise to me." He sat back in his chair and regarded them over his steepled fingers. "First of all, it was far from a "secret arrival". It was no secret, merely private business. I understand that there *was* a robbery attempt, which was thwarted. Only *one* shot was fired—at the robber—which may have missed entirely as no body has yet been found."

Brian sat, feigning only polite interest in the account as Jane scribbled frantic notes on her pad. Jane looked up sharply. "But the package itself, what is it?"

"Ah! Here, let me show you!" With joyful exuberance, he ducked behind his desk and pulled out the box. It had been opened, and the crinkled brown paper was folded back over it in an untidy fashion. He placed the bundle on the desktop, peeled the paper away from a cardboard box. He opened the shipping box, burrowed his hands deep into the protective padding of dried grasses and pulled out a small wooden box, covered in ornate carvings.

Brian and Jane leaned forward in their seats and Fisk laid the ornate box before them on the desk. "A new acquisition for my private collection," he grinned and slid the lid to one side as though it was on rails. Within the box was a round ceramic pendant, about the size of a pocket watch, on a frayed twine necklace. Fisk lifted it from the box with a gentle hand and displayed it proudly to his guests. On the pendant was a picture: the sun's beams fighting through the clouds to shine upon a hilly countryside, all this encircled by a ring of strange foreign letters. "It is a piece of Asian history! It is meant to have two brothers. Together, the Chinese call them the Keys to Wisdom!"

Brian hummed critically. "An interesting piece, Monty."

"Yes," Jane agreed, "But it doesn't look to me to be a key at all. What are they all about?"

"Once upon a time, the land now known as China was a collection of small kingdoms, lesser states, and warring tribes. They each had a different philosophy toward life, collectively known as the Hundred Schools of Thought," Fisk explained. "Then the first dynasty was installed, China was unified and the conquerors proceeded to promote their way of thinking, and eradicate all others. This procedure is known as the Burning of Books and Burying of Scholars. One such scholar, Mo Tzu, built a secret library to preserve the knowledge and wisdom of his philosophy. Then, he fashioned these pendants and presented them to his three most faithful followers before his death, promising that together they would guide one to his cache of wisdom. At least, that's how the fable goes. Of course, no such storehouse has ever been found."

Brian laughed, sat back in his chair. "A nice bedtime story! All that's missing is a curse!"

Fisk lowered the pendant back into its box. "It's funny you should say that, Byron. In fact, there *is* meant to be a curse! One of the carriers of Mo Tzu's keys was captured by the authorities and issued a curse upon the pendants. Anyone who possessed them, who had no intention of seeking Mo Tzu's wisdom, would be bedeviled by some sort of evil spirit. A yellow demon, or some such foolishness!"

An unearthly cry reverberated through the study and a furry humanoid beast dropped onto the desk. The three jumped back with a start as it screeched at them with a gray skull-like face surrounded by a mane of golden-brown hair. It stood about two feet tall, with long, thin limbs and a long catlike tail. With quick, jerky movements it scanned the desktop and seized the ornate box.

Fisk reached out with one urgent hand. "Now see here, you little thief!" The hairy monster hissed at him, bearing a pair of white fangs and Fisk drew back with a cry of alarm. Before the shock of its arrival could dissipate fully, the beast leapt from the desk, bounded across the marble floor, and jumped onto the sill of an open window. "The pendant!" Fisk exclaimed.

As though the industrialist's cry had broken some enthrallment cast by the creature, Brian leapt for the open window. Leaning out, he looked in all directions and found the impish simian picking out handholds among the wisteria and vines that covered a nearby trellis. It soon climbed over the gutter and disappeared. "Quick! It's on the roof!"

"This way!" Fisk barked as he led the charge into the hall, up the wide stairs and out onto a second-floor balcony.

Jane pointed off to their left where the monkey scampered across the dormers. "There it is!"

Brian climbed over the railing onto the shingles. "I'm going after it!"

"Be careful, my boy! I'll get the groundskeepers armed with the hunting rifles!" Fisk announced as he rushed back into the manor.

"Byron! What can I do to help?"

He stopped and looked back. "You'd best stay in the house, Jane, out of harm's way."

With a frown and clenched fists, she groaned in exasperation. Brian rushed over the shingled roof as she stomped her way back into the manor.

Brian traversed the sloping roof as quickly as he dared. Suddenly there was an inquisitive chattering above him. He looked up and saw the golden brown monkey watching him from the apex of a dormer. "There you are!" He jumped for the furry thief, but it retreated from view with a call not unlike mocking laughter.

He slipped, caught himself, then walked up beside the dormer, following the monkey. Brian climbed up to the peak of the second story roof and looked down the far slope where he found his thief sitting beside a pot-shaped ornament on the cornice. He crawled over the apex and down the incline, picking his way with quiet care. In moments he crept upon the distracted monkey, reached out one hand.

Brian grabbed it by the scruff of the neck as a thundercrack sounded on the ground below. In the same heartbeat, the cornice exploded where the monkey had been standing. Startled, Brian jumped, began to slide toward the edge of the roof. Instinct made him release the thief and save himself by grasping the nearby ornament. The monkey bounded across the roof, shrieking.

"Careful there, Tom," Fisk admonished the gunman. "You nearly got Mr. Twain!"

"Sorry, sir!" replied the servant, as he tried once more to get the monkey in his sights.

"Byron, are you all right?" Fisk called up.

"Fine, Monty!" Brian said with a reassuring wave. "Have your men route that beast back to this end of the house!"

"Will do!" the industrialist consented.

Brian climbed to his feet and set off after the monkey. A gunshot rang out to his right, beyond the peak of the great house. Then another shot, a screech, and the sound of raining shingles. The hairy thief appeared on the apex of the roof, and ran along the horizon of the peak as shingles exploded behind it. Brian ran along the roof, keeping pace with the simian burglar.

The shingles ahead of the monkey erupted with volcanic force, and the thief jumped with a cry of panic. Brian made a short leap up the incline and caught the monkey in his arms. The beast looked up at him with its skull-like face and let loose a spine-chilling shriek. The thief struggled to escape with enough force to throw Brian off-balance. Brian stumbled about in an effort to stay upright, but the broken shingles shifted beneath his feet. Both he and his hairy catch rolled down the incline and fell over the edge amid a shower of debris.

Brian Twain fell one story and landed in the soft loam of a flower bed, azaleas and begonias flattened beneath him. A quick assessment proved that he suffered no serious damage. He picked himself up and quickly spied the pendant's box a few feet away. He stumbled toward it when Jane's voice yelled out behind him, "Byron, look out!"

Brian spun about and gawked in wide-eyed shock at an advancing Chinaman with ten inches of sharpened steel raised for the kill. Jane clung to his back, both arms wrapped about the villain's neck. Brian noted that this was not the man from the freighter, though dressed in similar costume.

Brian let fly a roundhouse that connected with the villain's jaw and followed with a left hook. While stunned, the long knife was knocked from the murderer's hand with ease.

Undaunted, the Chinaman twirled around in a sloppy pirouette. The momentum swung Jane's feet out in a wide circle where her hard shoes struck Brian's head with lethal force. The Chinaman finished his spin and Jane's own weight pulled her off of him. The assassin advanced upon Brian, who clutched his head in agony, and dropped him to the flower bed with a single blow.

As Brian lay groaning in the dirt, the Chinaman stepped over him, bent down, plucked the ornate box from the ground.

"No, you don't!" Brian cried as he seized the brigand's ankle with one hand. The Chinaman fell into the loam with a cry of alarm. With a frown, the Chinaman tried to pull his leg free while rattling off his native tongue in an urgent tone.

Jane screamed as the skull-faced monkey bounded past her with the long knife in its paws. The monkey leapt onto Brian's back and drove the blade through his thin coat and into his flesh. Brian cried out in anguish, let loose his grip on the thug.

The Chinaman jumped to his feet and bolted across the gardens to an awaiting sedan with the box in hand. A sharp command prompted the murderous monkey to follow. The groundskeepers rounded the corner of the manor, with Fisk leading the charge. They leveled their rifles and fired as the fiend and his animal companion climbed into his car and sped away.

Brian watched the car race away with hatred in his heart. Then his eyes fell to a scrap of paper, incongruous in the trampled flower bed. He reached out, nabbed it, and held it tight in a clenched fist even as Jane demanded an ambulance.

◇ ◇ ◇ ◇ ◇

A few short hours later, Brian Twain was in a private room in Stockport General Hospital where Jane Wayland hovered over him like a mother hen. The knife had been removed from his back and given to the police, the wound stitched and bandaged. Brian was then placed in a room for overnight observation, and the nurses came and went in a steady stream under Jane's careful scrutiny. Eventually, a man in a white doctor's coat entered.

"Good afternoon, I'm Dr. Saunders."

At the sound of the name, Brian looked up with immediate interest. He didn't recognize the face with the bulbous nose and sagging jowls, but he knew the voice behind the disguise.

"You're not the doctor we saw earlier," Jane remarked.

"No ma'am," said the man in the white coat as he stepped up to the bed, grabbed the clipboard and began looking through the charts. "I'm a specialist on nerve damage. My colleague asked that I make the time to give your condition a quick appraisal." He looked up at Jane, smiled. "Miss, would you mind stepping outside so that I may conduct my examination? I promise it shall be brief."

Jane absorbed the worrisome prospect of nerve damage and quickly consented. The man in the white coat thanked her, held the door open as she left the room. Then he closed the door, pulled the shade down on its window and turned back to the patient. "I came as soon as I heard, Brian! What happened?"

Brian grinned and said, "Hello, Byron!" He lost the grin. "I'll tell you what happened: I was stabbed in the back by a monkey!"

Byron Twain frowned through his disguise. "A monkey? You'd better tell me everything."

Brian wasted no time in relating the adventure thus far. The account was cold and factual, a detailed history, with no words wasted for the sake of entertainment. As Brian came to the end of his tale, he reached out to the nightstand by his bed, seized a scrap of paper and held it out to his disguised twin. "Jane has threatened to watch over me all night long. You'll have to pick up the trail and this is the only clue I can offer you."

The man in the white coat took the paper and frowned at the name and address at the top of the page. "An empty receipt from the Jade Lotus Laundry?" He turned it over and recognized Montgomery Fisk's address, written in neat, penciled letters.

Brian nodded. "I believe the Chinaman dropped it in Fisk's gardens during our little tussle. It *could* lead you straight to him..." Then he slumped in his bed. "...or it could be a dead end."

Byron stowed the receipt in a pocket of the white coat. "I'll look into it. In the meanwhile, you heal up."

◊ ◊ ◊ ◊ ◊

The Jade Lotus was deep in Stockport's Chinatown, a neighborhood cramped onto the brick-and-stone quays across the harbor from the shipping docks where the *Gertrude Burrows* made port. It was a three-story brownstone with crumbling mortar, boards criss-crossed over the windows and doors, and a painted sign for the laundry which bore chipped letters and fading image of an exotic green flower.

Byron Twain—now clad in the gray hat, coat, and mask of the Sleuth's costume—skulked through the deep shadows of dusk seeking an entrance to the disused edifice. At the rear he found a pair of double-doors which covered a basement entrance. Close inspection revealed that although the boards were crossed over both doors, they were only nailed to one. To the casual passer-by, it offered the illusion that this entrance was barred like all the other portals of the building.

The Sleuth cast his eyes up and down the back street. Spying no lookouts, he entered through the sham-blockade and pulled the doors quietly closed behind him to maintain the illusion.

He descended the creaking stairs into a basement crowded with boilers, furnaces, and water pumps. The spaces between these dusty, rusting machines were filled with crates and stuffed sacks that were piled up like sandbags against a flood. Out of the corner of his eye, the Sleuth spied a movement off to his right. With soft footsteps, he proceeded to investigate.

A gray skull lunged out from behind a crate, surrounded by a mass of golden-brown fur. It screeched at him with sudden ferocity, and instinct forced him to step back. Before he could suppress this basic human urge, strong arms emerged beneath his own arms and reached up to his neck in a submission hold. Grunting in exertion, he struggled to break free, but failed. Unable to extricate himself, the Sleuth heard urgent voices behind him babbling in what he assumed was some Chinese dialect. There was a burst of pain on the crown of his head, and everything went black.

◊ ◊ ◊ ◊ ◊

The Sleuth awoke with a throbbing head. He wanted to rub the pain away and found his wrists tied to the arms of the chair he was sitting in. His ankles were likewise secured to the chair legs. A quick look around revealed that his chair was in a cement-lined depression—not unlike a swimming pool—with a drain in the center of the floor and a pair of pipes that stretched up to the ceiling high overhead. A set of narrow stairs led to an open walkway that surrounded the pit, but there were no other features.

A stern-faced Chinaman stood over him, with appraising eyes and a bottle of smelling salts in hand. Satisfied with what he saw, the Chinaman corked the salts, folded his arms into the sleeves of his black robes and called up to the walkway above.

Another Chinaman stepped up to the brink and looked down into the pit with hard eyes. Unlike his fellows, he wore a voluminous yellow robe that was covered with an intricate Oriental design in crimson thread. He had fat cheeks and a babyish face behind a long black mustache and a tall forehead that stretched up to his bald cranium.

The man in the yellow robe descended the steps and approached the Sleuth as the Chinaman in black bowed and backed away in reverence. The man in yellow regarded the Sleuth in silent contemplation for a long moment. Then, at last, he spoke. "Good evening." His voice was nasal, his tone curt. "When my servants first informed me of a trespasser, the news was not so engaging. However, once they described you, my interest piqued."

The Sleuth frowned up at him. "Who are you?"

"My name is Lao Shiang," the newcomer replied. "Sometimes I am called 'The Dragon's Claw'. You may or may not have heard of me."

"I'm sorry, no," the Sleuth admitted.

Lao Shiang smiled. "Fear not, I am not offended. Indeed, I strive very hard to remain anonymous and unknown in my endeavors. However, very little occurs amid the local criminal underworld without coming to my attention, hence my interest in you."

The Sleuth looked up sharply from his bonds. "What do you mean?"

"I deduce that you are this mysterious Sleuth whom I have heard about," Lao Shiang hypothesized aloud. "You have been connected to various crimes—many thwarted, and many that were successful. Yet you have never been apprehended, and I daresay that few can give a reliable report about you. You come and go like a phantom. Yes, I believe you are the Sleuth. Tell me please, am I correct?"

The Sleuth's eyes wandered about the dimly lit basin as he considered his answer. "Yes, I suppose you are."

Lao Shiang clapped his hands together in triumph. "I have wondered for some time now whether or not you truly exist!" he laughed. "The thought has occurred to me that you were merely an invention for the purpose of propaganda. Either invented by the authorities in a vain effort to dissuade criminal enterprise, or by the criminal element as a red herring to confound police.

"But instead you are real!" the Chinaman marveled. "If half of what I have heard of you is truth, then you are a most extraordinary person! It is an honor to meet you at long last!" He offered a deep, respectful bow.

"Funny way to show it," the Sleuth replied, tugging at the ropes that held him secured to the chair.

"I apologize for the necessary precaution," Lao Shiang stated, his tone devoid of emotion. "I have heard conflicting reports about your personal disposition. Although Commissioner Wayland publicly denies your existence, it is rumored that he has a secret file about you, and regards you a great criminal threat. Contrariwise, other rumors insist that you were instrumental in the downfall of countless criminals. So, you see, I have yet to determine whether or not I can trust you. Exactly whose side are you on?"

"I am on the side of justice," the Sleuth said in a defiant voice.

Lao Shiang sneered. "An unsatisfactory response, for justice is highly subjective. Its definition depends greatly on one's point-of-view. What purpose has brought you here to the Jade Lotus?"

"I have come to retrieve the pendant of Mo Tzu and return it to Montgomery Fisk, the rightful owner," the Sleuth declared.

The man in the yellow robe nodded and let loose a heavy sigh. "That is unfortunate, for it means we are at odds. I had hoped that you could be persuaded to work in accord with my organization?" He looked askance at the Sleuth, who offered a wry smile and shook his head. "A pity. Under different circumstances I suspect we could have worked together quite well. Instead I fear I shall have to kill you."

The Sleuth straightened in his seat. "Kill me?"

"Of course." Lao Shiang raised his arms and indicated the room around them. "This is a sub-basement beneath the laundry. This vat you are seated in is meant to hold seawater, pumped in from the harbor." He waved one hand to the pipes that ran from the pit to the ceiling. "It is then meant to be taken up through pipes to the laundry machines on the floors above. But we will only fill this basin, and you will drown as we abandon these premises permanently."

The Sleuth shrugged in his restraints. "Why leave? Once I'm dead, I won't be revealing your hide-out to anyone."

"True," the Chinaman mused. "However, from what little I have heard of your exploits, I deduce you have some organization—whether great or small, I cannot tell—at your disposal. Therefore, I must assume assistance in some form will come to this place in search of you. Only a fool would risk assuming otherwise. I am no fool, so we make haste to depart before your agents may come to your aid." Lao Shiang turned to the narrow stairs, paused, turned back and advanced on his prisoner. "But first I must satisfy my curiosity. If you will indulge me..."

Lao Shiang reached out with one hand, pulled the mask up onto the Sleuth's forehead. The Chinaman gawked for a long moment at the sagging jowls and bulbous nose that Byron Twain hid behind to infiltrate his twin's hospital room. Lao Shiang grunted thoughtfully and returned the mask to the Sleuth's eyes. "Your face is not known to me and not at all as I expected."

His curiosity sated, Lao Shiang turned on his heel and climbed the stairs. A subtle wave prompted his servant to follow him. The Dragon's Claw issued orders in his native tongue; the servant bowed and retreated beyond the Sleuth's limited view. The golden brown monkey scuttled up to Lao Shiang, chortled, held up the ornate box to its master.

"An interesting animal you have there," the Sleuth remarked.

The villain looked down at the simian, smiled, and took the proffered box. "Yes, he is a Sichuan golden hair monkey from the Shaanxi province. He has proven a clever pet, and has learned many useful tricks."

The squeal of metal on metal filled the air as a rusty valve was forced open after a long rest. Seawater poured into the pit from some opening behind the Sleuth. In a matter of minutes, the water covered his shoes.

"I apologize for the mundanity of this death," the Dragon's Claw lamented. "I feel an extraordinary man deserves a more worthy demise. Alas, I am pressed for time. Farewell, O Sleuth, may you go to whatever Heaven suits you best." Then he turned and walked away, followed by his pet.

Despite the rising water, the Sleuth smiled. For Byron Twain was an ardent student of escapology, and had studied the secrets of such men as Harry Houdini, John Nevil Maskelyne, and Major Zamora. Having his limbs lashed to a chair by mere ropes was no challenge to him. His nimble fingers worked the knots free long before the water had risen to his knees.

The Sleuth ascended the stairs, found himself in a subterranean storeroom. A rickety wooden staircase rose to the building above. Crates and barrels were pushed up against one brick-lined wall across the room from a tangle of pipes with a dripping valve-wheel. The chamber was lit by a single lantern that sat on a crate beside an arched tunnel.

Having heard no creaking complaints from the wooden stair, the Sleuth guessed that the villains had escaped through the shadowy tunnel. With nary a hesitation, he charged down the dark corridor as quietly as his squishing shoes would allow.

After twenty yards of bricks reinforced with wooden support beams, the tunnel widened into a vast chamber. The Sleuth gawked in astonishment at the wide, lantern-lit dock beside the subterranean canal. Lao Shiang waited on the pier, the monkey at his side, as two of his underlings prepared a small boat for castoff.

The Sleuth reached for his gun but found it missing. With a sneer curling his lip he charged across the short distance between him and the Chinese ringleader. The golden-haired monkey turned at the sound of squishing footsteps and screeched. The Sleuth brought his fist around and knocked the Dragon's Claw to the boardwalk as the monkey scurried away, screaming.

The two Chinese henchmen scrambled to the dock as the Sleuth scooped up the ornate box from Lao Shiang's hand. The Sleuth stood, threw a haymaker that knocked one goon into the canal. He ran back for the tunnel, pursued by the second Chinaman who was spurred on by Lao Shiang's wrathful command: "Kill him! And retrieve the pendant!"

The Sleuth was nearly to the tunnel when arms wrapped about his waist. The tackle threw him and his attacker off their feet. The Sleuth rolled onto his back, saw the Chinese thug springing up from the boards and diving at him again. The masked hero lashed out with both feet, striking the villain in the chest.

The henchman slammed into the wall beside the tunnel, dislodging a lantern. The oil splattered as the light clattered on the floorboards, setting fire to the dock, and the Chinaman's changshan. The Sleuth and the thug both jumped to their feet, pulled back their fists to continue the fight. Then the Chinese brute paused, eyes widened. With a shriek of pain he slapped at the flames on his shoulders in futility. Screaming, he ran across the dock and jumped into the canal, even as the other thug pulled himself out of the water.

Seizing the opportunity, the Sleuth darted into the tunnel as the fire climbed up the heavy support beams at the mouth. He ran for the sub-basement beneath the laundry. Halfway there, a sharp pain erupted on the back of his head. He recoiled in pain, crashed against the left wall. He paused for one deep breath, then urged himself to continue. He looked back to check on his stalker and a fist struck him between his masked eyes. The Sleuth hit the hard bricks again and fell to the tunnel floor, the box tumbling from his feeble hand.

Groggy, the Sleuth lifted himself up and reached out in a lame attempt to stop the Chinaman from plucking the box from the floor. The thug then uttered some pithy remark in his native tongue, and dripped his way back to the canal.

Powered by sheer stubbornness and determination, the Sleuth pulled himself to his feet and stumbled down the tunnel in pursuit. The pounding in his head was like a dozen drummers, each beating a different tune on his head. Ahead of him there was a thunderous crash. He looked up, tried to blink away the stars and saw the flaming support beams had fallen along with a heavy rain of brick and dirt.

As the cloud of concrete dust dissipated, the Sleuth saw one of Lao Shiang's dripping henchmen, an iron crowbar in hand. Behind him, the Dragon's Claw stood in the boat with the ornate box in his bony grasp. The Chinese mastermind barked out a curt order and the henchman, scowling at the Sleuth, dropped the crowbar in favor of another lantern. Without pause, the thug threw the new lantern at the debris, adding fuel to the fire, and then turned and rushed to the getaway boat.

Lao Shiang raised the box as though offering a toast. "I should have guessed that hasty deathtrap would be insufficient for the likes of you." His underlings scrambled about the boat, preparing for launch. "But in the end, your escape was for naught. In a way, I am disappointed, for I expected better. However, I suppose even the Sleuth must lose once in a while." Then he slid the lid off the box and gasped in surprise.

"Looking for this, Lao?"

The Dragon's Claw looked at the Sleuth, trapped in the tunnel behind the flaming debris, the pendant of Mo Tzu dangling from his fingers. Growling with lethal wrath, the crime lord looked about the underground dock with beady eyes. In a loud, clear voice Lao Shiang issued a statement in the language of his homeland.

The Sleuth could only wonder at his words for a fraction of a second. Then a ball of golden brown fury burst through the flames and landed on his chest. The impact threw him to the tunnel floor once more, this time with the sinister skull-faced monkey snarling down at him. The ancient pendant, too, hit the floor and with a *pop* shattered in two equal halves. Both the Sleuth and the killer monkey looked with curiosity and saw the folded scrap of paper that had been concealed within.

The monkey recovered first, screeched into the Sleuth's masked face, then snatched the antique note in its paw. It jumped up to a supporting timber, the Sleuth scrambling after it. The monkey leapt up and grabbed one of the beams on the ceiling. The Sleuth, still dazed, tried to wrap his arms around the furry thief, but failed.

The monkey jumped through the fiery blockage once more, scampered across the dock, and jumped aboard Lao Shiang's boat as it was paddled toward the nighttime harbor. The Sleuth watched with disappointed eyes as the Chinese crime lord took the historic note from his pet.

With a gloatful grin, Lao Shiang held up the note for the Sleuth to see, then eagerly unfolded it. The grin melted from his face and he crumpled the brittle note in one talon-like hand. Fuming, he glanced hither and yon about the subterranean canal as he thought, until his eyes fell upon the Sleuth, still watching intently from the tunnel.

"For the sake of closure, I shall tell you that I *have* been thwarted today, though not by you," said Lao Shiang at last. "Sometime in the long history of the pendant, some other found its secret before me, and in its place he left…" The mastermind cast a hateful glance down at the hand with the crumpled paper. "…a rather surly note. So, alas, my efforts here have born me no fruit. However, if you have truly come for the pendant, then I bid you take it and go." By now, his unlit boat slipped beyond the light of the lantern-lit dock, vanishing in the darkness of the subterranean canal. "I bear you no ill will, and apologize for your inconveniences. It was interesting to finally meet you, O Sleuth! Who knows? Perhaps we shall meet again in the future, under better circumstances! Farewell!"

The Sleuth squinted into the shadowy waterway but could no longer see the escaping boat, nor Lao Shiang's golden robes. With a sigh, he frowned down and snatched the two halves of the pendant from the floor. A cursory examination showed him that the pendant was undamaged. He deduced it was cleverly designed to be hollow, and was meant to open thus. With careful fingers he snapped the two halves together, marveled at the trinket for a moment, then slipped it into a pocket.

He frowned once more at the waters beyond the fiery dock, and nodded grimly to himself. For he expected to cross paths with the Dragon's Claw again, he was already planning it, and he did not expect the circumstances to be any better. A gut feeling told him that next time, it would be much worse.

EMPIRE STATEMENT

by David S. Briggs

Eighth wonder, they call me.
What a depressing number.
Have they no vision?
I've seen marvels enough to exhaust
more than my 20 fingers & toes—
Tyranosaurus Rexes feasting under the embers of sunset,
Pterodactyls nesting on cliff faces that dwarf the Earth,
waterfalls so tall they disintegrate to mist.
I've had tribes offer me their finest women
just to stop my roaring,
for I have a thing for small, hairless dames
—really tiny ones.
Something makes me want to care for them,
such small, fragile creatures among the beasts
forever snarling around me (all of whom
by rights should be extinct).
And her above all others, intoxicating blonde
I would follow anywhere.
I wish to be like her: small as my own hand,
able to curl beneath her skirt
to press my lips against her without crushing her.
Able to sleep in a bed that was made for us.
Able to slip inside this skyscraper
instead of scaling it
like a hunted squirrel, a homeless drifter.
I'm too big for this land,

(continued)

but you drugged me, dragged me here
without a clue what to do with me.
So now you've got a rampage on your hands.
I'm the last raging thing between progress
and the boundless sky
the last of my kind in a world where all the biggest things
have been felled.
And I don't care what happens anymore.
I only want to hold her here at the top of all things,
so come on now, throw everything at me.
Come on, you armored beetles, you dark shapes on the horizon.
Come on, you spitting bees.
I can swat you from sky with a single swipe
—do your worst.

KONG, STILL CONSCIOUS, REFLECTS ON HIS VISIT TO NEW YORK

by Jimmy Grist

for the poet William Trowbridge

I lay, as I am prone to lying, motionless—for a time.

In my ears was a sort of murk, through which blunted sounds echoed from nowhere and everywhere. I heard their whining sirens, their murmuring crowds, and something pithy about beauty from he who brought me here; here to this continent, to this city, careening eventually to this unnatural flat earth. I let my eyes remain shut, as some perspectives were not worth taking, though a part of me feared blindness. Tears had been beaten from me by the impact, and they could have just as easily been my jellied vitreous.

My body was certainly crushed, as were those beneath mine. It was an inauspicious place to be crippled. The tower, that wasp-ridden peak I'd failed to conquer and the axis of their phallocentrism, cast a cold shadow over my form. Extrasensorily, I could perceive their wee flashbulbs and vehicles, and the ripples of their voices. The voices particularly, incessantly.

I had cratered the asphalt in my own image, and my figure in their stone was nearly a place I could belong. I like to think this the real reason I lay for so long. No one had gifted me persuasion or occasion to rise. No one was going to do so.

I had never contemplated my own end, it seeming distant and irrelevant as the storms that form over the sea off my island. Yet in spite of my reluctance, there it was. The end hovered overhead, billowing with menace, stirring up my figurative beaches and eroding the face of my mountain. Without a cave in which to skulk, I was forced to think away the rain.

This seemed the first fitting time in my life for an introspective discussion of what would come next. Without intention, I had outrun instinct to find that I had no *plans*, per se, for the hereafter. But try as I might, a satisfying statement about death could not be had—for every valid thought dissipated when pursued, and every supposition was discredited by experience. On the cynical hand, should this be the *end* end—by which I mean the end of all me—I should hardly call myself satisfied. Much to the contrary, with due respect to all I had known and tasted in life.

At home in the tropics it was readily apparent, but even in their megalopolis it was true: there had always been an element of the prelapsarian to my existence. Like the pastoral literature favored among those urbanites, but with bone piercings and tyrannosaurs. Alas, what savage ceremonials were held in my honor. What skirmishes I waged with those rival king lizards. These people professing science should have understood the relativity of an act like *grazing*. For some it involved idylls, flour mills, rumination. For others it involved the wet *snickety-snap* that comes from unscrewing a dinosaur's head.

It's apparent to me now that these cultured little apes didn't see the similarities. In their bookishness, they delineated a false dichotomy—the bucolic and *the exotic*. And of the latter, I was a grotesque example. My arrival was not, it turns out, as a wonder of the natural world; but as a horror thereof. Something to be prodded and cajoled onto a boat, then maligned and instigated onstage. Shackled. Berated. The biggest of all, belittled. These lesser simians had it in them to know me, own me, and *name* me.

The dunces. I have no shortage of names for them. Rubes. Spatherdabs. Jackanapes.

At first, they seemed to me not so far removed from the people of my island. But where my islandfolk had reverence, these cityfolk had gall. Where my islanders saw me with humbling religiosity, these *citizens* saw crimson exploitation. Where my people called me king, these people called me—!

I could not utter it, for the very phonetics insulted. The raw sound of it was a slur, vile and monosyllabic.

It was here, fixated on their debasing language, that the vine of my thought snagged. But where my intellect stuck, my vehemence flourished. I seethed at them and their wilted winter, and seething kept my spirit ablaze. Even while the heat floated up from my body, my furor was my phlogiston. And as I lay beyond time in my capsule of combustible hatred, they attached machines to my inanimate corpus for its removal. I had been shackled in life, and so it seemed was to be shackled in death.

They lassoed my wrists and ankles with fat cords. The restraints terminated at the tip of stilted machines, laughable *cranes* wheeled rather than winged, as un-avian as could be imagined. Constructs singing songs of blackest smoke. Yet though the cables were resilient and the engines unreal, they overprided themselves and the products of their hands. My physicality was indisputable. It was my freight, after all, that had done the damage of my fall—not their bi-winged annoyances. My mass shuddered the creaking motors and their grumbling operators. Their whole endeavor was unnerved. And despite their efforts to the opposite, I lay undisturbed.

With the treatment of my corpse, I was finally given insight as to what awaited in the hereafter. Here was a disrespected end, bland and mechanical like the world that produced such pale, sunless people. And with body discrete from mind, I felt I had no preoccupation to keep me from waiting. My bulk had won me a paltry, momentary victory. But they would remove me somehow, even if it meant letting me succumb to slow rot and carting my bones from their city. For someone still inexplicably conscious, as I was, I need not explain this idea's lack of appeal.

But for now, their engines retreated. After some minutes unapproached, my fears did the same. I thought then with ambivalence of my unwilling companion: the fair one, the canary-headed friend. She had been a fixation of mine, admittedly, from the moment I parted the treetops and saw her bound at my altar. If I had known then the sensation of being shackled, would I have acted differently? Would I still have palmed her, as a possession, and carried her around like the shiniest shell? But then I meant only to protect, certainly, from the local brutes and the foreign pests.

Oh, she was like a drop of sun. *Musa paradisiaca*, a genuine plantain. In a sense I've not had, she gave me companionship there in the mountains. She saw that I was gentle, if provokable, and she understood. Even as I was subdued by their trickery, there was something apologetic in her hairless face. For what more could a great ape ask?

Freed temporarily—and pursued—I only sought her out in their city because I knew not where else to turn. Was it foolish for me to seek aid from one who had already proven powerless against their greed and disrespect? Undoubtedly. But I was a *sucker*, to borrow their term, one who sucks. A sucker for the romantic. I believed...

Well, I can't say *what* I believed.

Perhaps that too, in a roundabout way, was my present existential dilemma.

It had occurred to me more than once *before* my fall that I could have expired already, and that this American life had been the beginning of an unacknowledged afterlife. What was *she* if not heavenly muse, seraphim? What was their gray sprawl if not soulless absolution, a paved *purgatorio*? Without realizing it, I could be lying in a ravine back home, on my island, having slipped on moss and broken my neck or been caught unawares by a coordinated tyrannosaur strike. Certain vines had looked notably weak of late, and it was none too farfetched to imagine one giving way as I trusted to its swing.

Other possibilities arose. Perchance I had ventured into the sea and wound up speared on a coral reef, drowned in the undertow, or sucked into the abyss by a chill leviathan. Could an affliction have ravaged me? Something foodborne? Stemming from the possibility that I had been long dead, it followed naturally that I may in fact still be alive. What assurance did I have that this misadventure was not just a fever dream, and that my mind was not just flitting madly about within itself while my physical form lay snoozing in a nest of leaves?

It was with impeccable dramatic timing that the humans began a new activity. Unable to move me wholesale, they took it upon themselves to hack me into more manageable bits. As one would expect, the corporeal sensation of bodily mutilation poked any number of irreparable holes into my "It was all a dream" hypothesis.

With the same carelessness characteristic of their tongues, they began the prolonged and arduous effort of dismantling me. At several of my joints, I felt the itching bite of their tools: clawlike adzes, noisy pneumatic pokers, and long warbling sheets of metal that two men would tug back and forth, back and forth, tidal. Above my ankles they cut. Into my inner elbows and thighs. Against the grain of my hairy throat. My dermis peeled back before them, and the tenacious hair was sucked into the cuts and clotted, tinted red. Their teeth snagged on my muscle, became lodged, and even fresh laborers found themselves unable to continue the motion. All this without reaching my bone.

With little delay they roped me again. This time, there was unmasked brutality in the bonds they attached: graceless chains with links the size of coconuts. Two or three men at a time looped rings around my limbs, wedging them down into the saw wounds. And then they retrieved their engines. Not the tall, ill-balanced cranes—but the trucks and tanks and others for towing. They ran the chains to hitches and cleared the street. My brain must have been slowing significantly, for it was only as I felt a deep-seated tug from all directions that I realized: their intent was to draw me.

It was one of their most sinister modes of execution. Anchored force would be exerted by their vehicles, measured in units of equine power. And with enough application my arms and legs were to tear from their sockets and be dragged, disjointed, across their abrasive concrete to the city's limits. It was possible my torso would continue to thwart them, and I could will my blood to flow torrential on their busy city streets. But being drawn as planned, I would be the more powerless—stripped of limbs to shackle.

So though my body could do naught, I consolidated my consciousness against the rumble of their machines. Should I be rent asunder, my mind would remain concerted. The chains tightened and yanked, and cut to the quick my exposed tissue. My arms and legs were cranked. Something in my spine cracked, and my cranium jumped out the distance of one vertebrae. The power of their engines rattled through me, shaking loose the meat withheld by their taut metal. Bodily death felt as an inverted birth—slow molecular growth rivaled by the curtest shredding of all that was—and I doubted my quasi-survival.

Yet somehow, against their exertions I kept my bodily tenacity.

The humans were not done. They allowed me a brief respite for their deliberation. I knew what would come next. I had not spent long in their world, the realm of mustard gas and gunpowder, but I had seen enough to understand the extent of their technology. For all intents and purposes, I was an unwanted mountain amid their avenues. And they had a way of moving mountains.

It was a clumsy way. Unpredictable. Unadulterated. The only thing between trinitrotoluene's employer and giblets was a mid-length fuse, and I imagined their street and structures would sustain collateral damage. But my obduracy demanded *dynamite*.

They were a long time clearing the streets of civilians. The sunrise that saw me felled had swooped around the sky and disappeared behind their skyscrapers. But the sidewalks eventually emptied, leaving only a smattering of experts— demolitions men, civil engineers, custodial crew. They were much quicker in establishing barriers of stone and sand.

They bore into my side with a mammoth drill and inserted a bundle of explosives. A pair in gleaming hardhats carefully unraveled the gossamer fuse, then skittered around a building corner with the plunger in tow. This moment may very well have been the most ignoble treatment of all. I had been gored beneath the arm and plugged up with a log of dynamite; and rather than the fiercely intimate contact of saws and labor, there was only a thin impersonal line trailing from me to my demolisher, who hid behind artifice. I wanted to groan, but couldn't find it in such deflated lungs. To return to my earlier analogy of death as typhoon—I felt then as if I had been stationed all along in its calm, unnerving eye. But now the cyclone shifted, and I was in the storm's path.

The blast was like a thunder clap behind my ribcage, nearer to earth than ever it should be. The flash popped and lifted my right half off the ground. The sound reverberated between the walls, bouncing up and stirring the low clouds. Gravel and grit burst from the prick in my side, splattering surfaces and shattering windows. The coagulation liquefied anew. That patch of hair turned to dust. The skin cracked and disintegrated. My body lurched, collapsed, and smoked from this newfound, charred hole.

Thus it went. They blew me to their proverbial smithereens, to their ironical kingdom come. Every failed severance became an entry point for their endless stream of concussive fire, their chemical twigs snapping with such unbridled force. And then they returned with their hands, and finely detailed my demise. An explosion here and there, then a little off the top. The foreman barked orders like a four-legged feral. Just saw through that hank of curling flesh. Take a sledge to the ulna. Drop a wrecking ball on that damnable patella.

I entered a state of anti-bodily shock. Paradoxically, I was not present for my burial preparation. As my mass dissolved, so did their difficulty. Smaller units of *me* were thrust into dump trucks, tethered onto flatbeds, and lugged to their trainyard. I filled all the cars of a freight train, my body parsed out linearly. My center was gone. Here was a parade of nullified ferocity: muscles without might— eyes without sight—indeterminate wads of cauterized meat—a petrified snarl, hardly intelligible and obscenely fanged.

The grisly transport found its way to a landfill beyond the city's limits. It was their idea of the natural world, flat and dry and without canopy. The falsest representation of what I knew to be true. In great pits, they stowed me like the ruins of a past best forgotten. The evidence of a past ancestry, or—the more disheartening for them—of past fealty.

There I lay, just as I did after my fall, only buried and disaggregate and neutralized. But still motionless, oh so motionless, for a time.

It seemed as if that would be my end. Finally, for all the wondering, here my questions were answered. The end was to be a continuation of laying motionless, undisturbed. After the things the humans had done, a part of me cannot say it was disappointed for whatever solace—even were it void of rectitude.

But another part of me still, *still* refused to accept this as the point of termination. How obtuse an ending. How poorly wrought, I thought.

It had happened that way before. When they surrounded me with their fiery slings, I groped for a handhold and used it to rise wrathful from their earth. I scaled their steepest peak, rooted myself at the top, and roared a disruption of their entire civilization. My proudest moment yet, wherein I towered over their tower, and they were them but I was *me*. Defiant. Ruling. Though when they pelted me with their glowing brambles, their toxic words and tracer rounds, I succumbed.

That was all to be expected.

But given another chance—though who was I to assume another chance? A regent, that's who. A bloody vengeful monarch. I didn't need to be *given* another go. I took what I wanted, always in balance, and what in their bastardized nation-state gave them the right to overcome my decree? *This* time—nothing hypothetical about it—*this time* would be different. They would buzz around me once more, gnatlings that they are—yet their infinite bites would be rendered infinitesimal. I had seen the end they feared. I had breathed the very loam they loathed and to which they were doomed to return. And I knew my limits, had seen them violated, and finally knew with dark certainty that the limits of life and death did not exist. The body they thought broken could break no further. The spirit they thought departed was too enlarged, too embittered. My might had not expired. The humans would be hard pressed to deter me. They would be unable to cut me down. What was my goal? I no longer had any escape to make, any thing to protect. This time, I had palmed nothing and no one to stop me.

Or nothing to distract me. There was only rage. Rage filled me, rabid rage. It was rage that stoked the fires of my soul. *Rage*—a guttural growl of a word, a majestically expressive onomatopoeia of incontestable anger. The horned rage of one unjustly punished; the smoldering rage of one abducted; the haunted rage of one betrayed. Rage had freed me from their shackles once before. Rage would free me from death's pernicious bosom.

With quiet attrition, I reinstated governance over my ligaments. Those unsevered bowed in servitude. Though my veins had gone stagnant and clotted thick, I had no want of them. They became in my limbs like branches, and my muscle wiggled and squirmed and *clung* all at once to two skeletons.

Dirt crumbled from my reconstituted bulk as, for the second time, I rose enraged from their earth. I pounded my undying chest in the moonlight, and the beat of my fist echoed in halls once filled by a heart.

MEANWHILE, BACK AT THE LAB

by John Grey

Mad scientist in the windmill down the street
still uses guinea pigs in his experiments.
With his wild grey hair, wire lab coat,
frenzied speech including references to "being God",
he's such a Universal Pictures cliché.
He injects them with his "Fountain of Youth" serum.
Excuse me if I don't go gaga at the prospect
of everlasting rodents.

Loony doctors poke and prod their rat collection.
Just what the average household needs…
radioactive vermin.
Some try their insanity out on rabbits.
So cute and cuddly now has the strength of ten men.
Be first on your block
with a fur coat that stops bullets.

But chimps, that's a different story.
We're talking simian, higher primates,
brains in the range of 282-500 cc,
upright walk, able to carry objects in hands,
use tools and symbols…
we don't bother with guinea pigs or rats or rabbits…
we work on men exclusively.

Ham's Poem

by John Grey

When I think of all the chimps
that have never known a world
outside of rainforest canopy,
whose instinct tells them
the slow brown Congo river
is the outer boundary of all life—

not a one of them
has trained for months
at an air-force base,
pulled levers
in response to flashing blue lights,
been punished with electric shocks
or rewarded with banana pellets—

they only know communities,
alpha male, dominant female,
a hierarchal order that
defines their place within it—
no shiny white laboratories,
merely nests in tree forks,
no gathering of the best and brightest,
just parents and siblings huddling close—

(continued)

yes, when I think of the chimps
that live and die and familiar jungle,
that live off the fruits,
swing from the vines,
cackle together in that great primate chorus—

not a space mission
between the lot of them,
no project Mercury,
no Cape Canaveral blast-off,
no sub-orbital flight,
no splash down in the Atlantic ocean—

when I think of those chimps,
which is often,
I have a hard time
thinking of me.

AN ODE TO HAM

by James Frederick William Rowe

Intrepid gallant of the genus *Pan*
You were tasked to pierce the heavens high
Filling your charge with such dash and élan
Your hands were first to wave the world goodbye!
And when you returned to the atmosphere
The commander was first to shake your hand
In honour of the dangers you withstood!
Triumph is yours, astrochimp without fear
Without whom our rockets would ne'er be manned
You turned our space-flight dreams from should to would!

WONDERLAND BY NIGHT

by Sarah Hilary

I was with Johnson on his last day on earth. We were in Bernard's Surf, slurping oysters and beer. Bert Kaempfert was playing on the radio. Johnson was hitting on a brunette with a tired face who wasn't impressed by his stories. He was saying how he was in the Space Program. She didn't believe him, of course. This was early '61; hardly anyone was talking about the Program.

Johnson didn't like long silences. When he got to a gap in the conversation, he had to stuff it full of words, like a mobster packing pool balls into a sock. When the brunette began to yawn, he switched to something like the truth: "I train monkeys."

For "train", read torture.

It was Johnson who set the voltage, deciding how many watts were too many, how much was enough to make the chimps dance.

The chimps hated Johnson. You could see it in their faces. I wasn't much in love with him myself. A little man that fate had made a demagogue, a small-minded monster. You don't believe me, ask the chimps. Ask Minnie.

That's Minnie, with the wise eyes, sad.

I saw a picture of Edith Piaf once. She had the same eyes, all of her soul in there.

Minnie is Ham's understudy. She's the only female in the Program. Ham's on his way to being famous, our first astrochimp. Minnie's destined for an Air Force chimp-breeding project. I know, ain't we the heroes of the Western World? Darwin would've loved us.

Minnie's going make a great mom, though. Best I've ever seen. You ask me, she's going to be here long after the rest of us are gone.

I sometimes sit and look her, and I think, "You've travelled further than anyone. Further than Ham." She looks back at me and I feel bad for being all serious, so I say, "You're far out, Min. That's all I'm saying. Far out."

All this time, training for space travel, but never leaving home. Never getting to see where her mate ends up, what's out there, all those miles away.

I said this to Johnson once. He just laughed and upped the voltage. "Dance for Uncle Sam, you little banana-crapping bastards."

Minnie hates to see Ham hurt. She shakes her fists at Johnson whenever the guy gets close. He'll stand in front of her cage, cracking nuts in the hard palms of his hands and tossing them up into his mouth. I sometimes have trouble figuring out who's the monkey, her or him.

Minnie's the only female who can't walk away from Johnson. He spends hours talking to her, never anything nice. I remember this one time he talked to her about Laika, the Russian space dog. He pulled a chair close to her cage and sat, feet up. He had small feet, and wore sneakers in the lab.

Minnie turned her back on him, but it didn't put Johnson off.

"Laika was a stray. Mongrel bitch, part husky. We called her Muttnik."

The chimps were getting fretful, the way they always did around Johnson. He wasn't bothered, kept running off his mouth. "She got all hot and stressed up there, in space."

Johnson made a noise like rain hitting big leaves, a sizzling sound that scared Minnie into her corner. "Hot dog." He kicked at her cage. "Fries."

"Cut it out," I told him.

I should've done something, but I didn't. As Johnson kept reminding me, I don't have shit for authority in this place.

It's my job to keep the cages clean, feed Minnie and the others, change the straw they sleep on. Johnson paid me less attention than he paid the chimps.

He was training the chimps to perform basic tasks, like pushing a lever within five seconds of seeing a flashing blue light. If they failed to push it in time, they got an electric shock to the soles of their feet. It was what we had to do, but Johnson needn't have got such a kick out of it.

Once Minnie went into the chimp-breeding program, Johnson would take her babies away, one by one. Make them dance. She knew it. Call it premonition, call it female intuition. Maybe just call it the smell of Ham's feet, burning. That was all the clue she needed, to what Johnson was going to do.

He'd have made her watch it, too. When he attached the electrodes, adjusted the voltage. She knew how much was too much, when the twitching turned to jolting and the jolting to screeching.

In Bernard's Surf, Bert Kaempfert was playing on the radio: *Wonderland by Night*.

"I train monkeys." Johnson scratched himself with a pool cue.

"Get outta here," the brunette told him. When he didn't, she got up and walked away.

Johnson went back to the lab. He often slept there; we both did.

I liked the quiet, and the way the windows stuffed with stars, like the whole world was lit up. Like *we* were the distant galaxy and out there—*out there* was where it was all happening. Exploration, discovery, unity—you name it.

Anyway, that was it.

Johnson's last night on earth.

The next morning they asked me, "Was he depressed?"

"He never mentioned it."

"Must've been," they said, "to take that way out."

"I guess."

"What a way to go."

They didn't like the smell, wrinkling their noses.

Johnson, fried.

I said, "Can I get back to the chimps?"

Minnie was very quiet, holding the bars of her cage.

To look at it, you'd have thought the cage was locked.

I caught her eye as I re-fastened the latch. Bright eyes, like the brunette in the bar. Too bright to be fooled by Johnson. All her soul in there, shining out.

I thought, *They'll keep this quiet, you won't see this on the news.*

I was right. It was like Johnson never existed.

Expunged, is the word. I looked it up.

Years later, when she passed away, they laid Minnie to rest with Ham at the International Space Hall of Fame in Alamogordo, New Mexico.

Unofficially, Johnson was cremated. They shot his remains into space, on a shuttle that never made it back. He's burning there still, a star that's taking centuries to die. A dim, dancing speck in the night's sky.

MAC AND STEVE

by Terry Alexander

"Right this way Mr. Cooper. Mr. Smithson has been expecting you." The butler was an odd duck, bald on top with bushy hair around his ears and the thickest eyebrows possible on a human being. They looked like two fuzzy caterpillars took up residence on his forehead. "May I take your pet while the two of you discuss business?"

"This is McBride. He's my partner, not a pet." Steve pulled a peanut from his jacket pocket and passed it to the monkey riding on his shoulder. "Mac is a black-headed Spider Monkey. They're one of the most intelligent members of the ape family." Quick hands took the offered treat. Mac cracked the legume open and quickly devoured the delicacy.

"If you say so, Sir." The butler quickened his pace, leading Steve to a white door at the far side of the room.

"Tell me, Sunshine, do you have a name?" Steve smoothed his hair over the top of his left ear, hiding the upper portion. Years ago in a bar fight in Chile, an unhappy customer bit the upper third away.

"King, James King." He nodded slightly, keeping his eyes glued on Mac.

Mac whinnied like a horse and made some complicated hand signals. A smile crossed Steve's face, he nodded. "Yeah, you're right."

"Did that creature communicate with you?" King's eyes bulged, mouth hanging open. "What did he say?" He recovered his wits quickly.

"He said you're a nervous man, and you haven't been around monkeys before." Steve passed into the large den. A lone man sat behind the desk; a green shaded gambler's lamp illuminated the shiny surface.

"Mr. Cooper, I was hoping you'd accept my invitation." Lucius Smithson jumped to his feet. He limped around the desk, his right hand extended in greeting. "I see you've brought your associate. Please sit down. Would you care for a drink?"

"Naw, I'm good, thanks." Steve collapsed in the overstuffed chair facing the desk. Mac climbed from his shoulder to sit on the chair arm. He turned to Steve, his digits flashing a message.

"Mac said you have a nice place. He'd like to see it in the summer when the fruit trees are bearing."

"Bring him back at harvest, by all means." A wheezing breath passed Smithson's lips. "I want to hire you, Mr. Cooper."

"Is this about the Drummond murder?" Steve pulled a second peanut from his pocket and offered it to Mac. "According to the papers he worked for you. His murder's still a mystery. The man's alone in a storage barn. No windows, no one around, and somebody blasted him."

Smithson nodded. "Levi Drummond was my foreman for two years. He forgot more about the orchard trade than I'll ever learn. Someone killed him over a year ago. The police aren't any closer to closing the case now than they were then. Drummond's kids deserve some closure."

"If you don't mind my saying so, you're a wealthy man. Why are you dabbling in the orchard trade?"

"Retirement, Mr. Cooper. I've left the family business. My son and daughter run Smithson Trucking now." He paused for a moment. "When I was a kid, I spent the summers with my Grandfather. He owned a peach orchard. It was his dream job. I guess a little of his dream rubbed off on me."

"If I take the case, it'll cost you a hundred dollars a day plus expenses." Steve rose from the chair. Mac climbed up his sleeve and rested on his shoulder.

"That's kinda steep." Smithson opened the lap drawer of his desk. He pulled five one hundred dollar bills from a money box. "That should keep you going for a few days. Come back when you need more. Are you familiar with Preston?"

"I worked a case here a few months back." Steve folded the bills and slid them in his shirt pocket. "Peanuts ain't cheap, you know." He walked toward the door. "Where did you pick up your wound?"

"D-Day, Omaha Beach. I was one of the lucky ones, I lived through it." Smithson nodded. "We all have our wounds, Mr. Cooper. Just like the ones you received in Korea."

"I'll be in touch." Steve's hand closed on the brass knob. The door opened easily at his touch. "Did Drummond piss anybody off before he was killed?"

"David Russell, but I don't think he'd do anything like this."

"You never know, Mr. Smithson. You never know." The door closed silently behind him.

◊ ◊ ◊ ◊ ◊

"I can't get over that monkey. The way it signs is just weird." Blackheart Benny Cavanaugh pulled the Drummond file from his cabinet and tossed it on the battered desk. Benny served as Preston's coroner. To those that knew him well, he was Blackheart Benny. "That'll be fifty bucks."

"My God, that's highway robbery. You only charged thirty-five last time I was here." Steve opened the file to a stack of black and white photographs. Different angles of a prone man, a dark stain covered his chest. "And I've told you before, Mac's my partner. He belongs to himself."

"Inflation hurts everybody. What can I say?" Blackheart smiled. "Drummond was killed with a .32 revolver, close up. Powder burns all over his shirt." Benny pulled a bag of peanuts from his coat pocket and offered them to Mac. The monkey opened the bag, and devoured one peanut at a time. "Didn't you tell me your partner found Mac, when the two of you were in Chile? What happened to him?"

"He's dead." A frown crossed Steve's face. "Who found the body?"

"One of the pickers, guy named Richards or Richardson. That should be in the file or don't you like to read." Benny took the opposite chair, his elbows resting on the scarred desktop. "Funny thing about that, Drummond walked to the barn about seven that morning. They found him inside thirty minutes later. All the pickers said no one went to the barn but him."

The monkey tapped Steve's shoulder, and made a series of hand gestures. Steve nodded.

"What'd he say?" Benny asked.

"He said that whoever killed Drummond was waiting for him in the barn." He pulled a magnifying glass from his jacket and studied the photographs. "He also said you talk too much."

"Humph," Blackheart grunted. He cast a hard look at Mac. The monkey opened his mouth and showed his teeth. "That's what Captain Martin thinks, but no one left the barn and none of the workers heard a shot."

"They didn't find the weapon. I suppose they did a through search." Steve closed the file with a snap. He reached for his wallet and peeled a fifty from the interior.

"Mansfield led the search. You know how that guy is?" Blackheart stuffed the greenback in his pants pocket.

"Yeah, he's a regular bull." Mac hopped to Steve's shoulder. He crushed the empty bag into a wad and threw it in the trash can. The tiny hands moved like lightning. "Yeah, that's where we're going."

Blackheart shook his head. "Is he really signing, or is this just a big con?"

"What do you think?" Steve checked his hair on the left side, making sure it covered his ear. "You owe me, Benny. There wasn't anything useful in that file."

Steve and Mac walked into Justin Smithson's fruit storage barn an hour later. The sunlight struggled to reach twenty feet inside the structure, leaving the majority of the interior in perpetual gloom. "Climb up to the rafters. See what you can find. I'll check down here and see if Mansfield's goons missed anything."

Mac nodded and leaped to the ceiling runner. His prehensile tail acted as another hand, as the monkey climbed higher. A smile touched Steve's lips. He closed his eyes for a moment, recalling the police photograph. "The body was there." His eyes scanned the dirt floor, and walked to a support post near the entrance. Steve studied the floor and the condition of the post, a faint stain discolored the wood a foot above the ground. "I didn't see that in the picture. It could be anything, doesn't have to be a blood."

A loud shriek sounded from the rafters.

"What did you find?" Steve climbed to his feet. His left knee popped audibly.

Mac appeared within seconds, a chrome snub-nosed .32 gripped in his tail. He dropped the pistol in Steve's hands, flipped in the air and landed on his feet. His fingers moved quickly.

"Slow down a little. You're talking too fast."

Mac's expressive face wrinkled into a frown, as he slowed his hand gestures. "Really," Steve arched his eyebrows. "The roof air vents. Could someone my size climb up there and crawl through them to the outside?"

Mac shook his head. Steve pressed the cylinder release and counted the loads. One bullet had been fired. "Could I reach the vent?" Mac shook his head again.

"Can I help you?" A thick man with a crooked nose, wearing a plaid shirt and bib overalls leaned against the barn door. "I saw your car and figured you might be lost or something."

"Naw, we're working for Mr. Smithson." Steve slipped the .32 in his jacket pocket. "We're looking into the Drummond murder. Who are you again?"

"David Russell. I own the orchard about a mile up the road."

Steve nodded. "Do you remember where you were when Drummond got whacked?"

"Levi, his first name was Levi." Russell stared at Mac. "What kind of monkey is that?"

"Black-headed Spider." Steve answered. "You didn't answer my question."

"It was harvest season. I was getting my crop gathered. I had my pickers out in the field." He rubbed his nose with a scarred hand. "I saw a few Monkeys when I was stationed in Africa during the war. They're smart. You can train them to do almost anything."

"How well did you know Levi?" Steve used the dead man's first name.

"He was one of my best pals. We grew up together, went through school and joined the military after Pearl Harbor. Man really knew his way around an orchard."

"What're your feelings toward Smithson?"

"He's a sorry piece of trash. My orchard is my life. Smithson offered to buy me out and I wasn't in the mind to sell. He bought the place next to mine and hired all the most experienced hands." Russell shook his head. "He paid better wages; really put me between a rock and a hard place." He turned to leave. "You know what the kicker is? Smithson doesn't care if he shows a profit. It's his hobby."

"He told me his granddad had an orchard when he was a kid."

"Yeah, he did, used it as a cover to run bootleg whiskey." Russell hesitated at the doorway. "After Clara died, Levi wasn't the same anymore; he drank too much, started reliving the war, seeing dead people in his dreams. I hope you find his killer." He disappeared into the bright sunshine outside. "But I'd pull out of this job if I were you."

Steve eyed the door for several seconds. "What do you think?" he asked Mac.

The monkey shook his head and made a series of hand movements.

"Me, too, and if I couldn't get through the roof vent, he damn sure couldn't." He pulled a peanut from his pocket and passed it to Mac. "What say we find a good restaurant and sit down and talk this over?"

Mac nodded, displaying his teeth. He brought his hand to his open mouth several times.

"You're always hungry."

The sign above the wood frame building read 'Shirley's Fine Food'. Steve parked his old Chrysler next to a new model Ford Edsel, one of the hardtop convertibles. The roof lifted up from the body and slid into the double hinged trunk. "Looks like someone hit the big time around here."

Mac nodded in agreement.

"Let's get some lunch, before we go to the police station. What are you hungry for?"

The monkey shrugged.

"Well, you can make up your mind when we get inside." A small bell above the door chimed as they escaped the afternoon sun. Three men sat at a wall booth drinking coffee. A burly cook wearing a greasy hat and a dirty white apron busied himself at the grill. A dowdy blonde waitress leaned on the counter.

"Hi, Guys," she said. "Grab a seat and I'll be right with you. What are you drinking?"

"Coffee for me and a small glass of water for my friend," Steve answered. He chose the table opposite the coffee drinkers, so he could keep everyone in sight.

"What the hell is that thing?" The cook gawked at Mac. "What the hell are you bringing that chimp in here? Damn thing probably has fleas."

"Mac is a black-haired Spider Monkey. He takes his hygiene very seriously. He's a lot cleaner than a lot of people I know." Steve slid into the booth. Mac stood in the seat across the table.

"Pipe down, Roscoe. Old Mullins brings his dog in here every other day." The blonde approached the table with a steaming cup of coffee and a glass of iced water. "Who gets what?" She asked a dimpled smile on her face.

"Damn it, Shirley, we'll get a bad reputation, if we let everyone bring their pets inside," Roscoe shouted.

"Hell, Roscoe, that little critter may bring a little class to this joint." A chorus of chuckles came from the far table.

Shirley placed a menu on the table. Mac snatched it up. He ran his fingers down the page, stopping at the salads. He pointed to an item and hopped up and down. "Looks like he made his choice," Shirley said. "What about you?"

"Cheese burger, no lettuce, extra pickles."

"You bet. Have it ready in a few minutes." Shirley removed the menu and took the order to the cook.

One of the locals left the table and approached them. "Is the circus coming to town? You fellas some kind of act or something?"

"Nope," Steve smiled. "We're detectives. I'm Steve Cooper. This is McBride. He likes to be called Mac."

"I'm Mike Taylor. You've got to be kidding me, you two are detectives. Where's Joe Friday?" The old timer laughed. "What are you boys investigating?"

"Good joke." Steve joined in the laughter. "We're looking into Levi Drummond's murder."

An ashen pallor colored Mike's face, his eyes widened in surprise. He closed his open mouth and swallowed. "Levi Drummond," he repeated. "Mind if I ask who hired you?"

"Justin Smithson."

His eye quivered with a nervous tic. Mike leaned on the table. "Take my advice. Eat up and get the hell out of here. We don't cotton to your kind around here."

"And what kind is that?" Steve blew the steam away from the cup and sipped the hot brew.

"The kind that snoops around where they ain't wanted." Mike regained his composure. "Give Smithson his money back and get out of here quick. Don't find yourself here after sundown." He turned and stalked back to his table.

Steve glanced at the opposite table. Mike quickly engaged in whispered conversation with his buddies. Within seconds, hostile stares were directed their way.

"The locals don't care for us," he whispered to Mac.

Mac nodded, his fingers tracing symbols in the air.

"We can't pull out. We need the money." Steve shook his head. "Why is the food taking so long?"

Shirley carried a battered coffee pot to the far table. "Care for a refill, boys?"

The man they spoke to earlier motioned her over and whispered in Shirley's ear. She immediately cast Steve and Mac a hard look. Turned to the pot-bellied man and nodded. The group rose from the booth. The large man pulled a five dollar bill from his pocket and tossed it on the table.

Shirley crossed the floor toward them, her face pinched in a frown. "You two finish your drinks and get out."

"What about the food?" Steve asked.

"Kill the order, Roscoe," she shouted. "Our guests ain't staying."

"Damn it, Shirley. It's nearly done."

"You eat it then, our customers are leaving." Her left hand fisted on her hip. "Get out of here, now. Get out of Preston."

"I always heard that country people were a friendly bunch." Steve reached for his wallet.

"We are mostly. Keep your money. You got that from Smithson and his money ain't wanted around here." Shirley turned away, striding toward the counter.

Three shotgun blasts erupted outside. Steve dropped to the floor, his hand circling the grip of the .32 snub. The sounds of car doors slamming and gravel thrown from rear tires soon followed. "What the hell is going on here?" Steve climbed to his feet, the revolver gripped tightly in his fist.

"The boy's are just giving you a little extra incentive to leave. Take it from me, next time they won't shoot in the air." Roscoe circled the counter, an old fashioned double barreled twelve gauge with cocked hammers centered on Steve.

"I get the message." Steve stuffed the pistol in his pocket. "We're pulling out." Mac hopped to his shoulder as they walked toward the door.

"Don't hang out around here," Roscoe shouted. "Did you hear me, Boy? Get out while you can."

The bell chimed above Steve's head as the pair left the café. He walked slowly to his car. Mac jumped from his shoulder and scampered to the passenger side while Steve climbed behind the wheel.

Mac turned to face him. His fingers moved with lightning speed.

"Yeah, they know who killed Levi Drummond, and they don't want us to find out who did it."

The monkey flashed more intricate patterns in the air.

"No, we're going to stick with this case. I want to find out what they're hiding."

Mac opened his mouth. He touched his lips three times in quick succession.

"Yeah, I know you're hungry." He pulled several peanuts from his pocket and tossed them on the seat. "That should hold you until we find a place to get some chow."

◊ ◊ ◊ ◊ ◊

"We're lucky we found a grocery store that hadn't heard about us, or we'd be going hungry." Steve parked the Chrysler in front of room thirteen of the Regents Motel, a run down building on the outskirts of town. He'd spotted the Edsel in his mirrors on three occasions since they left the café.

Mac climbed through the car window and perched on the roof. A grunting noise came from his lips.

"Yeah, I saw them, too." He lifted two bags of groceries and carried them to the door. "Hey, unlock this, will ya." He dangled the key from his left hand.

The monkey snatched the key away and slid it in the lock, the door swung open easily. A musty odor filled Steve's nostrils. He fought back a sudden urge to sneeze. "Get my pistol out of the glove box. Might need it if visitors come calling."

Mac scampered to the vehicle. He returned moments later with Steve's .38 and his jacket. He hopped to the bed with both items and laid them on the pillows.

"We'll drop the .32 off at the police station tomorrow. Talk to Mansfield, see if he has any useful information."

Mac shook his head, his mouth open teeth showing. His fingers moved swiftly.

Steve glanced at the open door. Mike and his buddies from the café blocked the late afternoon sun.

"Can I help you?"

"Maybe, I didn't make myself clear down at Shirley's. It's not healthy for you here." Mike moved into the room. He swung a ham sized fist at Steve's head.

He ducked under the looping blow and landed a hard strike to the intruder's bulging gut. The breath burst from the big man's lungs. He bent double holding his stomach. Steve drove a knee into Mike's flabby chin. The pot-gutted man fell forward on his face, blood bubbling from his split lip.

A brass-knuckled right landed on Steve's cheek. Stars exploded in his head, the flesh split to the bone, gushing blood. A man wearing thick glasses grabbed his hair and drove a fist into Steve's nose.

Mac leaped on the third man's shoulder. His sharp teeth closed on his cauliflower ear, biting a chunk away. Steve fell to his knees, unable to see through the tears misting his eyes. Blood covered his cheek and face. Thick Glasses kicked him hard in the jaw. Steve flopped to his back and lay still.

Mac jumped to the bed, his hands closed around the pistol grip. A solid fist landed on his jaw, knocking him to the floor. "Damned Monkey." The man wiped blood from his ear. "Bruce, get Mike on his feet and get him to the car."

Rough work-scarred hands fisted in Steve's hair and pulled his head off the floor. "Take this as a friendly reminder. Forget this Drummond business and get out of town in the morning."

"Ernie, give me a hand. I can't budge this tub of lard," Bruce shouted. "Hurry up. We need to get out of here."

"Remember what I said. Forget about Preston, and get out while you're still able." Ernie released his grip. Steve's head bounced on the pastel linoleum.

◊ ◊ ◊ ◊ ◊

Steve gritted his teeth as Mac stuck the needle through his flesh and stitched the split cheek together. "We're definitely on to something," he said. "I need to talk to one of those good old boys."

Mac tied a knot in the string and bit the remainder of thread away. The monkey's fingers weaved into motion.

Steve nodded. "Some lettuce and cabbage in the bag; eat all you want." Steve winced as he gained his feet. "I'm gonna clean up. Make me a sandwich, will ya." He stumbled to the restroom.

He gazed at his reflection. The beginning of a fresh bruise colored his chin. Dried crimson circled his mouth. Steve wet a washcloth and dabbed the blood away. He opened his mouth and pressed his bottom teeth gently. "That one's a little wobbly." He tossed the red stained cloth into the sink.

"Finish eating." He emerged from the bathroom. "We're going to cruise town for a little while. We might run into those guys again."

A chill wind blew from the north, as they drove the main drag of Preston. Steve spotted the Edsel parked with three other vehicles in front of Sonny's bar. He flipped a U at the city limits and circled back through town.

"Those fellas are likely in there enjoying a cold beer and drinking to our health." Steve passed the tavern and turned right at the next corner.

Mac grunted, his tongue protruding from his mouth. His fingers moved in precise gestures.

"We're not going in. We need to park somewhere and keep an eye on the door." Steve licked his bruised lips. "I want to talk to one of those boys one on one."

Mac nodded. His small hand closed on Steve's sleeve and tugged. He pointed across the street. A gas jockey was locking up the DX station for the night.

"Good idea. We'll park next to the building." Steve nodded. "That'll give us the perfect vantage point."

They parked in the shadows next to the red and white structure. Steve patted his pockets wishing for a cigarette and reminding himself he quit for a reason. He sat quietly as dusk turned to full dark.

Mike staggered outside an hour later. The fat man nearly fell when he stepped off the curb and leaned on the hood for support. Finding his keys hiding in his pocket, he opened the door and settled behind the wheel.

Mac grunted, his hands swatted the dash.

"I see him." Steve turned the key, the Chrysler's engine roared to life. He popped the clutch and burned rubber across the empty street. "Get in." He pulled the .38 from the seat and leveled it at Mike's head. "We need to talk."

"What..." Mike gulped. "What are you doing here?"

"Get in, fat boy, or I'll drop you right where you are." Steve cocked the hammer. "Move, right now."

"Look, I'm sorry about what we did, but we can't have someone poking their nose into this. Levi Drummond is dead. Let him rest in peace." Mike lifted his hands. His drunkenness vanished in an instant. "We can't let the truth come out." His hand lingered on the door handle.

"Shut up and get inside," Steve mumbled. "We're going for a little drive."

Mike swallowed nervously and lowered himself into the car. "Look, we had a reason for what we did. You don't need to be dredging up any information on

Drummond."

"Mac, get in the back seat. Grab the .32, if he moves, blow his head off." Steve watched as the monkey clambered over the seat, the double click of the pistol sounded a second later. "He can't miss at that distance. Sit back and enjoy the ride."

Mike closed his eyes and nodded. "Where are we going?"

"Back to the fruit barn." The car backed into the highway, Steve pressed the gas pedal to the floor leaving a trail of burned rubber and smoke behind.

◊ ◊ ◊ ◊ ◊

"Get inside," Steve prodded Mike's ribs. "We need to talk." The Chrysler's headlights illuminated the open door and twenty feet inside.

"Look, you need to back off. I'm sorry we beat the hell out of you, but you need to forget about Drummond's murder." Mike leaned against a mid-span support.

"You know who killed Levi Drummond, and you're going to tell me." Steve slipped the .38 into his waistband. He drove a hard fist into Mike's ample gut. The big man fell to his knees, gasping for breath. "Now, who killed Drummond?"

"I can't tell you that. We promised, all of us. Isn't it enough that the man's dead?"

Steve kicked the man's ribs. A barely audible snap came to his ears. Mike gritted his teeth. He rolled on the ground holding his side. "Who killed Levi Drummond?" Steve shouted.

"I can't tell. I can't." Mike cried out. He rolled over and pushed himself up to his knees.

Steve unleashed a straight right that caught the larger man in the mouth. He collapsed in a heap, spitting blood and teeth. "No more, no more," Mike sobbed. "Please, no more."

A warning howl erupted from Mac's lips. Steve turned to see Bruce and Ernie inside the door. The latter trained an automatic on his middle.

"You two don't take hints well." Ernie snarled. "You were told to leave Preston. Take that pistol from your waist and put it on the ground."

Steve moved his hand slowly. His thumb and forefinger squeezed the grip and lifted the .38 clear. He bent and placed the revolver on the uneven soil. Behind him, Mac moved silently into the shadows.

"What are we going to do with these two?" Bruce asked. "What?"

"I don't know." Ernie shook his head. "We'll figure something out."

"We can't kill them. I'm not going through that hell again." Drops of blood flew from Mike's lips.

"We ain't got a choice, Mike. If they live the whole story comes out." Ernie cocked the hammer. "We ain't got a choice."

An animal shriek filled the air. Mac leaped from the rafters, his open mouth closed on Ernie's nose. The teeth sank deep into the soft flesh. "Get this blasted monkey off me," he screamed.

Steve dove into the darkness. His hands closed on his jacket and the .32 revolver inside. He yanked Mike's head back by the hair and pressed the pistol to the fat man's temple. Mac jumped from Ernie's grasping hands, returning to the rafters.

"Now," Steve's raised voice echoed in the barn. "If anyone tries anything, old Mike here is going to be the first one going to hell." He cocked the hammer. "Now which one of you killed Levi Drummond?"

"None of us." Ernie wiped the blood away from his ravaged snout. He centered the pistol on Mike. "I'm sorry, Buddy. I really am."

"Ernie, NO! Please don't do this!" Mike blubbered. "Don't do it."

"You can't do this, Ernie." Bruce grabbed the pistol barrel. "You can't kill Mike, damn it. We've drank coffee together for the last five years."

"Even if you get lucky, and the bullet goes through this bag of guts, I'll kill you before I take my last breath," Steve warned.

"Hell, that peashooter's been in the rafters for over a year, it may not even shoot," Ernie snarled.

"Care to find out?"

"Put the gun down, Ernie," Mike begged. "Please, put the gun down."

"Daddy, put the pistol down." A young woman walked into the barn. "It's over with. In a way I'm glad. The truth will finally come out."

The lights from the Chrysler placed her face in shadow. "Who are you?" Steve demanded. "Why are you here?"

"I killed Levi Drummond." She stepped to the center of the barn and tugged the pistol from Ernie's hand. "I graduated high school last year. The whole class got together for an end of summer party. We came to this barn to drink and make out."

"Thelma, don't say anymore please," Ernie begged. "I don't want you locked away in prison."

"I was drunk. I stumbled outside to puke." She stopped speaking for a moment to dry her eyes. "Levi Drummond showed up. He was mad as hell and ran the rest of the gang off."

"So you killed him for that. You killed him for ruining your party." Steve climbed slowly to his feet, the revolver centered on Ernie's chest.

"I killed Drummond because he raped me."

"I won't let you go to prison." Ernie wrapped his arms around his daughter. He turned to Steve. "I did it. I killed Levi Drummond."

Thelma broke away from her father's embrace. "Drummond found me out back sick as a dog. He was on me before I knew it, tore my pants and underwear away and pinned me to the ground. I tried to fight him off, but I couldn't do it. I was too drunk."

"Don't talk anymore, Baby." Ernie grabbed her hand. "Don't say another word."

"It has to come out. I stole dad's gun and came back to the barn during harvest time. I hid in the rafters early one morning and waited for him to come in here. The trucks were running outside. I knew those engines would cover the noise. I dropped down and shot him in the chest. He kicked for a few minutes then he went all still. I crawled back up top, hid the pistol in the vent and crawled to the roof. I jumped to the ground on the low side and ran through the woods until I got home." She turned to face Steve. "You can take me to jail. I'm ready."

"You have me confused with the police. I'm a private detective." He handed the .32 to Ernie and retrieved his .38 from the ground. "I'd get rid of that, if I were you. Take a torch to it and cut it into small pieces."

"You're not going to tell the cops?" Thelma asked.

"No, you've been through enough. Prison's not the answer here." He turned toward the darkness. "Come on, Mac. It's time to go home."

"How can I thank you for this?" Ernie stepped forward; he held his bleeding nose with one hand and pumped Steve's hand with the other. "After everything we did to you. You're not going to turn Thelma in. How can I thank you?"

"You'll need to see a doctor for that. Makes us even for the brass knuckles. If you're ever in LA, you can buy me a steak dinner."

Mac descended from the darkness to Steve's shoulder, signing with his fingers. "Yeah, we're out of work again, and we'll have to return some of Smithson's money." He walked into the Chrysler's lights, circled to the door and sat behind the wheel. The engine fired up. He reversed the large automobile, made a u-turn and drove away from Preston.

Back Story

by Beth Ann Spencer

Frame 352 of the Patterson film purporting to show a
Bigfoot near Bluff Creek, California

Through the trees a fire winks.
The moths are plentiful as stars,
as the bats wheeling after them
radioing joy.
He is dressed in motley,
his eyes dull coals of fear that flare
with each snapping gust.
In his hands a glinting flask
travels often enough to his mouth
that I begin to thirst.

Why has he come but to search for me,
his strange attractor,
and why have I but to burn
with the bulk of me
his reason down.

Still, I wait through the night,
watch him undress,
and with his pale cock
above its pale wattle
piss out the flames,
watch the moon

lay her bright cape on the river,
drag it west.
Before dawn I go to him,
blow upon the ashes of his dreams
until his eyelids flutter,
then I vanish
leaving my prints
near his groaning blanket.

I am bathing when the jays alert me.
In the time it takes a hawk
to fall upon her prey
I swim to the sandbar
and haul myself into the sun
his lens dishes out.

From myth to possibility
I sear my way.

Bigfoot Takes A Lover

by Beth Ann Spencer

It's not hard to imagine why she did it,
only what took her so long.
We couldn't have lasted a week
in those woods
alone

imagining her at each new sound,
her ripe scent.
She had been alone a long
time. It was summer,
hot.

The town went crazy afterwards.
Any town would.
Love is one thing but this?
We can't stand for it.
Naked

into this world and out. His wife said
Bigfoot unzipped the tent, plucked him up,
carried him off. He was 23,
on his honey-
moon.

No sign of them since. Sometimes we think
we hear them singing, but
that's not possible…a beast craving
a man or vice
versa.

Singing in Place

by Beth Ann Spencer

I call this to the Yeti
inside four walls of avalanche
~ Wislawa Szymborska

I am drunk, what do you expect?
Try as I might, I can hit but one note
at a time. But Yeti, listen to the monks
of Tibet and tell me you don't hear
the voices of your ancestors.

They would tell you, Beware
the urge to show yourself again.
If you returned to these woods
you'd be shot—or sedated, collared
and tracked back home.

The kindness of your face
is no defense, nor your loneliness.
The palace of wisdom
has manacles just your size
whatever it is.

Consider the Lord God Bird,
sixty years among the dying hardwoods,
safer as myth than miracle. Knock
knock, we're all there, chattering
our wonderment. Is that what you want?

(continued)

Yeti, we've got Oprah here,
Yeti, we play FreeCell, wear
the latest brands, harken to catastrophe
between news of the Dow
and smoke signals from the Vatican.

Fly from us while you have time,
while the icecap remains.
On clear nights tune in to the monks
singing in place. Those notes above
the drone? Prayers for weary travelers.

Keep to your castle of snow
and brush away your prints.
Truth is a pathless land.
Each temple has a gun to it.
And an avalanche above, waiting.

THE GREAT GERTIE

by Caroline Cormack

There was a gorilla sitting opposite me. This is less astonishing when you know that I was in her cage at the time.

I hadn't been expecting a gorilla in the cage. She (according to the sign on her truck, her name was Gertie) was supposed to be performing in the big top. Had I known the cage was occupied I probably wouldn't have entered. I say probably because while, ordinarily, whether to enter a gorilla's cage is a fairly easy decision to make, there were men with guns and baseball bats chasing me which meant it wasn't necessarily the worst of my available options.

I wracked my brains for any information I might have learned previously about how to behave around gorillas. Nothing. A finishing school education is worse than useless in these circs.

I didn't have time to think about it much then because I was trying not to panic about sharing a small enclosed space with a huge gorilla, but I was wondering why the men were chasing me. I was up to no good but nothing they could have known about.

The problem with my hiding place (other than the gorilla) was that I wasn't actually hidden. The truck was at the back of the park and the barred side was facing out of the field rather than towards the fairground. It was secluded but anyone walking past would see me.

I heard voices on the other side of the wooden wall of the truck. Gertie could hear them too, and she wasn't pleased.

"Did she go into the truck?"

Gertie started to thump the wall behind her, growling deep in the back of her throat. Gertie had been a formidable sight when she was sitting quietly, now she was starting to get angry she was truly terrifying.

"Don't think so, boss. She came down this way but I didn't see her after that."

"Who else was here? Did anyone see where she went?"

Gertie really didn't like the boss. Every time he spoke she got more worked up.

"No, boss."

"So, not only were you morons careless enough to let someone come down here, you didn't even manage to see where she went."

"Sorry, boss."

"Go round there and look!"

I was about to be found. As far as I could tell the only hiding place inside the cage was behind Gertie, which meant I had a big problem. No way I was moving closer to those huge hands of hers.

"No way! You can fire me if you want but I'm not going round there. That gorilla damn near ripped Colly's arm off last night."

"I can do more than fire you, you idiot, now get round there and check if there is anyone in that cage!"

I guessed the boss was making his point with the gun I'd seen earlier. I had a choice: being found by the armed gang or being torn limb from limb by a gorilla. Gertie had so far not shown any aggression towards me, whereas the men most definitely had, so gorilla it was. Trying not to think about what might happen to me, I quickly scuttled across the cage.

Gertie had all her attention focused outside the cage, trying to grab at the man coming round the front of the trailer. I crouched down behind her and tried to keep her between me and the men in front of the cage.

"Nah, she's not in there," the boss said, "Look at Gertie, she'd be doing her nut if someone was in there with her. That girl must have doubled back. It doesn't look like she knows about the secrets Gertie's keeping for us."

Interesting.

I heard the men walk away. I quickly backed away from Gertie, trying to get to a safe distance while keeping her between me and the front of the cage as far as possible in case anyone was looking. But then she took me by surprise. Rather than tearing me into little pieces, she calmed down and looked at me impassively.

Score one for the sisterhood.

Now it looked like she wasn't going to kill me I felt sorry for her, stuck in this cage. When this was all over I'd call the RSPCA and see if they could do anything to help her.

I opened the side door a crack and listened for signs of anyone waiting for me. All was quiet. I left the truck and hurried away from the area.

There was a high wall running around the grounds so I couldn't make a quick exit out of the back. I made my way around the edge of the grounds to the main gates where I found a long queue of people and cars. Security guards were searching everyone before they could leave.

"What's going on?" I asked one of the security guards who was working the queue, keeping everyone in line.

"Theft in the main house. Bunch of jewels gone missing." he said.

When I got to the gate, they went through my bag and scanned me with a metal detector wand. Neither guard enquired as to why I smelled quite so much like gorilla.

Once safely back in my hotel room, I made the phone call I'd been wanting to make since meeting Gertie.

"You told me that cage would be empty!" I yelled as soon as Nick, my partner, answered the phone.

"And hello to you, too. Nice day?"

"Lovely, aside from the gorilla in the cage that you said would be empty."

"It should have been," Nick said, "The gorilla show is always on at seven. They must have cancelled it for some reason."

I had a fair idea what that reason was but I didn't want to discuss it with Nick. Now I knew that Nick had made it safely back, too, I wanted to get off the phone. I was tired and smelly and wanted a long hot bath.

"Listen, Nick, I'll call you later, okay?"

"Wait, before you go. Did you…?"

"Yes, as planned."

"Okay, I'll catch you later."

Charming, he was more concerned that I'd done the job properly than about my safety. As a thief he was topnotch but as a boyfriend he was decidedly second-rate.

I ran myself a deep bath. As I sank back into the bubbles, I considered the day and its rather dramatic end.

Nick had started planning this job after he saw a poster advertising the circus's summer tour including a week spent in the grounds of Shanly House near Canterbury in Kent. Nick has wanted to rob Shanly for longer than I've known him. They have jewellery on display which had some decent stones that would provide a nice return even if they had to be taken out of their settings. He'd learned the routine of the place and knew he could take the items without being spotted.

The only bit he had never figured out was how to get them off the grounds. Shanly sits in the middle of a large walled estate giving the owners plenty of time to shut the gates if a theft was discovered. The security was fairly lax inside the House because there was no way to get off the estate.

The circus would finally give him his way out. If he could hide the gems in one of the circus vehicles, the circus would carry them over the threshold and he could pick them up at the next stop.

It wasn't risk free, of course. The circus would get searched once the theft had been discovered and even if the police didn't find the jewels there was always a chance that the circus staff might.

Earlier that afternoon, Nick had arrived at the house and walked around looking like a bored husband killing time while his wife looked at the exhibits. Although he appeared to be wandering aimlessly, he was following a carefully planned route that would get him to the jewellery rooms just after the staff had led all of the other tourists out ready for closing up the house for the day.

His end all went well and, as we passed each other on the stairs, he slipped the jewels into my bag. He continued to browse around while I, who hadn't been near any of the jewellery displays, went out into the grounds and to the circus.

Gertie's surprise appearance had thrown me more than a little, but I had managed to hide the leather pouch of jewels as planned. Inside Gertie's cage there was a narrow gully running around the top of the walls that was deep enough to hide fairly small things placed there. It wasn't particularly secure, if anyone happened to put their hand on the same spot they'd find the bag immediately, but it was the best place we'd been able to think of without involving any members of the circus crew.

Soaking in the bath, I thought again about the circus goons and why they had chased me. One of the men had referred to Gertie keeping their secrets. They must have come after me because they thought I knew about those secrets. It sounded like Nick and I weren't the only ones to think a gorilla's cage was a good place to hide things.

The plan was for Nick to retrieve the jewels from Gertie's cage after the circus had moved to the next town on their tour the following day. As I towelled off after my bath, it occurred to me that Gertie might be able to do me another favour.

◊ ◊ ◊ ◊ ◊

The police let the circus move on after a day's delay. There was nothing on the news about the jewels being found. Given my thoughts about what else might be in Gertie's cage, I wondered how the circus hands had managed to keep the police from finding anything. Maybe the police didn't search that hard. Gertie certainly was a very effective gate keeper.

I hadn't told Nick about the men with guns or what else might be hidden in that cage. He was a great crime partner and an okay boyfriend, but I didn't see why I should share everything with him. I needed to return to the cage and I had the perfect reason to insist that it should be me that pick up the jewellery.

Blessed Gertie.

Nick and I met in a coffee shop near the new circus site.

"It's not that I don't trust you…" Nick said, protesting my suggestion that I retrieve the jewels.

"It's exactly that you don't trust me," I interrupted, but I knew trust wouldn't win me this argument. I knew he wouldn't be swayed by an emotional appeal so I focussed on the success of the job. "The noise Gertie will make if you even get close to her cage will bring the entire camp running. I'm the only one who can get in and out without being spotted."

Nick sat back and drank his coffee. Pushing him at this stage would just make him more suspicious so I stayed silent. A finishing school education may be useless on the ways of gorillas but when it comes to getting your own way it's top notch.

I noticed Nick hadn't made any protestations about my safety. Whatever happened at the circus, I decided, Nick and I would go our separate ways after this. When he couldn't even be bothered to pretend to care about my well-being, it was time to go.

Nick put down his coffee mug and looked at me closely. "I'll know if any of the jewellery is missing. I know exactly what I stole, remember."

"Of course."

Now to hope that Gertie would be in a good mood.

◊ ◊ ◊ ◊ ◊

Gertie's cage was once again parked right at the back of the field, with the open caged front facing out towards the open fields opposite. I suspected that this was as much to hide the coming and going of people in her cage as it was due to her less than sunny disposition.

There was no-one around as I walked down the field trying to look like an innocent audience member who'd wandered off. Of course, if they caught me down by Gertie's then they wouldn't care who I was, they'd be after me just as they had been last time.

Gertie was sat in her usual spot in the corner of the cage, watching a whole lot of nothing go on outside. I entered the cage through the same small door I had used last time.

"Hey, Gertie, old dear," I said softly, "Hope you still like me."

She didn't react to my presence other than to watch me as I reached up to grab the bag of jewellery. It was still there, thank goodness. I stuffed it in my rucksack and looked around the cage trying to decide where I would find the goons' hiding place. I was sure there must be something here. Why else would they have cared so much about someone getting close to this cage that they came after me with guns?

The obvious place was the little gully around the top of the cage. Taking a deep breath and praying for a lack of spiders I reached up and ran my hand inside it.

Bingo.

I found nine untidy piles of used notes held together with elastic bands. I stuck them in my rucksack without attempting to count them. Cash was what I had hoped to find. When I'd tried to work out what the goons might be up to, drug dealing seemed the most likely. I figured they hid the cash in Gertie's cage until they could launder it through the circus's takings.

I hadn't been in the cage very long and Gertie hadn't moved so I figured I was safe to sneak out again. As a sentry against the arrival of unwanted men, she was hugely useful.

"Bye, Gertie." I was sad to leave her. It was sentimental nonsense I knew, but she'd saved my life and she'd been the reason this job had been a success. I was sure that I had been nothing more than an interesting diversion for her, but nevertheless I had grown attached to the magnificent old lady.

There was nothing I could do for her right then. I snuck back out of the cage and pushed my way through the hedge at the back of the field and walked quickly away from the circus.

As I walked along, I thought about what I was going to do next. I'd already decided to split with Nick. It was tempting to leave now and take the jewellery with me, but I didn't fancy looking over my shoulder all the time worrying about him finding me. Plus he could come in handy again in the future. Foolish to burn bridges when you don't have to.

I surprised myself by considering going straight, but the more I thought about it the more I thought it was probably time. I hadn't been caught so far, which couldn't last. And what a way to finish, with a gorilla as a partner in crime! I'd never top that. Which reminded me, I had a call to make.

"Hello, RSPCA?"

Monkey Business

by Cecelia Chapman

My husband left me for another woman. He cleaned out our bank account, packed his belongings and left while I was out. So I took off traveling and bodysurfing the most eastern Caribbean islands.

I found odd jobs doing office work, making flyers, painting fabric and t-shirts. Making my own prints and drawings for sale. Jean and her husband Neville rented me the shanty behind their home when I started doing their book work. They were busy as groundskeepers and guardians of the Primate Research Center sending tiny caskets of drugged spider monkeys to first world countries for laboratory purposes.

One afternoon I fell asleep on Jean and Neville's big house porch. I woke to the full moon pulling itself up from the sea. Female and children monkeys screamed in delight as loose males jumped up and down on their cages. Children darted bat-like in the dusk. Low tones drifted down the porch between Jean and Mr. Hewitt, a policeman from District F, her cousin from the other side of the island.

"You haven't seen her since? Did she mention any plans, a trip? What was she wearing?

"No. She walk from the house in she gold bikini, big plastic rings..." Jean made big rings with her fingers, lips and eyes.

"What house?"

"The house they say she burn...Meurice, he call me, he say he look everywhere..."

Hewitt studied his notebook, "You're the last to see her..."

Hewitt turned to Neville who just came in, "When did you last see your brother?"

"He come by before yesterday to check the drain pipe spilling into his trees."

Judge Holder lived next door. He recommended Jean and Neville for the position of groundskeepers of the island heritage house. It included the monkey caretaker job that simultaneously cleared the animals from ripping up cane fields and farms.

"Did he mention traveling plans? Was he carrying anything?"

"No, no."

"What was he wearing?"

"He judge suit, you know."

"He never arrived at court."

"You saw Desmond Brown cleaning trees here early yesterday?" Hewitt looked to Jean.

"I asked Desmond to clean those coco trees and pick a few nuts, then I gone off to the shops. When I come back he gone." Jean said, then added. "He eyes so red I afraid to send him up the tree." Hewit studied his notes.

"Well, that leaves Beverly Cole. Her manager called us. Her neighbours took in her children, her sister's got her sick mother. Who saw her and when?"

"Monday," Neville pointed, "cleaning the road by the large cages over there."

Derek screamed upstairs. "There's a monkey loose up here." We all looked to see a large monkey jump from window to tree.

"Close the screen and go to bed, Derek," Neville yelled.

Everyone looked to Hewitt.

"That's it?" Jean asked.

"Yes." Hewitt said.

Loud waves woke me early. Surfers and small boats dotted the sapphire coast. Waves like little mountains rose up out of deep Atlantic waters, slow-moving crests rolling onto soft, sea-moss reef. I took the day off, bodysurfing at dawn, then again in late afternoon, all the while watching for Desmond, and the others.

Desmond built the bamboo shanty I lived in when he was fishing and working with Neville. Later he moved home to care for his mother. He carried each floor-stone up the cliff. He cut each bamboo in the bush. The hut captured cool sea-breezes yet was sheltered. And private as a place can be where when you come home your collins is vanished. But the next morning it returns to your yard with a pile of sugar cane and coconuts.

By sunset I was sipping green coco with rum while roasting a breadfruit. Steamed okra, peppers, onions, fresh tumeric and fresh thyme lay ready. Coconut meat was grated and soaking in an iron pot. The lid was placed over a banana leaf so flies wouldn't dive in, covered with the broken half-lid I threw down the cliff and broke two days ago after receiving divorce papers claiming I abandoned the marriage.

After eating I lay in my hammock in a drunken rum coma and watched the moon climb. Neville and a friend talked on the porch for a long time. Later I heard Jean and the children coming home from dinner at her mother's. Pails clanging, doors slamming, glasses clinking, lights blinking.

I fell to sleep again until the brilliant moon startled me awake. When I swung out of the hammock to go to bed I stumbled. Thoughts raced through my mind: I live too alone, too unloved, I need security, a home, a schedule, a good job, maybe children, a therapist, insurance, yes, a mortgage, debts, a cheating husband with horrible in-laws and I'm drinking too much rum. The life of an artist was harder than I could possibly have imagined. And I wanted to know things...like what happened to those people and more than anything, now what was going to happen to me?

"Sssssssssst..."

"Here, Lady." A monkey was at my shoulder, to steady me, whispering, "What you want?" His tail swept my cheek. "What you want, Lady?" The monkey repeated, looking me in the eyes.

"I...I, I..."

"Yes, you, Lady. What you want? I give you wish, anything you sweet heart desire. What you want? A man? You want a nice man? Good job? Some big jewelry? Money? Clothes? House? A trip? Fame, power? A nice lady like you deserve her heart wish. You want a Jaguar? What you want? You get it." He rifled through my peanuts and grabbed sugarcane, ripping it clean with his teeth.

"I...I, I..."

"O.K., Lady, you get it. I see you a interested lady, a lady what wants knowledge. You wise. You gets you wish. Later, wise lady, I see you later." The monkey melted into a tree.

I sank into the hammock and closed my eyes. But on my eyelids I saw the shimmering blue and white beach, as if projected onto a billowing sheet or wind-filled sail. Angela walked on the sand with Meurice following behind her. She was toying with him. Her flirtations with men irritated him, then she ignored him. Or she took up political causes to annoy him. Meurice, assistant to the Prime Minister and married to his sister with eight children living on the other side of the island, entrepreneur, arms dealer, was devoted to Angela. He gave her anything she wanted. Usually money. And when he travelled abroad he took her with him. He built Angela a house that burned down when it was completed. Angela travelled to Cuba, then returned to rent a house on the beach. The sea faded and the wind-whipped canvas filled with figures. Angela tied on a bed in a hotel room, gagged, eyes bulging. Two men slashed at her suitcase. One man counted the money he found. The other pulled her gag, holding a knife to her throat.

"I support your...cause...the money is for your people who suffer...you..." Angela's hoarse voice cracked.

"We suffer nothing," the man laughed spitting on her. "I want to know now where is the rest?" Then he nodded at the other man. The hotel room faded from my vision.

Dense, rolling smoke filled my eyes, throat, nostrils, I heard the monkey chuckle. Coconut-curry, damp wood, and hemp. A hut materialized from the smoke, with a turbaned man holding a large walking stick.

"...enter dread...jah rastafari. Irie, brother, come forward."

Desmond carried an empty burlap sack inside the hut. The man sat on the bed pointing his stick at the heap of plants on the floor. He offered Desmond a splif and a coco, and stirred a bubbling stew while Desmond filled his bag with herb. Smoke billowed and stung my eyes...then slowly thinned to reveal a gully of hacked plants behind the shanty. I smelled wet dirt, gasoline and blood. Armed men packed plants in a helicopter walking around Desmond's body.

Howling with laughter, clutching his sides, the monkey fell off his branch.

Black acrid cane smoke poured into my nose and still-watering eyes. When my vision cleared I saw Beverly on her road job. She was hacking at overhanging bush, hooking it with the tip of her collins, and tossing it into her trash bag with great grace. I saw her moving up and down the byways picking up litter, waving at tourists in their rented mini-jeeps, helping people off the bus with their loads, holding traffic for children, chasing goats from the streets. She took care tying Mrs. Holder's rose bush back from the crosswalk and moved broken crate parts from the road.

Cane-smoke rolled in and rolled out. When it cleared, I stared. Beverly? She was styled, polished, finished. Like the model that rented Mrs. Bannister's plantation each year. Reflected in a large mirror I saw faces behind her. A hairdresser grabbed her hair, a stylist unzipped her, an assistant handed her papers, a pen, a driver appeared with a messenger, a make-up artist approached her with a huge brush, a waiter handed her tea, a writer stood to the side nodding at everything the manager was saying to her. They all talked at once. One of her cell phones rang, then the other. A microphone was placed in her face, a camera.

"She lovely lady, she get what she want," The monkey sighed.

Wind filled the sail, then flapped and unrolled to reveal Judge Holder sitting in his courtroom. Bewigged, heavily robed, he looked tired, uncomfortable, miserable, hot. The scene faded into heavy mist, the roar of smashing waves, followed by a long silence. Slowly the quiet was filled with the ticking of the antique clock being re-set by Mrs. Holder in their dining room. Judge Holder's vexatious wife watched his every move with her tiny eyes as he ate. The mist returned hiding the room. Sea-foam splashed me and when my stinging eyes re-focused I saw Judge Holder crouched low in a banana boat. I recognized the boat. It was Rocky's, a friend of Neville's from another island. Rocky cleared the harbor watching Holder as he steered, and I could tell he loved him. Quickly the boat was lost on the horizon.

Strange Companions at London Zoo

by Carrie Ryman

The gray cement floor at London Zoo was agleam with a fairy dusting of rainbows. Boris Freeman cringed. He thought it looked more like something you'd see in a glitzy nightclub or beneath a little girl's dressing table. He gritted his teeth, bending lower over the wide broom and pushing it past the wall of the gorilla exhibit. Ever since the gift shop started selling those wretched pink and blue elephants, the place was always covered in that ghastly glitter. Boris took comfort in the fact that he'd be back to his beloved night shift the following day. Only one more hour. One more. It was the mantra that carried him through until closing time. His nerves were raw from the constant cacophony of squealing children who littered the building that day.

"A bloody field trip," said Boris to himself. Day shift was deplorable. First, there were the infinite sites of vomitus to which he was emergency-paged. Boris thought the snake exhibit would be the more deserving location of such voluminous retching. And he would happily say goodbye to the trash cans in the ladies room, which incessantly reeked of wet nappies.

His sweeping came to a halt when his eye caught a movement behind the glass exhibit. The young mountain gorilla, who had arrived a week ago, was one of the most celebrated acquisitions of London zoo. Some *balda* in management decided that all new primates would be given names that began with the first letter of their species, thus making it easier to catalog them. So the head veterinarian made a game of it and named her simply "G." That eventually became "Gee." This new naming business was rubbish and set Boris' teeth on edge. He didn't know why it upset him so much. The only thing that usually got him riled up was when his neighbor, Mrs. Beastly, fell asleep with the telly on.

"You deserve a better name. Guenevere or Galena would have suited you perfectly," said Boris, in a soft voice. Gee was delicately preening her tummy near the front of the exhibit. "Or, better, forget the first letter thing. They should have called you Anastasia." The name evoked royalty and his own Russian ancestry. He took off his cap, rubbed his shining pate and returned his attention to sweeping. It was not his job to assign monikers to the mammals. His job was to clean up after them.

"The messiest animals aren't the ones inside the cages, but the ones standing upright on the outside," he said with a wink toward Gee, as he shuffled past. She lifted her head, and flashed her ivory teeth, as if she, too, was amused by the sentiment. A throng of visitors hustled in the direction of Gee's display, and Boris realized that Gee's smile had been a threat display. She scurried to the back of her cage and crouched with her back to the audience.

Boris remembered the anticipation he felt upon reading last month's *"Zoo Noos"* bulletin. It said that the mountain gorilla's delivery to her new home would be the morning of April 5th. Boris promptly circled the date in red on his kitchen calendar. He had just finished Dian Fossey's book, *Gorillas In the Mist*. He enjoyed almost everything he read, but the books about these sleek African primates intrigued him. He needed to find a way onto day shift. After a night at the pub, Aaron, the first shift janitor, agreed to switch hours with him the week of the gorilla's arrival. Boris didn't normally care for the spike-haired lad, or the piles of dirt he left for Boris to clean on night shift, but the lad was quite agreeable once you got a coupla pints into him. Time passed as slowly as cold treacle as Boris waited for the big day to arrive.

Boris recalled how bug-eyed he had been that first morning, with one eye on the empty, gray exhibit and another on his broom and dustpan. It was half past seven, several hours before opening, and he was happy he would not have to fight through the crowds to get his first glimpse of the mountain gorilla. His vigilance paid off as he watched the door at the back lift up. One small gorilla emerged from the dark hollow of the back quarters. Boris' eyes kept wandering back to the now closed door, half expecting a companion to join her. She sat with her back against the back wall, arms encircling her plush body. Her crouching form was swallowed up by the enormous stone cage which was empty, save for a few trees, a bail of hay, a rubber tire and a streak of sunlight from the glass ceiling. The door opened again, and an aluminum tray containing something green, along with a few banana slices and stalks of celery, was set inside. Gee ignored it.

For the first few days, Boris noticed that Gee rarely approached the front of her cage, and stayed hunched in one of the back corners during open hours. Boris found himself chastising children, and more than a few adults, who rapped their knuckles on the glass to get the Mountain Gorilla's attention. He wished he could say something to the ones who contorted their faces or rudely thrust their tongues out at Gee, but he knew that making faces wasn't against the rules. At least the other primates at the zoo had companions to distract them. The zoo currently had six Western Lowland Gorillas, but from what he had read, the two species did not interact well so Gee was given her own cage. Boris sighed. This little lady was given a life of solitary confinement. He knew what it meant to be alone.

His reverie was disturbed by the monotonous bleeping of a golf cart rolling past. Boris was just sweeping up the last centimeter of frightful pink and blue fairy spittle when the zoo attendant settled onto the stool next to Gee's exhibit. He had seen her there before and had heard that the saucy little minx was a student at the Royal Veterinary College. The girl reminded him of berries, sweet and ripe for the picking. Her blonde hair and perky B-cups pointed his way invitingly. He was focusing on her left breast, in particular, which bore the name, "Patrice," when a pronounced throat clearing brought his attention back to her face. The girl smiled and blew him a kiss. Boris wished he was not retiring in a few weeks. He gave her a grin that was both wolfish and sheepish and smoothed down his spidery, silver uni-brow with one finger. He doffed his cap to her and began to empty trash cans. Boris listened to the monologue she gave twice each hour.

"Welcome to London Zoo. Gee is a five-year-old female *Gorilla beringei beringei* or Mountain Gorilla. She comes to us from the Virunga Mountain Range in Uganda, East Africa. She is just over one meter tall and weighs nearly 65 kilos. At maturity, Gee will weigh approximately 130 kilos. Though Mountain Gorillas are extremely powerful, they are very gentle and social animals." Boris chuckled to himself when Gee seized that particular moment to hurl her food tray against the back wall. The round metal tray clattered to the floor and spun on its edges for what seemed like ages. Banana slices rolled in every direction like tiny wagon wheels. Patrice paused, smiling, and then continued, "Due to deforestation and poaching, Gorilla populations are facing a rapid decline throughout the world, and Mountain Gorillas are dwindling the fastest, with only seven-hundred remaining." Patrice paused to take a sip of Irn-Bru and then stood up, mic in hand, walking toward one of the last groups of zoo patrons.

Boris groaned at the sight of a toddler dragging yet another pink and blue elephant. She waddled toward the exhibit with her mother in hot pursuit. "Kitty!" Boris' heart melted when he heard the child's adorably mistaken moniker for Gee. The little girl's eyes were fastened on Gee as she tried to climb up onto the shelf that ran around the exhibit. Her mother pulled her away. Boris felt sorry for the little girl until she emitted an ear-splitting wail. Then the child's mother gripped her hand and hurried toward the exit. A trail of pink and blue glitter was left behind like breadcrumbs. Boris grumbled and reached for his broom and dustpan.

Patrice ended her oratory by waving the fan of colorful literature toward the backs of departing patrons, and then sighed heavily, returning to pack up her station. As she did, Boris got the inside scoop about Gee. According to Patrice, poachers slaughtered Gee's entire family. Many days later, wildlife researchers found the orphan gorilla nesting only a few meters from the site of the grisly murders. "Murders" was the exact word the girl used. She obviously felt strongly about the welfare of animals. A wave of guilt hit him. In future, he would make a concerted effort *not* to ogle the girl's chest and bottom. He said goodbye to Patrice and started to pack up his janitor's cart. He glanced at his furry spectator again and smiled.

"How are you, luv?" Gee saw him standing next to the glass, paused and then lumbered closer. She sniffed a spot that was about a meter from the periphery of her cage and then planted herself with grace on the floor. She watched Boris. Boris watched her. There was something significant in her caramel-colored eyes. But Boris couldn't say exactly what it was. Something meaningful. Something clever. Gee leaned closer toward him, looking more intently into his eyes. It was impossible not to recognize high intelligence when it presented itself, and it lived in this animal. "Are you lonely, little girl? Miss your mummy?"

The knowledge of Gee's history stirred pictures in his head. A jade green forest. A waterfall spilling from a chocolate brown mountainside. A dozen or more inky, plush creatures tumbling and frolicking together. His heart went out to her as she sat all alone in her cage. Boris pulled a handkerchief from his pocket and blew his nose. Sometimes he hated this job, he thought, as he wheeled his cart into the janitor's closet. As his retirement approached, he found himself becoming quite misty-eyed at the silliest things. Retirement was a good thing. It would mean he'd have all the time in the world to read.

Boris, a closet librarian, read everything he could get his hands on. But Boris didn't share his bibliophile habits with anyone, especially at work. In fact, except to the zoo's feathered or furred residents, he spoke only a few words to anyone. Boris sometimes wondered if his love of words was the reason he expended them so sparingly and only on the most worthy ears. He made an occasional stop at the pub, but not for the social aspect. Like any man, he enjoyed a pint or two. But after downing his ale, Boris was quickly out the door again.

The next day was Saturday, and Boris was having a lovely dream about bashing in pink and blue elephant heads when the phone rang. He stumbled into the living room and knocked over a huge stack of books before grabbing the receiver. The man from London Zoo personnel sounded quite desperate.

"Aaron just rung us. Says he has the influenza and is quite incapacitated. We'll need you to come in and cover his shift. Can you do a double?"

What a cock-and-bull story, Boris seethed, on his way back into work. Aaron was a blithering idiot. Everyone at the zoo knew the wanker wasn't sick. He had been flapping his cakehole all week about the lunch date he had on Friday with a lingerie model named Trixie whom he intended to shag. Apparently lunch turned into dinner, and the date concluded as expected.

It was a rainy and especially harrowing day at the zoo. He had to mop and remop the entrance. And the loo suffered from numerous clogs. The last of the zoo patrons left, and Boris had just enough time to grab a bag of crisps from the employee vending machine before heading back for his second shift.

The night was blissful and uneventful. The animals were given their evening meal and safely locked away in the back areas by 7 PM. This gave the cleaning crews a chance to go into the front areas and sanitize them. As Boris passed the gorilla section, he noticed that Gee was still out in her main area. It was half past eight. Odd, he thought. She saw him and immediately repositioned herself only inches from the glass and then pressed her long, black palm against the surface. It was such a human gesture. The gesture of a loved one saying goodbye from a departing train window. She held it there for a few minutes, looking intently at Boris. He sat down on the ledge next to the glass.

"Hello, little girl. How would you like to come home with me tonight? I'll share what's left of that delicious steak and kidney pie that Mrs. Beastly baked for me." The gorilla yawned but kept her hand against the glass. "What? Not a meat lover? Ah, yes, I forgot. You're a strict vegetarian. Well, then, perhaps I could whip you up a mean bowl of banana porridge. Would you fancy that?" Boris didn't know why he was so talkative whenever he was with the animals. Somebody had to do the talking, he guessed. Gee leaned her shoulder against the glass, her eyes alert and poised on him. He could see a few fine silver hairs that intertwined with the dark ones along her coal black body. Premature aging from all the trauma, he surmised.

Boris noted how few lines crisscrossed the palm of her hand and wondered why he had always assumed that a gorilla's skin was leathery. Up close, it looked butter soft. He lifted his hand and placed it on the opposite side of hers. He pressed his shoulder on the glass, too, and rested his head on it, watching her. And then he was close enough to see the vertical trails of misery that darkened Gee's cheeks. Boris went rigid. He had always been able to ignore the emotional aspect of caring for caged animals, but the urge to smash the glass and set her free was hard to resist. The poor thing needed love and companionship. If she were a human child, she would barely be out of nappies.

"I wish I could help you, luv. I really do. If it were up—" A sound interrupted him, and Boris turned to see the security door to the back area swing closed. Had someone been standing there all this time? He hoped it wasn't anyone important, but jumped up to get back to work, just in case. Then he noticed the door at the back of Gee's cage slide open and a tray of food was slid inside. Gee ignored it, pressing her face against the glass. Boris headed to the next exhibit to clean, hoping his absence would encourage her to eat.

Boris and Gee developed the routine of old friends. Every evening he took his dinner break beside Gee's cage. He was enchanted the first time she picked up her tray from its place near the back wall. He expected her to throw it again. Instead, she pushed it or carried it, albeit a bit awkwardly, across the cage and set it down on the floor by the window. Sometimes a few bits of celery fell off, and she knuckle-walked back to retrieve them. Gee, apparently, preferred to eat in the company of others, and Boris had become her chosen dinner partner. Boris wondered how she did at breakfast when he wasn't there, and he worried a little. But her fur gleamed, and her eyes were bright. She was the picture of health, as far as he could see. They would eat, and Boris would tell her all about his day.

He told Gee about Mrs. Beastly's latest home-baked treats or the long wait at the tube station or about the people he saw in the queue waiting for the train. He described the catered press party that the zoo had to promote the new Siberian tiger exhibit and what a gala event it was. Gee casually emptied her tray like she always did and sat listening. Or at least, it seemed like she was listening as Boris began to tell her about the amazing book he had just started.

"It's about meteors, you see…they're up there," he said, pointing toward the glass ceiling of her cage. Her eyes followed his finger, and she pressed herself closer to him and lay down. She often fell asleep next to him, and Boris wondered how long she stayed in the front after he left. She was gone when he returned to clean her cage toward the end of his shift. He always saved her cage for last. It seemed the zookeepers were letting her have more freedom, allowing her more time to acclimate to both the front and back sections of her cage. It gave them more time together.

But that time was bittersweet, because April 30th was approaching fast. Thirty-seven years at London Zoo. Yes, he was quite ready to say goodbye to the mop and broom forever. He planned to celebrate his retirement by not cleaning his own flat for a month. He would read a book a day, sleep in every morning and eat whenever he chose. And he wouldn't step foot in the tube station again, except maybe to visit Gee. The child gorilla was the first thing he thought about every day when he awoke. He couldn't wait to get into work so he could check on her. *What a charmer she is, that Gee.* It would never be the same, coming as a regular zoo visitor, fighting to see her between bobbing heads…and who knew if she would even come close to the glass again with all the screaming children and cameras flashing at her?

◊ ◊ ◊ ◊ ◊

A bluetit pried a thistle seed from the tube feeder that hung outside Boris' second story flat. The two-note call of her mate reminded Boris of a squeaky swingset laden with child. Boris put down another book he had lost interest in reading and sipped his Rosy Lee tea. *Enchanted Seas* should have been fascinating stuff. But his heart felt like a teacup without a saucer. One could still have tea without it, but it just wasn't the same. There wasn't that satisfying chink of the spoon hitting the plate or the fragile resting place between sips. It had been over a month since he retired from the zoo. And he felt listless for the first time in ages. He had been so busy wading through his retirement and pension paperwork, he had not been back for a visit. Perhaps it was for the better, he thought, make a clean break of it.

He spotted the Cancun brochure that was wedged between the *Evening Standard* and the book about Mayan culture that he had finally finished. The bottom half of the brochure had turquoise water framed by tropical fuchsia flowers and said: TO PARADISE. He knew the top half said: ESCAPE. A place in the sun to sip a fruity drink and smoke an imported cigar. An all-inclusive week in Cancun was exactly what he needed. He had invested his money wisely, so there was nothing stopping him. He had no children, no nieces, no nephews, no worries.

Boris picked up the brochure and stared at it. The sound of honking from the street below penetrated his reverie, and he peered out the window. A decrepit plaid-trousered codger inched a metal zimmer across the intersection. He stopped to rest frequently. The sound of horns screeched from beneath slick silver bonnets of cars, driven by slick young executives, impatient to reach their slick offices. The old man stopped, his mouth hanging open. That will soon be me, Boris thought with a grimace. And then the phone rang.

"Mr. Freeman? I hope I'm not bothering you." The caller identified himself as Ian MacDowell, the head veterinarian at the zoo. The man's lilting Irish brogue was thick, and Boris wondered if he misunderstood the title. *Why is he calling me?*

"No, of course not. What can I do for you, Mr. MacDowell?" Boris tried to sound casual, as if men of such caliber called him every day.

"It's our Mountain Gorilla, you see. She's gone off her food, and will drink very little water. Frankly, we're concerned. She's become quite lethargic. And then there's the lowland gorilla that we brought in for company. We thought perhaps a younger gorilla would be a suitable companion, but she completely terrorized Gertrude." He sounded quite deflated, even for an Irishman, Boris thought.

Did the man say Gee is not eating? Boris felt a lump growing in his throat. "I'd like to help, but…You *do* know that I worked for the janitorial department, don't you?" Boris wondered if there had been some mix up in the personnel files.

"Yes, of course. Let me explain, Mr. Freeman. I've been told how close you and our gorilla were and—"

"Her name is Gee," Boris couldn't resist. The "our gorilla" was beginning to get to him.

"Oh, yes. Gee. Of course you would be on a first name basis." He chuckled, and Boris did not join him, nor did he see the humor, so the man continued. "Well, one of my assistants, in primates, Patrice Matthews, has told me how much Gee has taken to you, and was doing quite well until you left. Miss Matthews said that our gorilla, uh, Gee, became quite agitated when you didn't show up for work at the usual time. She tried to console her, but then they had to restrain her for a few days for fear that she'd hurt herself."

"Is she alright? How bad is it?" Boris asked in a hushed voice.

"Mr. Freeman, she's not doing well. Indeed, we have to take whatever measures are necessary to ensure that this animal's, er, depression, is lifted so she can make a full recovery. I realize you are no longer employed with us, but the fact of the matter is that this animal is in decline. Would you consider coming back on a part-time basis as a partial caretaker with Gee? If it works out, I assure you we can pay you well."

MacDowell asked Boris to come in at his earliest convenience, which, for

Boris, was immediately. He hung up the phone, pulled on his jumper and headed for the door.

The admissions attendant at the main entrance to the zoo recognized him and waved him through. Boris nearly trampled a tour guide and his entourage as he hurried down the corridor that lead to the primate building. Patrice was waiting for him at the security door when he arrived at Gee's cage. The cage was empty.

"Thank you, thank you for coming, Boris. Gee will be so happy to see you!" She gave him a huge hug, and then led Boris past the side door that joined the front of each exhibit and into what he secretly called "the inner sanctum." They walked down a short, very white corridor. Boris peeked into a few doorways to see metal counters topped with glass containers and a few cages. He heard the familiar, high-pitched screams of the chimpanzees and the guttural voices of the other primates. Then Patrice came to a stop in front of an aluminum door and peered through a little portal at the top.

"Gee's awake," she said, turning back to Boris. "Now, let me just give you a few guidelines, as these are very strong animals. Even Gee, in her weakened state, could break your back if she wanted to." She paused and searched Boris' eyes for a sign of fear or hesitation.

"I'm fully aware of the danger," Boris said firmly. "Please, just let me see her."

"Alright then, we'll go inside. Just please don't move quickly, do not turn your back on her at any time, and most importantly, do not look her straight in the eyes. That's a sign of challenge in the gorilla world." Patrice rested her hand on his shoulder. "Don't worry. I can sedate her quickly if she has a stress reaction or becomes aggressive. But the more prepared you are, the better. If she does well with you today, the next step will be trying to get her to eat something. Now, Boris...I want you to warn you. Gee's not the same gorilla she was a month ago. She has lost some weight, and she's very lethargic." Patrice rubbed circles on her forehead.

Patrice began to open the door and then jerked it closed again, asking, "You're not sick, are you? Some human diseases can transfer to primates, so I need to be sure." She seemed to be stalling, perhaps having second thoughts. Boris assured her that he was completely healthy, had all his shots and all that, and then Patrice opened the door. Boris squeezed past her to see his friend huddled on a gray blanket on the floor. She looked much smaller than he remembered. He felt a tremor in his chest.

"Don't approach her. See if she comes to you," Patrice whispered, standing close by. Gee lifted her head, but didn't move. He could hear a little sound escape her throat. It sounded like a wheeze, but he wasn't sure. Boris waited for what seemed like ages, and then spoke to her in his usual story-telling voice.

"Hello, luv. It's your old pal back again. Oh, I missed you like the dickens." Boris moved a little closer and then crouched down to her level. And then he saw a flicker of recognition in her caramel eyes, a drift of spirit returning. She furrowed her brow and lifted her arm to stretch across her head, as if in puzzlement, her eyes meeting his. He averted his eyes downward, as he had been instructed, though he thought it was silly. She made another wheezing sound and a long groan. And then she moved forward.

"Easy now," Patrice said. "She's most likely just coming in for a closer look, so stay put." Gee was slow in coming to Boris, but her motion was deliberate. When she got within reach of Boris, she extended her hand toward him. With her fingers pointed downward, Gee touched his knee and rested it there. She sat down next to him and began to whimper. Don't look at her, he thought, don't look. He didn't want to be thrown across the room by an enraged female primate. Gee made a clicking sound and then leaned her face closer to his.

"Hello, sweetheart. How's my girl?" Boris said softly, his eyes still observing the floor. He slowly lifted his hand up on to his knee, and then touched hers. She wrapped her fingers around his, pressed her shoulder against him. A soft cooing sound came from her lips. And then he had to do it. It was a trust issue, and he knew he had hers. He peered straight down into Gee's eyes. They were red-rimmed and explored his own, searchingly. And then he was huddled into a gentle fur embrace that was Gee's gift to him. Complete and utter trust. He felt it in her touch, saw it in her eyes. Gee remembered him, and her warm reception proved he had been forgiven. "I take it our dinner date is back on, then, eh?" He laughed, sliding his arms around her then. A soft purring vibrated her chest. "Oh, Gee, you are a charmer." Young, caramel brown eyes peered up to meet old, dimming gray eyes. No glass between them, no barriers, thought Boris. He marveled at the bond they still shared. Patrice coughed in a funny way. The kind of cough someone makes when they are trying not to cry. He looked up to see her beaming with delight.

Boris pondered on his own emotions which flooded him as he sat there, embracing and being embraced by a child gorilla. And he realized the joy he felt was akin to something paternal. He loved this gorilla more than he could ever imagine loving a daughter. Gee reached up and touched his face with her leathered palm, and yes, it was soft as butter.

DILEMMA

by Cheryl Elaine Williams

I have a talent that I share with nursing home cats. I can smell death on a patient halfway down the hall. Lately the scent of death has hung heavy over a private patient of mine, my quadriplegic younger brother Brad. The odor is all around him and you can't miss it when you walk into his townhouse unit. The scent is as overpowering as skunk spray and just as nauseating.

Hey, I don't like acknowledging what I sense about my brother, but there it is. My sniffer tells me death is coming. Brad has held on for fifteen years since his motorbike accident. You could say he's been dying ever since he lost control over his limbs. He's had a couple close calls with breathing problems, and lately I've been listening more attentively to how he breathes. It's normal, nothing to call the doctor about. But then again, he doesn't breathe with the same sense of life he had before.

I'm hearing it. The rhythm's not there. Is he giving up? No matter what the pulmonary physician says, things are just different with him, I'm telling you. And it breaks my heart. I don't want my one and only brother to die. He's a rebel and a fighter and I hope to pull him through this, whatever it is he's going through inside that weakened body of his. Brad's thirty-nine years old and I want him to see age forty.

That is, if he himself really wants to hit that milestone. It's all up to Bradley Michael what he wants to do. In any case, he keeps me, Big Sis, his caretaker nurse, hopping. Every morning I head across the street from the townhouse I share with my husband to Brad's smaller unit at the end of our cul-de-sac. It's a lovely housing plan, quiet, minimal traffic. Brad as a quadriplegic can live here independently— with a little assistance from his animal friend. That's Percy, a trained companion monkey that the Animal Friends of the Disabled assigned to him.

And guess who's caretaker of both Brad and Percy?

It always falls on the available female in the family to do it. I'm not complaining.

I'm doing this for Mum and Dad who have to be watching down on us from Heaven. I only hope the angels are keeping score, too, because it's a back-breaking job for me. Brad pays me from his disability check. I sit with him four hours a day and then do another four hours at Hilltop Retirement Residence. That's where Brad should be but none of us can afford the four thousand a month fee. All our extended family, who live too far away to help, call me a saint. Saint Maggie.

If it makes them feel better, I'll claim the title.

Another day starts. "I don't know how you do it," says my husband Jim as I head out the door. He'll be off to his own job by the time I give Brad his morning bath. Then I have to make breakfast for both Brad and the monkey. That's part of our arrangement with the animal charity. The monkey needs a Mama, too. I have to guarantee that the animal's physical and emotional needs are cared for. That's only right.

Percy's the dearest little capuchin monkey. Think of an organ grinder monkey and you have a good mental picture of him. Light tan face, chest and upper arms. The rest of his body is dark brown like he's covered with a friar's robe. The brown 'skullcap' on top of his head makes him cute as a button.

Brad's monkey companion is good for incidentals. Fetching a drink from the fridge, picking up something that fell on the floor, changing the DVD's in the DVD player. While I monitor their interaction, I make mental notes for my weekly report to the charity organization. I also do light housework for Brad and clean out Percy's large and comfortable cage which takes up the back corner of Brad's living room.

Both of them are like 'kids' to me. Another day is starting. I don't mind that the caregiving is starting all over again.

"Hello, hello," I called out as I unlocked the door to Brad's unit. I could hear Percy chittering from inside his large cage in the living room. That made me smile.

"Morning, Mrs. Keller." The night sitter met me in the hallway. Jeffie was a young college student who we hired to stay with Brad at night. His main duty was to turn him over every half hour so he didn't get bedsores. He was also strong enough to help Brad onto the commode and he had CPR training, if needed.

"How's Brad today?" I asked, hoping this morning would bring a good report. Instead, my insides clenched as I watched Jeffie struggle to give an answer.

"Um, not as good as yesterday. He's—not talking. I mean, nothing happened during the night. He slept okay." Jeffie gathered up his jacket and textbooks from the hall table. "You'll have to look at him. He's a little 'off'."

"Oh?" I walked into the living room area where my brother lay under warm blankets, secure in a high quality hospital bed. "Good morning, Bradley Michael. How you feeling, brother?"

No answer. His eyes were open. They even blinked a few times, so I knew he was awake. But how alert could he be?

"I tried to get him to talk." Jeffie followed me into the sick room. "He's like you see him. He wouldn't sit up. I tried to get him to sit up, but he fought me on it."

"He fought you on it? So he showed a little activity, right?"

"Yeah, and then he went into how you see him now."

"Did he now." I leaned over the sidebars of the bed and gave my brother a smacking kiss on the forehead. "There's my favorite guy. Good morning, Brad. You know I love you, buddy. Lots and lots."

No answer. "You ready for breakfast? I was thinking oatmeal and syrup."

No response. His mouth twitched, but his gaze looked beyond me. His eyes focused on the ceiling. I wondered if he was seeing anything at all.

They get like this when they're giving up on life, a little voice reminded me. Memories of patients in the past. When the threads are life were about to be cut.

I turned to Jeffie. "What about Percy? Did Brad want to see Percy at all?"

"Uh-uh. I told him Percy was bouncing around his cage. I said I'd go bring him out." Jeffie raised a hand in the air and let it fall. "He didn't give me an okay. So I have to leave the monkey in the cage, right?"

"Right. We can't force the monkey on him." Not on a dying man, the thought came to me.

We both turned toward the monkey cage. The little capuchin hung on the bars, gazing out at us much like a baby standing in a crib, begging to be picked up. Percy wanted to be let out and given some love. The eighteen-thousand-dollar monkey, for that's what his training had cost to turn him into a caregiver companion, now wanted his share of caregiving.

"Sorry, Percy," I said. "We got us a problem here." I laid a hand on Jeffie's arm. "Could you stay a few minutes more, please? I think Brad should go to the emergency room. I'm not fooling around with this. I want him checked."

"Good idea," Jeffie agreed.

"The 911 people may have questions to ask you."

"No prob," Jeffie said. He checked on our too-quiet patient, then made a face that I took to mean it was all too big for him, which I thoroughly agreed with. I reached into my jacket pocket for my cell phone. Mercy Hospital was ten minutes away and the local police station had an ambulance on site with emergency technicians ready to respond to any call.

As I made the call, Jeffie ambled over to the monkey cage. "Bad news, Percy boy. Your friend's going away." He reached through the bars and rubbed Percy's black cap of fur. The animal clutched at the young man's fingers with his light-colored paws, seeking consolation.

Amazing, I thought, watching them as I gave details to the dispatcher. The monkey looked as sad as the humans around him were surely feeling.

I stuffed the phone back in my pocket. "I should get a bag ready for Brad." My mind was reeling. I couldn't think clearly.

"I think he knows," Jeffie said, indicating the monkey.

What, that my brother was dying? Yes, animals were extraordinarily sensitive to such things. It was entirely possible. "He looks damn sad," I whispered.

We kept our voices down. My brother lay close by and neither of us wanted to say anything that he might overhear. "Is this it?" Jeffie mouthed silently, the movement of his lips exaggerated.

I felt my stomach turn over. "It's very bad," I mouthed back. "I'll, uh, keep you informed. I'll call you later today. So you know about—tonight."

He looked at me like he knew he wouldn't be coming over to work that night.

The monkey screamed then. I knew his species could get loud, but this was the sharpest cry I had ever heard come out of that animal's mouth. This was all I needed, to have the caretaker monkey disturb the peace of my poor brother.

"Hush a boy, baby." I hauled butt over to that cage. "How are we, baby?" I found myself reaching through the bars. "You want out, I know. But I can't take you out, sweetness." It was morning and he wanted to run free. "The ambulance people are coming. Sorry, Perce."

The animal grasped my fingers, then kissed them with his wet lips. Oh, it was going to break my heart, it was.

"I guess I could take you out. If you behave." For one last look at his friend. This could be it. The last meeting.

The final goodbye.

My eyes started to tear over as I opened the cage. The animal jumped right into my arms. Percy held on for dear life and I cooed to him, telling him everything was alright.

"I'll take care of you, sweetie," I promised him. "There will always be someone to take care of you." I carried him over to Brad's hospital bed. His inert form lay there like a lump of lead. Had he had a stroke? I stopped with Percy at the foot of the bed and didn't go any further. I felt not to take him too close. The animal was agitated enough and I didn't want to risk another scream possibly agitating Brad in whatever state he was in.

In whatever dimension of life he was in.

And then the strangest feeling came over me as I held Percy to my chest. There was more life in that bundle in my arms than what remained in the twisted body on the hospital bed.

Sad. I bit back tears.

The monkey wasn't fussing, so I took a hesitant step closer. "You want to see Bradley? You want to see him one more time?"

The animal balked. He obviously smelled death the same way that I did. He climbed up onto my neck and hid his face. I understood this perfectly. Percy did not want to get closer to a dying being. He had taken his last look. In his own way, he had made his peace with his human companion.

"Brad loves you, Perce. He loves you."

I gave a long sigh, then carried the capuchin back to his cage. He allowed me to put him inside with no argument or complaint. He swung over to his food dish and picked at the goodies inside. I thought he looked relieved to be back in a familiar place.

"Good boy, Percy. You've been a good boy for Bradley." I dabbed at my nose with a tissue. "Thank you, sweetie. You've been good to us and we thank you."

I was speaking for myself. The monkey didn't pay me any more mind.

My brother was admitted to hospice care. He passed away two weeks later. My husband and I took turns in caring for the monkey until the animal homecare team could arrange a pickup for him. He's now been placed with a disabled teenager across town.

I figure she's a lucky girl to have him.

If An Infinite Number of Monkeys...

by Pete McArdle

This could be my big break, thought Chad, an interview with the great Norman Gross, billionaire author and recluse, the most prolific writer in English history. Chad was a decent writer himself, he had a flair for the right words and phrases, and no problem churning out pages. He simply couldn't get the publishing hierarchy's attention; he had lousy people skills and not a single connection.

But now things would be different. He'd nailed a plum assignment for *People* magazine, a day with the literary lion in his East Hampton mansion. In addition to scoring a national byline, Chad would get to sit at the knee of a master storyteller and soak up his style and M.O., share some food and some laughs and who knows, maybe Gross's agent or publisher if Chad were lucky.

As he packed a small valise with his tape-recorder, sweater, allergy pills, tissues, notebooks and pens, Chad felt like pinching himself to see if he was dreaming.

"O-o-w!" he cried, rubbing his skinny bicep. That overly enthusiastic pinch was going to leave a mark but it confirmed his fabulous, amazing, life-changing luck. Time to hop in his old jalopy and head for the Hamptons!

◊ ◊ ◊ ◊ ◊

The first surprise Chad had at Norman Gross's waterfront mansion was the greasy, rumpled affect of the man who answered the door and motioned him in. He was more than a hundred pounds overweight, his hair was frightful and he smelled of garlic, tobacco, and sweat. The second surprise was that this was no hygiene-challenged domestic; the man was, in fact, Gross.

"I know," he grumbled as he led the young journalist into a sparsely-furnished room overlooking the ocean, "I've let myself go. And never quite got around to changing that photo on the dust jacket of my books. That was me a quarter century ago."

"Well, Mr. Gross, you certainly don't look, um..." said Chad, digging himself into a deep hole. "*Hey*, look at this view!" Cheeks aflame, Chad rushed over to the picture window and beheld the majestic sun-splashed Atlantic.

"Yes, I love the water, always have," said his malodorous host, appearing at Chad's elbow. "Instead of bathing, I swim in the cold briny deep, at least once a week."

"That often?" said Chad, immediately regretting his tactless remark. No wonder he couldn't get ahead.

"How 'bout a glass of Scotch?" said Mr. Gross, blithely ignoring the fact that it was not yet ten in the morning. "And please, call me Norm."

"Er, no thanks, um…*Norm*, alcohol gives me the runs. Do you have any sparkling water?"

"Nah, I never buy that crap, I drink my water straight from the tap," said Norm, walking over to the bar and filling a glass with amber liquid. "They say Hemingway loved his Glenfiddich neat. And if it's good enough for Papa, well, it's good enough for me!"

"Ha, ha! Perhaps I should call you Ernest, then," said Chad, his laughter dying as the other man's expression remained unchanged.

"And what's your name again, young fellow?" said Norm, taking a healthy belt of his drink.

"Um, Chad. Chad Fairchild."

"Seriously?"

"Uh, *yeah*, that's my name."

"Amazing," said the great man, absent-mindedly stroking his beard. "I've written more novels and short stories than any man alive, and not once have I named a character 'Chad'. Not once!"

He drained his glass, picked up the half-empty bottle and poured himself another. "Are you sure I can't interest you in a drink, son?"

"No, Norm, uh, really, I'm fine," said Chad, nervously adjusting his glasses.

"Then what can I do for you?" said the literary icon, looking out the window with a thousand-yard stare. His hairy gut peeked out from under his sweat-stained undershirt.

"Um, I'm here to interview you for *People* magazine."

"*People* magazine, eh? And what does that tawdry purveyor of pablum want to know, my favorite sex position or the title of my latest release? That's easy, they're both 'The Missionary'."

"Ha, ha! 'The Missionary', I get it," said Chad, reaching for his notebook and pen. "A heart-pounding exploration into the darkest recesses of—"

A murderous glare from his subject cut Chad short. He took a deep breath and determined he was not having an asthma attack, just a severe case of hoof-in-mouth.

"Seriously, Mr. Gross, er…*Norm*," he said, "the world knows your work but next to nothing about you. The magazine sent me here to learn who you are and how you do it. Frankly, I'm most curious to know your views on writing, what the process of writing means to you, how you find your muse."

Norm walked over to a wooden box on the bookshelf, took out a half-smoked stogie and lit it up. "It's all been done, my boy," he said, pulling on the cigar and blowing a big cloud of smoke into Chad's face. "There's nothing new to write, it's all just a rehashing of the same old stories."

After a brief fit of coughing, Chad wrote in his notebook, *It's all been done* and *Next time, don't forget your rescue inhaler.* He cleared his throat and asked, "But how do you do it? That's what everyone wants to know. How does the legendary Norman Gross keep turning out classics, what's the secret of your amazing fecundity?"

Gross cracked up, cigar smoke spurting out his nose. "Fecundity? I'm not sure I know the meaning of that word but I *like* it, it sounds dirty." He took a sip of his Scotch and wiped his mouth with the back of his hand.

"I like you, kid, so I'm gonna show you how I do it. But this is strictly off the record, are we clear on that?"

Staring into the man's bloodshot eyes, Chad felt a pang of fear, or perhaps it was just indigestion. "Crystal," he said.

"Good, now follow me." The man walked over to a wood-paneled wall, pressed a button and a door miraculously appeared, the door to an elevator. "Now listen, bubbeleh," said Norm as they got on the elevator, "keep your hands in your pockets. The bastards bite."

Norm punched a button and the elevator dropped like a stone, finally stopping at a floor far below the Earth's surface. The elevator door opened and Chad and his mentor stepped out into a scene of complete and utter chaos: a room full of monkeys. As the Macarena blasted from hidden speakers, an orangutan ran circles around the room, a howler monkey swung from the chandelier, and two chimpanzees played ping-pong with a paddle in each hand. The room stank of urine, scat, and spoiled fruit, some of which adorned the carpet, walls, and ceiling, and a huge, lowland gorilla was somehow managing to nap in the corner.

"This is the rec room," yelled Norm, ducking as half an apple flew past his head. "But what you want to see is in here." He led Chad though a door and down a long, blissfully silent corridor.

"Everything's sound-proofed," the legendary author explained, "or else you'd lose your friggin' mind. Here we are."

A pair of double-doors slid open and Chad entered a large room that looked like nothing as much as a busy newsroom at a major metropolitan newspaper. Industrial-strength fluorescent lights shone down on a honeycomb of at least a hundred desks and swivel chairs, and the only sound was the loud staccato tapping of keys. But instead of intrepid cub reporters and hard-boiled journalists, these seats were occupied by monkeys, whaling away on old-fashioned typewriters.

"Gotta use typewriters," said Norm, "they type too damn hard for computer keyboards."

Chad stood there, mouth agape, until he saw a bearded tamarin pluck a flea from his neighbor's head and swallow it. He closed his mouth and through clenched teeth said, "Norm, what on Earth are they doing?"

"Why, they're working, me fine bucko," said Gross, grinning widely through a cloud of cigar smoke. "Slowly adding to the collected works of Norman Gross. This is one of fifty production rooms in the facility, ten-thousand monkeys typing in twelve-hour shifts."

"Typing?" wheezed Chad, suffering significant asthma symptoms thanks to the wealth of monkey dander. "Typing what?"

"Oh, pretty much anything. Poetry, love stories, textbooks, whodunits, and of course, a huge amount of garbled nonsense. You name it, they do it." Norm took a moment to pick his nose, then stared at the dried, crusty treasure before wiping it on his pants leg.

"I gather the monkeys' work at the end of the week and edit it. They're good for five-to-six books a month. I publish the good stuff under my name and the genre work under pseudonyms. We give the textbooks to schools and send the completely unintelligible crap to the literary journals."

Chad was speechless, not to mention slightly short of breath.

"So, go ahead, young Master Fairchild, have a look around," said his portly host, flashing crowded, tobacco-stained incisors.

Young Master Fairchild walked away in a daze before turning down a side aisle and looking over the monkeys' shoulders as they worked.

A pygmy marmoset typed: *Blln sune92 m skk!*7 Ij&43*

A spider monkey wrote: *His heart pounded frantically as he slipped his hand down the back of her white lace panties.* The cheeky furball winked at Chad as he walked away.

A black and white Colobus stared at blank paper, undoubtedly blocked.

And from a tufted capuchin, this: *It was a new dawn for vampires and werewolves. They would have to unite against the blood-sucking lawyers or face extinction!*

Chad could not believe his eyes as he toured the room. From a thousand furry fingers came nonsense and iambic pentameter, total garbage and rocket science, wasted paper and porn, some of it quite good. There was an elderly lemur wearing a green eyeshade whose work would have been perfect for *Reader's Digest*.

So this was how the greatest author of our time did it, and Chad had agreed not to tell a soul. Gross stood by the entrance, smoking his cigar and absent-mindedly scratching his ass as Chad came upon a wizened baboon in the corner. He watched as the old baboon wrote: *It was the best of times, it was the worst of times, it was the age of wisdom, it was the age of foolishness...*

"Why, that's truly fantastic," said Chad regaining his voice. "You're a genius!"

Thanks wrote the baboon.

"Um...you understand English?"

Duh! typed the monkey, rolling his eyes.

"By any chance, do you know how to text?"

Double-duh!

Chad took a quick peek at Gross—he was busy drinking from a pocket flask—and slipped the baboon his cell. "This is my work phone, my personal number's on there under 'Fairchild, Chadwick'."

Chadwick? Are you serious?

"Don't *you* start," rasped Chad, and then softening his voice, he said, "And what's your name, old fella?"

Tap-tap-tappety-tap-tap: *Aristotle.*

"*Really!*" said Chad.

No, just messing with you. The name's Barry.

"Well, Barry, it was very nice meeting you. And I look forward to texting you," he said, resting his hand on the beast's hairy shoulder.

Like that, Barry snapped and Chad jumped back, cursing and howling and waving his bloodied hand.

Norm came waddling over, gave the baboon a dirty look and escorted the bleeding, wheezing interviewer out of the room and into a different elevator than the one they took down. "I told you they bite," he grumbled as the doors whisked close.

Later, Chad sat on a couch in the study, having been inoculated for tuberculosis, a bag of frozen peas on his heavily-bandaged hand. Although it was only a little past noon, his host was totally plotzed, already well into his second fifth of Glenfiddich. It was clearly time to go.

Chad thanked him, although there was practically nothing he could use for his magazine piece, and said, "There's just one thing I don't understand, Norm. The monkeys were going wild in the rec room, pounding their chests and throwing shit at me. How do you get them to behave so well when they're working?"

"Simple, my boy," said Gross, grinning crookedly. "Their collars contain tiny two-volt batteries." He removed what looked like a pager from his belt. "They sit still and type—twelve hours a day, seven days a week—or *zaap*, they get a nice little shock for their trouble. I got the idea from a Peter Gabriel song."

Chad was aghast. His idol was a drunken lout, a phony, and worst of all, a user and abuser of monkeys. Chad handed the man his frozen vegetables and left without a word.

Later that night as he lay in bed, unable to sleep, Chad received a text message from Barry, the silver-haired baboon: *Sorry bout the bite. Its act U ly a sign of affection.*

Chad replied: *H8 to C U pissed off!*

Barry: *LOL! Seriously...You must help me escape, I h8 it here. I'd B good 4 U, I'd B surprisingly good 4 U.*

Chad: *Is that frm W. Side Story?*

Barry: *No, Evita. I jst luv Madonna.*

Chad: *LOL!! Barry, I think thish is the beginning of a B U tiful friendship.*

Barry: *Here's looking at u kid! 2moro midnight, on the beach.*

◊ ◊ ◊ ◊ ◊

Chad pulled into the driveway a little too fast and skidded to a halt perilously close to the garage door. The Lamborghini *Diablo* was clearly going to take a little getting used to. He hurried inside, up the spiral staircase, past the glass-enclosed living room, finally arriving at the combination kitchen/patio on the roof.

"Sorry I'm late," he said, setting his packages down on the stainless steel counter, "but these nitwits at the grocery store kept pestering me for my autograph."

"No worries, mate," said an electronic voice with a passable Aussie accent. Barry's hand was a blur as he typed on a small laptop. "What's for din-dins?" said the tinny voice.

"Well, I'm having a nice steak with a tossed salad and baked potato. And for you, I got some fresh boysenberries, two dozen crickets, and a freshly-killed rabbit I found by the side of the highway."

"Ah, nothing like a little bruised hare on the barby, eh?"

"And that's not all," said Chad, hastening over to the table and lounge chairs where Barry sat, all decked out in flowered Jams and gold Ray-Bans, watching the sun set over the placid Pacific.

Chad reached into a paper bag and pulled out a bottle of Dom Peringnon, '07.

"To celebrate our latest bestseller, 'Bond Time for Bonzo', the heart-warming story of a poor circus chimp who makes it big on Wall Street!"

He popped the cork, filled a couple of flutes to overflowing, and handed one to the baboon.

"To Bonzo!" toasted Chad.

"And to us, mate!" chirped the laptop, as man and beast clinked glasses and took a sip of the bubbly.

"Oy, that's a wee bit of wonderful," said Barry, typing furiously. "But I thought alcohol gave you the shits."

Chad plopped himself down in the lounge chair next to Barry's and patted his burgeoning gut. "Actually, I'm developing a taste for it," he said.

gorilla

by Christine Hamm

He says, *Gorilla, huh!* as if it were something with a mind of its own. The gorilla is not real; the gorilla is made out of rubber, synthetic hair and dark. The gorilla has real action eyes! They blink up and down when you snap your head back and forth. The gorilla tastes like Old Spice and hair cream on the inside, with a faint odor of Amstel and burning leather.

When the gorilla feels something bite the skin under his shoulder blade where he can't reach, his fur ripples. It's actually a series of muscles contracting and releasing along his spine, but it looks like a breeze snaking up a grassy hill.

Most mornings, you find the gorilla quivering in the corner of your bedroom like a wild animal, his breath rasping and faltering. You pull the covers up over your arms and neck; you pretend not to notice.

My Darling, the Gorilla

by Christine Hamm

He rips the door off the hinges at 4am—it's not even locked. He
stumbles and hits his
head on the chair. He lies still, his mouth slightly open. I can smell
the piss on his pants—
there's a yellow trail of translucent vomit down one arm. His eyes
are so swollen they
look like leaking red fruits, as pulpy as plums. He makes himself a
bowl of blackberry ice
cream and falls asleep. He tips over, wakes up; he steps on the cat's
tail, he steps on the
cat. He leaves the refrigerator door open, knocks milk all over the
red-tiled floor. He
turns on the gas stove. He tries to light a cigarette and sets his
beard on fire. Milk
footprints follow him into the bathroom. He tries to make a knot
of the shower curtain
and hang himself, he tries to take off his shoes and pants at the
same time. He ends up
face down in the tub, scrabbling and slipping. He pauses: his breath
is wet and heavy.
After a moment, he asks for a beer.

gorilla girl

by Christine Hamm

for Frances Murphy

I'm not going to end with the punchline, "and the gorilla girl is a
man" because it's more complicated than that. Like many girls, she
was born into a body she didn't recognize. One that
grew hair across her mouth, one that grew large, pale and mottled,
pushed out full flaps that could pass for breasts, that were breasts.
She liked to wear a dress: who doesn't? She favored pink and peach,
gauzy sleeves, pearl necklaces, and a saucy small hat, perched at
an angle. She decided to make the best of the beard that surprised
her each morning—pincurls, styling gel, a contract with the circus,
with the traveling freak show. It's not easy being a gorilla or a girl:
eventually, after climbing all those skyscrapers, swatting all those
biplanes, they're going to catch you. They're going to catch you
on the subway steps, or outside a restaurant smoking after ten.
Eventually, the cops and doctors will part your legs in a courtroom,
and on a metal table, will unbraid the mystery buried in all that fur.

Fascination

by Mike Berger

Stately. Slender;
the apotheosis of
elegance.
Classic beauty.
Sharp nose and high
cheeks with a
voluptuous lower lip.
Her smile was wry.
Something earthy
drew you in.

We went to an elegant
restaurant.
It was dark and subdued
with flickering images
dancing in the candlelight.
Soft music hung in the
perfumed air.
Raven hair caressed
her cheek, a foil to big
brown eyes. When she
smiled she wrinkled
her nose.

I was surprised when she
ordered a T-bone steak,
medium rare. We laughed at
not being able to see our
food or the color of the wine.
Suddenly!
The fascination came to a
crashing halt. She bent low
revealing her breasts; they
were covered with tangled
masses of hair.

The Man Who Brought The Monkeys

by Henry Sane

Like most of my friends, I remember hoping every day that summer—the summer of my tenth year—we'd get a special visit from the man who brought the monkeys. When August came around, I felt sure that, once again, he'd skip over our neighborhood, leaving me and my friends to go monkey-less for a third year in a row. (Living in south Florida, it is needless to say that it was torture not to enjoy some monkey refreshments every once in a while!)

Finally though, just when the talk of "back-to-school wear" was starting to come up in advertisements and dinner conversations, our prayers were answered.

It was the hottest day of the summer—one of those days when I swear I could see ants sizzle on the pavement outside my bedroom window—when I saw the Monkey Man's big rainbow-colored truck round the corner and head down our back alley street. If only I could express the joy I felt when I saw that happy little truck—and then when I heard the first notes of that merry, repetitive tune!

Wasting no time, I grabbed the money I'd been saving in my top drawer and raced out of the house, hoping for my friends' sakes that they too had heard the familiar tune and that their mothers would let them out into the blistering heat for just a few minutes without sun block (such a delay could cost them precious seconds, and the Monkey Man never stayed around for very long).

When I stepped outside, my knees buckled as the aroma of the Baboon Floats and Gorilla Kabobs wafted under my nose. I realized for a fleeting moment that life felt like a dream—but that smell! It was enough to slap you in the face, shake you around and assure you that you were most certainly living in reality. I have since come to realize, so many years later, that that was, without a doubt, the most real moment of my entire life.

As I approached the curb, I met with my friends, looking around to make sure the whole gang was there. There was Freddy, Pitch, Walt, Lance, his little sister Becca, Chris P., Chris K., Mattie, Ham, Little Mikey, Geoff, Jesse, Melissa,

Gretchen—even my old Uncle Abe came galloping out from our house and joined us like he always did when he saw us out playing kickball in the street. Everyone— except of course Mitchell, whose parents sent him to his aunt's house in Virginia for the summer—was accounted for. I was delighted that almost all the kids I was closest to—Uncle Abe included, being such a kid at heart—could share in this magical experience with me.

It only took a few seconds for the monkey truck to reach us. Within a few yards of our waiting post (beside the "Speed Limit 20" sign outside my house), the truck pulled to a stop amidst the bustling crowd, sending visible shivers through every nerve of each surrounding child. Even the parents, who came wandering out of their houses after us, seemed to recall the joy of their own respective childhoods.

Without delay the Monkey Man, whose pleasant demeanor was apparent even through the reflective windshield, left his driver's seat, disappeared momentarily into the back of the monkey truck, and reappeared at the side window, indicating he was open for business, willing and ready to cool off the burning masses. As he shuffled about, setting plastic jars of kabob sticks and monkey toppings upon the window counter, his thin silver mustache twitched ever so slightly, accentuating his glowing smile, which grew bigger and bigger as he watched us all rush madly toward the window, hoping to be first in line. Leaning half his slender body through the serving window, he exclaimed merrily, "No need to push and shove! I've got a full supply on board, so there's plenty to go around! Now," he said, looking about with a hint of playful mystery, "who's up first?"

Naturally, everyone shouted at once, "Me, me, me!"

But as I could have guessed, no one knew yet what they wanted. Therefore, I contented myself to hang in the middle of the pack with Uncle Abe, pondering over the menu board's many options while the kids in front of me blurted out their orders..

"I'll have a Chocolate Chimp Sundae!" cried Gretchen.

"Marmoset Marmalade for me!" shouted Pitch.

"Gimme a Gibbon Ribbon Rainbow!" exclaimed Lance.

"I wanna Lil' Lemur Pop!" Becca yelled to her brother.

"Big Baboon Float! Big Baboon Float!" bellowed Ham, who was obviously sick of being spoken over.

"Gelada Gelato here!" declared Chris P.

"Gelada Gelato for me, too!" dittoed Chris K. (who always got what Chris P. got).

"I'd like just a small Ape Shake, please," said Geoff in his quiet, polite way.

When all the initial orders had been placed and fulfilled, I found that as we had been inching forward (Uncle Abe and I), we were suddenly at the front of the line. At last I had the Monkey Man's full attention.

"And what can I get for you, young fella?" the Monkey Man asked me, smiling brightly.

Despite studying the menu board's every detail for several minutes, I still hadn't decided what I wanted. Everything looked so good! After several seconds of hesitation, Uncle Abe said jovially, "C'mon Davey, quit holdin' up the line! Monkeys don't come and go for you alone, ya know!"

Everyone laughed, including the Monkey Man. I laughed a bit, too, but my appreciation for Uncle Abe's silliness was stifled by my resolute concentration on the menu board.

"Now, now," the Monkey Man said gently to Uncle Abe. "I'm sure he'll make up his mind soon, won't you, young fella? Tell me, what's caught your eye above all else?"

A little embarrassed, but still willing to satisfy the Monkey Man's request, I told him there was something on the menu board I'd never before seen or tasted. I asked the him what it was, pointing to its picture.

"Oh, the Tamarin Dream?" he said. "It's brand new and it's simply delectable! It's a small, orange monkey that is just bursting with flavor! It's like a monkey parade came waltzing down your taste buds! You have to try it! You just have to!"

With a huge smile and several exaggerated nods, I agreed, my eyes all the while dancing madly behind closed eyelids. Without hesitation, the Monkey Man turned to his store of treats and fetched the Tamarin Dream, passing it down to my eager little hands, which accepted the gift with the utmost delight. As I studied my delicious-looking treat, Uncle Abe ordered an extra-large Gorilla Kabob, paid the Monkey Man for the both of us (I'd forgotten in all my excitement), and directed me out of the way so as to allow the next customers to take our place.

By the time we had moved out the way, I still hadn't tasted my Tamarin Dream. I was in too much awe of its appetizing features—and from what I saw, I was sure this would be the most exquisite thing I ever put my tongue to.

But oh, how looks can deceive!

I took one bite and, within an instant, was horror-stricken. The monkey treat, as if out of some terrifying tale of the unknown, *came to life*.

When I look back on that unprecedented moment, I still have trouble believing it actually happened—

The Tamarin Dream—a *monkey*—came to life in my very hands! (I repeat it to emphasize that, despite the obviously supernatural implications, this was *reality*).

Out of instinct I screamed, dropping the monkey to the pavement, watching in pure baffled fear as it scampered away and up a nearby oak tree, finally coming to rest on one of the more elevated branches. Uncle Abe, having seen the whole thing, could only stand by, frozen, speechless, white as a ghost. The surrounding parents reacted similarly, while their children suddenly burst into pitiable shrieks and wails, many of them tossing down their own monkey treats for fear of an equally terrifying result.

The Monkey Man, however, having heard my piercing cry, immediately exited his vehicle and came to comfort me. The calmness of his disposition suggested that this had happened before and, more importantly, that he knew how to handle it.

As the reality settled in, many of the parents—Uncle Abe included—started hurling vicious insults at the Monkey Man, demanding answers from him, wondering how he could be so careless as to let a tainted shipment of monkeys get into his store, and how he could then sell such a frightful treat to an unsuspecting child.

But no query or insult was too great for the Monkey Man. In a display of unparalleled charisma, he stood upright in his lanky posture, gripped the lapels of his jacket confidently and spoke in an authoritative yet consoling voice that at once hushed the panicked masses.

"Good people!" he exclaimed merrily. "Come now and listen! Allow me please to explain this strange phenomenon that has just occurred! I promise there is no cause for concern, for while this is indeed a very rare scenario we've all just witnessed, I assure you there is no danger in a monkey that should suddenly come to life! While I cannot explain the cause of this unearthly occurrence (nor can any scientist of notable repute), it is simply something that happens every so often. But look now! Up there, in the tree—the monkey simply sits there, keeping its distance due to a level of fear that is of a far more severe nature than what any one of us could ever know."

Following his suggestion, we all looked up and, just as the Monkey Man had said, the monkey remained frozen in place as would any creature afraid for its life.

"Now if you will observe…" the Monkey Man started.

The Monkey Man, with the unadulterated attention of the crowd now upon him, then grabbed hold of the tree's massive trunk and, like he were the most agile of youths, propelled himself up the tree with such energy that if one had blinked, the act of ascension might have been missed entirely. Before we knew it, the Monkey Man was upon the same branch as the living monkey treat. With great balance, the Monkey Man then fished into his pocket for some small morsel, which he held out as if attempting to coax the monkey toward him. As we watched in anxious throes below, we could overhear the Monkey Man say calming words, as if the monkey treat could understand the sweet nature of his tone. Then, carefully, the Monkey Man began to shimmy across the long branch toward the frightened monkey. When he was within a few feet of the little monkey, he extended the morsel he'd removed earlier from his pocket until it was easily within the grasp of the timid creature. The Monkey Man remained perfectly still as the monkey began to edge slightly toward him. The monkey, with obvious caution, examined the morsel he was offered and reached out with what appeared to be conscious hands to take the morsel and shove it inside of himself as if he were eating it.

Truly it was a moving and unforgettable performance!

The monkey, having finished off the morsel, was suddenly very lively. He danced and sang out happy-sounding notes, to which the Monkey Man responded by offering yet another morsel from his pocket. The monkey, as before, accepted it with what I perceived to be delight. The next morsel, however, the Monkey Man held just out of reach of the monkey, persuading it to follow him as he shimmied carefully back down the tree. When they reached the ground, the Monkey Man gently lifted the tamed creature and held it like a baby, feeding it several morsels, which caused it to make many pleasurable sounds.

By this point, the crowd had amassed around the Monkey Man, who bade us keep quiet so as not to startle the fragile monkey treat. He held his companion down low for the children to catch a glimpse up close, and we all instantly felt secure by its obviously placid demeanor. As I gazed down upon it (this was perhaps the strangest moment of all), I swear I remember seeing what appeared to be a *face* on the monkey treat, which then produced a gaping smile and innocent, sleepy eyes to represent its apparent complacency. After several minutes of silence, the monkey, curled into a little ball, was completely motionless; and once again, it looked like a normal monkey treat, lifeless as it should be.

Fixed still in a state of dreaminess, my friends and I all looked at each other and realized what a truly special moment we had all just shared in.

◊ ◊ ◊ ◊ ◊

From that point forward, the visits from the Monkey Man held a new sort of allure and wonder for everyone in the neighborhood. Before that memorable day, the monkey treats were delightful in and of themselves; but from then on, there was a new feeling, an encompassing whimsy that perhaps, just once more, someone's monkey treat might actually come to life and give us another grand performance. Sadly though, the magic of that day would never be repeated.

Still, I've never given up hope. For even to this day, as I delve further into the riper of my years, I still listen out for the man who brings the monkeys, hoping that the next time he comes around, my monkey treat might, just maybe, come to life once more.

THE LOST APES

by Viktor Kowalski

In every ape's lifetime there comes a time of great weariness, a time of burdened brow and cloudy thoughts. Such time was now upon Clay, the rightful ruler of all ape-kind not by birth and heritage, but by fist and fang.

Clay sat upon his rocky throne and the weariness claimed him. He rested his chin upon his hand moodily as he contemplated the red roads that he had taken to ascend and keep his rule. Before his mind's eye passed a panorama of his human servants giving him offerings in fruit, always keeping behind the bars that encompassed Clay's mighty kingdom. Clay had, on many occasions, tried to impart some of his wisdom on his human servants but his efforts were fruitless. He had come to realize that his mighty oratory skills were far beyond the capacity of feeble human's minds to understand—Clay remembered all the times he had stood upon a large rock delivering his decrees, and the humans hid their ignorance behind derisive laughter, their minds unable to comprehend the truth behind his words. They carried strange hand-held devices which clicked and flashed bright lights at him.

He also remembered Glaber, the ambitious and devious throne usurper he had to best in ape-to-ape combat to protect his throne. But now all this merged into a meaningless panorama of shadows and dreams, as Clay gazed dreamily at his kingdom and his subordinates.

"What bothers you, oh great King?" came the screeching voice to his right.

"I'm in a state of pensive disarray."

"Eh?" blurted Reggie the chimp.

"I'm weary, Reggie," Clay sighed dejectedly. "The burden of kingship weighs heavily on my broad shoulders."

Reggie was basking in the afternoon sun, lying prostrate on the green grass beside Clay's massive form. Presently he rose to his feet and eyed his King.

"My lord, you're tired of the life of the court. Come with me to the great trees and let us roam them for a while."

"Nay. Those things cannot lift my spirit. I shudder at the task at hand, and doubt that I'm ape enough to do it."

"A task, my King?"

"Aye," said Clay. "Look at those apes yonder, my subordinates."

He swept his large hand over the sunny plain and pointed his finger at the bunch of primates that were drudging along with a slow gait, their faces expressionless and their limbs dangling limply.

"They have that look in their eyes."

"What look, my King?"

"The one of apathy and dullness. They grow lazy. Their apish soul is not a wild fiery blaze, but merely a waning flicker of a flame. Where has their zest for life gone, Reggie? Their live and breathe, aye, but alas, they are dead inside. They are not truly alive, but just sleepwalking. The worst of it is, they are unaware of their own mindless condition. But I can see it, reflected in the emptiness of their eyes. Just as I have seen it mirrored many times on the faces of the humans that visit me. It's a most terrible fate to live in a walking daze. Shall ours be the same as theirs?"

"But, that's why you're here, King. You'll teach them."

"It matters little, good Reggie. I have tried to teach them wisdom, but my words fall on deaf ears."

Reggie fell silent, his big eyes blinking and his mouth parted in a confused "o". Clay looked down at his companion gravely, and shook his head. Reggie was an old friend, but Clay knew the chimp's mind was not cast in the same mould as his own. Reggie had a good and loyal heart, but no deep broodings were meant to be contemplated by the somewhat dim-witted chimp.

A clamor rose from a group of apes who started bickering over some fruit. Clay watched wearily for a while, and then spat in disgust. Growing tired of the sight, he retreated to the back of his habitat—that is to say, his royal quarters— with rest on his mind, and hope that dreams may cast a light on the way out of his predicament. The heat was intense even in this late hour of the day, and so he was driven to find refreshment in the small lake nearby. The lake's surface glinted brightly as Clay loomed over it to quench his thirst. He could see his image reflected in the shiny surface of the lake and his mind wandered.

The lake seemed like a mirror to another, stranger world, and Clay found himself lost deep in thoughts as he gazed in the dark brown eyes of the ape that grinned at him from the other side of the surface. An eerie sensation traveled along his spine and Clay felt as if his spirit started to leave his body. He tried to move and shake it off, but his body would not obey his commands; deeper and deeper his mind sank into the two brown orbs that now seemed to merge into an endless abyss, drawing Clay's very essence into it.

Grey mists obscured his vision, and through them Clay caught glimpses of dark shapes gliding like ghosts upon water. The sky was dark and menacing; tall, exotic trees loomed over him and cast deep shadows over the land. The ground was carpeted by a low, thick growth of vegetation. Clay's vision slowly cleared and he started to make out the dim shapes scrambling around him. He recoiled in surprise when he recognized them to be apes—like himself, but gigantic and powerful were they; apes of another age, more ancient and more savage. These were apes of the Wild, untamed and full of life, unhindered by the confines of civilization that, Clay knew deep in his soul, had taken the apish vigor out of his brethren. He knew all this, not by rational thought, but some dim and ancient instinct.

Now the apes fought terrible grey monstrosities with fierce determination. These foes were—Clay understood it—an ancient breed of primates, lost and forgotten to ape-kind, now reemerged in a last attempt to stall the crumbling of their dying race by stealing the offspring of the younger races. They were terrible and brutal, smiting and gnawing their way through the ranks of the beleaguered apes which huddled in a circle around their young in a desperate last stand.

It was then that the red mists of fury descended on Clay's mind. He knew not these apes, but he felt a strange kinship with them; mayhap they were his wild ancestors or his brethren from beyond the chasms of Space and Time. They were Life, and the grey monsters were Death. Inside his soul and heart he felt his wrath towards the foul attackers rising, and he leapt to the defender's side, bellowing a challenge that reverberated with savage ferocity.

Clay sprang among the grey apes with such speed and ferocity that he resembled a tiger, but an ape. He tackled one foe and started to beat his head with his mighty fists closed. The grey ape roared furiously and locked his arms around Clay's body, and Clay witnessed the brutal strength that lay in the monster's sinews. Breath was instantly squeezed out of his lungs, and his head swam with pain. Bolts of agony spread through his chest like wildfire as he struggled to release himself from the iron grip. Here were not the rotting muscles of the civilized apes he was accustomed to dealing with; here was the raw and desperate strength of the Wild that sought to extinguish the flame of life that burned inside of him. Clay struggled in vain to free himself, and just as he was on verge of expiration, he heard the fearful cries of the younglings pierce the clamor of battle.

He felt red fury surge from his soul, and in a burst of apish rage he broke free from the death-grip, landing ferocious punches against his opponent. The flurry of strokes would have felled a weaker ape, but the grey beast shrugged them off and circled Clay in an attempt to come up from his behind. Clay snarled his defiance and once again sprang at his opponent, arms spread wide, heedless of his injuries. Blow after terrible blow struck the bulk of the grey ape, and each time a grunt of pain broke from his throat.

At last, the intensity of Clay's hatred took its toll on his foe, and the grey ape bellowed awfully. He leapt away from the fray, hurt and bleeding, limping away in haste. This seemed to turn the tide of battle. Demoralized, the others soon followed, and in a few moments the glade was occupied only by the black apes who snarled after the retreating forms of their attackers. Clay faced the haggard defenders; their bodies, although larger and of shaggier fur, were very much like his, and their faces bore the familiar visages of warmth and friendliness, in stark contrast to the blind ruthlessness of the grey apes.

The apes regarded Clay curiously, but remained silent. Clay didn't know if they could speak his language—or any language at all—since they seemed to belong to an ancient breed, probably one of the first Old Apes that inhabited the misty lands of A-fu-ri-ka, the birthplace of his ancestors. A large gorilla, bearing fresh wounds from the battle, separated himself from the huddled bunch and warily approached Clay.

As long as he lived Clay would never forget that moment; each remaining day of his hard life he would be able to vividly recall the feeling of fierce pride swelling inside his breast as the gorilla laid his paw on his shoulder, and nodded his grim appreciation. No words were necessary; no words could even begin to describe the storm of emotions brewing inside of Clay that almost made him shed a tear at the fate of his mysterious brethren. He marveled at their courage and will to stand against insurmountable odds.

The gorilla backed off, and soon the pack started to disappear into the grey mists. With them, the whole world started to reel and shatter and Clay soon found himself pitched into a black abyss.

◊ ◊ ◊ ◊ ◊

A distant sound echoed through the gulfs of Time and Space, a sound both terrible and weird, yet somehow recognizable to Clay. He felt drawn to it, like a moth to the flame—but more like an ape to a banana—as he slowly regained possession of his own mind.

"Aie! The King is dead! Aie! Aie!" Reggie shrieked like a mad hill-ape, drawing the attention of a large number of other primates to the prostrate form of King Clay, who lay near the shimmering pool, eyes closed and his body unresponsive.

"Aie! Who will lead us now? Oh, great King! Woe to us all! Aie!"

"Cease your bellowing, you blundering fool," the King's voice rasped through half-parted lips. "You sound like an ox, not an ape."

Clay slowly rose to his feet and stretched his mighty limbs. He felt pain in his joints and muscles; pain borne of great exertion that seemed elusive to his mind yet somehow known to his soul.

"Oh, great King! What happened to you?" shrieked Reggie. "I observed you from that tree yonder as you went to drink from the lake, and as I watched you stare into the lake I seemed to temporarily lose my sanity—as it has been known to happen on some occasions—for I saw your form slowly drained into a whirlpool that opened up to swallow you. As I rushed to your aid, I had lost the sight of you, and when I neared the lake, I found you lying on the grass—apparently dead!"

"I live!" roared Clay, and the primates shrank back in fear. A soft murmur passed between the slowly growing circle of spectators that had gathered around the King.

"Reggie, what you saw was not due to lapse of sanity, although such instances were indeed known to happen to you. My dream-like experience is best to remain untold, for it cannot be explained by words, nor understood by reason. But know this!"

Clay faced his subordinates who eyed him with alarm and suspicion, but were still transfixed with the resonance of his words. He regarded them grimly.

"I have seen the other side of the Veil that we apes call life; I have treaded on strange, misty shores and battled an ancient menace side by side with our long-lost kin. I, King Clay, have seen the face of the primordial apes, those your mothers used to scare you when you misbehaved. I felt the evil strength of their blood-stained hands upon my flesh. I know not how I came to be there, or how I made my way back, but my path is now clearly laid out in front of me.

"You walk like dumb brutes and waste away your days in spiritless passivity. You have food and water a-plenty and yet you quarrel over trivialities and fight among yourselves like base animals! Bah! But no more! You are dogs, and I must make you apes. By my hand will I mold you into proper apes, worthy of our ancestor's legacy, so I swear."

The apes gazed in complete silence and mouths agape, uncertain what to think or feel, although in their countenances was evident a deep and mysterious understanding of the King's cryptic words.

"All hail King Clay, the ruler of all!" shouted Reggie.

A cheer went up from all the apes.

King Clay thumped mightily at his wide chest, letting out a long and powerful grunt from the depths of his lungs, and in that grunt was a note of power and hope, but also a subtler one, a hint of sadness and want of things that once were but may never be again.

THE TASTE OF GOLD

by Bernie Mojzes

Now, you know how people are. They come up with all these crazy stories, allegories for knowledge and wisdom and all that crap to pass on to future generations down the ages. Brahma dreams the universe into existence. Prometheus steals fire from the gods. Thor sneezes out a big glob of snot and names it Iceland. Yeah, so maybe I made up the last one. Who knows? Maybe a couple hundred years from now it'll turn up in someone's thesis. Just hope no one asks where the British Isles came from.

There's a thousand of these stories, a million. All spinning tales of fantastic beings who embody the best and the worst and the most extreme of what constitutes being human. Every tribe has its own set—one god to embody each archetype. And only ever one god per archetype.

Or that's what they'd like you to believe.

I know better.

◊ ◊ ◊ ◊ ◊

It all started one night, sitting in McShea's with some friends from my writing group. I was nursing my third shot of Jameson's while everyone else extolled the virtues of a particular local brew with the unlikely name of "Gold Monkey." Except for Greg, who has a thing for Dead Guys. Don't ask.

Anyway, I'd been reading up on trickster gods for a story I was working on and had stumbled upon a reference to Sun Wukong, the Monkey King of Chinese mythology. Not at all what I needed for my Coyote story, but by my fourth shot of Jameson's, I'd come up with a brilliant idea: I was going to send a bottle of Gold Monkey addressed to Sun Wukong, People's Republic of China, with no return address. Yeah, I know, right? But that's not the brilliant part.

The brilliant part was I was going to send an empty bottle.

See, the Monkey King is a god of immeasurable appetites. Don't believe me?

Look him up. Sending a single bottle is a taunt. Sending a single *empty* bottle? Ha! I scribbled my idea on a napkin and promptly forgot all about it.

And the other thing I forgot? It hardly seems worth mentioning the raven that sat on the sill of the window next to our table, watching us through the glass with clever eyes that reflected the flickering neon *Coors* sign that hung above it.

"I think it wants my fries," Barb said.

She was wrong.

◊ ◊ ◊ ◊ ◊

So here's where it starts getting weird. And I totally don't blame you if you don't believe me, but this is the absolute God's honest truth, so help me Bertrand Russell.

Two days later, I got an email from one of the people in the group.

"Is there a reason you stuck your Monkey King napkin in my purse?" she asked.

Monkey King napkin? It took me a minute, and then I remembered. No idea how it got in her purse, though. No idea either how an empty bottle of Gold Monkey Ale ended up in the back seat of my car, with a black feather, a couple tufts of grey fur, a condom wrapper, and an earring I didn't recognize. I told my spousal unit it must have been some neighborhood kids. She said we'd talk about this again. Later. Making the best of things, I found a nice gift box, packed up the bottle, and shipped it to China.

◊ ◊ ◊ ◊ ◊

It was a few months before I next had any direct involvement in the events that followed, but I don't see any value in making you wait that long. Long story short: Sun Wukong received my package and flew into a rage over his inability to extract even the tiniest drop of the succulent beverage whose mere scent drove him into a frenzy of desire. He immediately set off to find the source of this most inaccessible of delicacies. His first stop, both because it was closest and because it was the only visa in his passport that hadn't expired, was Japan, where he had recently gone to feast on fugu liver sushi.

Now in China, everyone knows about the Monkey King and his capricious and enormous appetite. No one, not even the hardline Communist airport bureaucrat who processed his boarding pass and scanned his carry-on luggage, tried to prevent him from bringing his empty bottle of Golden Monkey onto the flight. And *she* didn't even believe in him.

Arriving in Tokyo, Sun Wukong breezed through customs. They didn't believe in him, either, and had little respect for the ancient superstitions of another land, but they still had yellowing posters of the Monkey King hanging in employee lounges and washrooms next to the labor regulations posters and the signs that read, "All Employees Must Wash Hands Before Returning to Wok." And while someone had gone so far as to draw a Fu Manchu mustache on the posters, everyone took the warnings seriously: "VERY DANGEROUS. DO NOT ATTEMPT TO APPREHEND." Over which someone had scribbled in red marker: "Give the monkey what he wants."

But nobody could. He stopped passengers, airline attendants, baggage handlers and one somewhat bemused teenaged schoolgirl who slapped halfheartedly at a wandering tentacle that kept slipping out of her purse to fondle strangers, asking—no, demanding—that they tell him where to find the Gold Monkey.

"Gold Monkey?" said the girl. "I..." She stopped a moment to snatch the tentacle away from a passerby and shove it forcefully back into her purse. "Stop that right this instant," she said, speaking into her purse. She turned back to the Monkey King. "I can't take him *anywhere!* Anyway, I don't know anything about this monkey of yours. Have you checked the zoo?"

That, Sun Wukong realized, was probably the best advice he was going to get from the people here. He bowed to the girl and her tentacled friend and headed off in the direction of the information booth to hail a taxi.

Imagine his surprise when he saw, standing in front of the information booth, a sleekly beautiful woman. She was tall and thin, with an unusually long face and a pointed nose—certainly not the sublimely beautiful moon-shaped face of classic literature, but stunning nonetheless. She wore a form-fitting white dress, with a fur draped over her shoulders. She held a placard with his name written in an impeccably calligraphied hand.

This in itself was something of a surprise, but the true surprise was something that no one else in the airport could see: she was a fox. He approached her cautiously, for foxes are tricky creatures, and many a man has lost himself in their enchanting eyes, and bowed.

She smiled, and returned the bow.

"Welcome to Tokyo," she said. "Your presence here brings me great joy. I am honored to finally meet you."

Sun Wukong returned the compliment, though he remained suspicious. He was always suspicious of tricksters. "Please, do not take offense, but I wonder what it is that brings you here?"

"Oh, I am here to meet you. I heard that you had come here seeking the perfect beverage. I am, if I may say most humbly, quite an expert on such things, and put myself in your service."

The Monkey King's eyes lit. *That* is what had once filled the empty bottle which he carried: the perfect beverage. It was these three words that sealed his fate, that caused him to change the nature of his quest. Before, he had been motivated by a mild curiosity which, had he been distracted away from the object of his desire by something like an excellent noodle shop, or a beautiful fox, would have been forgotten as quickly and as thoroughly as if it had never existed. But the *perfect beverage?* For that, he would travel to the ends of the earth.

"Lead on," he said.

◇ ◇ ◇ ◇ ◇

Throughout that day, and the night, and the following day, the fox woman led the Monkey King from bar to bar, from restaurant to nightclub, from brewery to sushi bar. None carried the elusive and distinctive label of the Gold Monkey, and the Monkey King left all of them disappointed, if a bit more drunk than the last. For what was the point of being in a bar with a beautiful woman on one's arm, if not to drink?

It was growing dark as the fox woman led Sun Wukong from the last of the purveyors of spirits, fine or otherwise, to be found in Tokyo. She steered him around cars, both parked and moving, and into Kiyosumi Gardens, where she helped him into a park bench. He sagged, flowing into his seat, and his eyes drooped.

"Where next?" he slurred.

"That's it," said the fox woman. "We have exhausted Tokyo."

"Impossible." The Monkey King waved an arm at an uncaring Tokyo skyline.

"Perhaps," she said, her voice soft beside him, "I might be of more assistance if I were to see this precious bottle of yours." She sat on his lap and nuzzled his ear.

Sun Wukong reached into his robe and produced the empty bottle. The fox woman took it from his resisting fingers.

"I think this monkey looks like it might come from Africa," she said. "I think it is an African monkey. Have you looked there?"

"What?" The Monkey King leaped to his feet, dumping the fox woman on the ground. She landed on all four feet, and her tongue shone pink behind sharp, white teeth and long, red fur. "Africa? Yes, yes, it does! I must go there at once!"

With a great leap that shook the ground and set off car alarms throughout Tokyo, the Monkey King set out on his way to Africa, somersaulting through the night sky.

The fox woman lay on her back in the soft grass and flipped through Sun Wukong's passport, marveling at the places his appetite had taken him, and laughed.

◇ ◇ ◇ ◇ ◇

It took the Monkey King a long time to get to Africa. First he was drunk, and set off in the wrong direction and got lost. Then he was hung over, and didn't go anywhere. He just pressed his head against the ice and threw snowballs at the penguins for making loud noises. But eventually, he made it to Africa, where he was sure he would find the elusive Golden Monkey.

He arrived in a land that was warm and dry, a high plateau of grasslands and spreading trees. Large cats prowled the tall grasses, while monkeys danced in the trees, mocking him and each other. Yes, this most certainly was the home of the Gold Monkey. He followed the scent of a cook fire until he came to a small hut sitting beneath a large tree. An old man sat on his heels by the fire, slowly turning a spit. The meat sizzled and dripped.

Sun Wukong bowed to the old man, although he saw that the old man was a spider.

The old man smiled, and his eyes twinkled. "Welcome, stranger. Are you hungry?"

Which is, you must admit, a silly question to ask the Monkey King.

They ate not in silence, because there was quite a bit of lip-smacking and exclamations of satisfaction, but without words. When the meat had been consumed and the bones cracked and sucked clean of marrow, the Monkey King sat back against the tree and rubbed his belly.

"As great a meal as served in the best restaurants of Tokyo," he said. "What was it?"

The old man smiled at the compliment. "The finest sort of prey, slowly roasted over an open fire, delicately garnished with pollen from the tree above, and a bit of dirt and ash that got stuck to it when I dropped the spit." He clasped his hands together over his belly. "The monkey is a most ingenious creature, and very difficult to catch, unless you can trick him with his own cleverness. This adds to its flavor."

This gave Sun Wukong some pause, if only for a moment. While the monkey they had eaten had clearly been an animal, and not a person—and certainly not a god—it still felt somewhat like cannibalism. Still, it had been delicious, and something he had never tried before, so he decided not to worry about it. On the other hand, the old man who was a spider clearly knew who he was, and either didn't have the sense to fear him properly, or felt that he had nothing to fear. One thing was certain: the old man who was a spider had laid a trap for him, and was confident enough in the outcome that he as good as boasted about it.

But what to do? He could kill the old man, and roast him over his own fire, and feed him to the monkeys. It seemed a fitting response, but without knowing the nature of the trap, it seemed unwise to incapacitate his only source of information. After all, the man was a spider, and could have poisoned him with the monkey meat. And while poisons had never affected him before, a man who was a spider might actually succeed where others had failed.

Or perhaps the old man simply wanted him to think that he'd been poisoned, in order entice him, through his own reactions, into some other trap.

Or perhaps…

No, he could spend all day second and third-guessing himself. Without more information, that was pointless.

"You know who I am," he said.

"Of course. You are the magnificent Sun Wukong whose greatness is sung far beyond the shores of your own land. I recognized you immediately."

"And you? Have you a name?"

"Oh, yes!" said the old man. He looked at his hands and wiggled his fingers. "More than I can count, apparently. You can use any of them, or one of your own choosing, it doesn't matter to me."

The Monkey King had no intention of being outwitted by a spider, and would not be taunted into a guessing game. "I have not come here to play games, spider," he said, letting the old man know he knew what he was. "I have come here seeking the Gold Monkey. What do you know of this thing?"

The old man scratched his head, and rubbed his chin. Then he scratched his head and rubbed his chin at the same time. He did this for several long moments before exclaiming, "Ah, yes, now I remember! The Gold Monkey! How could I have forgotten?"

"You have heard of it?"

"Yes, yes, of course. It is very famous. I will tell you how to find it."

The directions the old man gave were long and detailed, and full of vivid descriptions, like, "Travel a hundred or maybe a hundred twenty miles, give or take, along that road until you see a baobab tree that looks like my thirteenth wife, *if* you go around off the road and look at it from the other side. You might need to squint a little. Turn left there. That would be before the Olympic committee outrageously accused her of steroid use. If you turn left at the tree that looks like my thirteenth wife after she *stopped* taking steroids, well, you'll never find it."

By the time the old man had finished the first third of the directions, the Monkey King's head was splitting. By the time he had finished the second third, the Monkey King had forgotten the first third, even though the old man had made him a doll of his thirteenth wife, constructed of twigs and twine, two cotton balls and a nutcracker for legs. "She was a runner," he told the Monkey King, as he fit a kola nut in the doll's crotch and cracked it with ease. He sighed. "She had amazing legs."

◊ ◊ ◊ ◊ ◊

"You will need this," the old man had said, after he had finally consented to acting as guide on the quest for the Gold Monkey. He handed Sun Wukong a tan hat with a wide, slouched brim. It did not look good on him, giving his skin a sallow tone, and making his wispy beard and fine, silk robes appear ridiculous and pretentious in comparison.

"I do not want it."

"It's necessary," the old man said, adjusting it on Sun Wukong's head so that it sat at a rakish angle, low on his brow. Then he handed the Monkey King a leather bullwhip. "Also, you will need this. You will never find the Gold Monkey if you are not prepared."

They traveled for many days across the hot, dry African plain, and Sun Wukong grudgingly conceded the usefulness of the hat under the equatorial sun, and of the whip in driving away poisonous snakes and lions, though not the necessity of either. He was, after all, a god, and could certainly have found some other way to deal with such unpleasantries.

They followed a river down the plateau into the lowlands, avoiding the desperately poor men and women panning for diamonds, and the armed men who watched over them. They were of little interest; Sun Wukong had his eye on a greater prize. They made their way past elegant resort hotels and military bases, subsistence farms and refugee camps, and a Baobab tree that looked very much like the old man's thirteenth wife, and eventually into the dense jungles of the Congo.

Sun Wukong had been bitten or stung by thirty-seven different kinds of bugs by the time they reached the Congo River. By the end of this stretch of the adventure, he had been assaulted by over two hundred distinct species of insect, nine of which had yet to be discovered and given Latin names, and by one arachnid. Neither the hat nor the whip were of any assistance. The bugs crawled under the brim and bit him on the scalp, and when he snapped one enormous hornet out of the sky, a swarm rose up behind it and chased the Monkey King into the river.

The old man laughed then, and laughed again as he burned the leaches off Sun Wukong's flesh. "If you keep feeding the bugs like this," he said, "you'll be half your size by the time you reach the Gold Monkey. Maybe it would be wisest to hire a boat to take us up the river. It will be faster, and there are fewer insects on the open water."

Sun Wukong agreed, and they hired a boat and set off upstream that very day.

The old man who was a spider watched very carefully, and noted both the place where the Monkey King hid his purse of gold coins, and also where he later moved it when he thought no one was looking.

◊ ◊ ◊ ◊ ◊

They ate well during their weeks on the river. The old man had a net to which the fish practically stuck, so there was no shortage even with the Monkey King's prodigious appetite. They supplemented this with food brought to them by traders in canoes and dinghies, who would swarm from the beaches at the sight of a boat. They brought fresh fruits and vegetables, and a variety of unidentifiable meats.

After three weeks of puttering slowly against the current, the old man pointed toward the shore at a clump of bushes that appeared indistinguishable from any other clump of bushes. "This is the place," he said. "From here we must travel on foot."

The jungle was denser here than along the coast, and there were no paths. Sun Wukong tore at vines and brambles until his hands bled. Low hanging branches swept his hat from his head time and again, and the whip coiled at his belt snagged on the underbrush every other step.

"A machete would have come in handy right about now," he said. "Why didn't you give me one of those, instead of this stupid hat and whip?"

The old man stepped easily through the broken foliage, chuckling lightly. "It wasn't necessary."

Their progress through the jungle was torturously slow. The old man kept them fed, catching birds and snakes and monkeys in his sticky net, and though they sometimes traveled less than a mile in a day, they never went hungry.

At long last, they came to a hill—broken rock that rose out of the jungle like the rubble of some vast, ancient structure. Behind a curtain of moss was a tunnel. Should I tell you of the traps and pitfalls that awaited the Monkey King on his quest? The poisoned darts, the iron spiked pits full of snakes and spiders, the collapsing ceilings and pressure-triggered spears? It would be anti-climactic, after having faced down a centipede the size of his forearm. Suffice to say that they came at last to the surface, in a bowl of green carved from the center of the mountain. As dense as the jungle beyond the tunnel, trees filled the valley and creepers reached up the sides.

But in the center, untouched by the foliage, stood a giant statue. It rose, gleaming in the sunlight, above the towering tree-tops. Its eyes glistened ruby-red, its teeth were diamonds the size of your fist.

"Behold," the old man said, "the Gold Monkey."

It looked nothing like the Gold Monkey on the label of the empty beer bottle still concealed in Sun Wukong's tattered robes.

"Now," the old man added, "all you need to do is toss your hat over that motion sensor over there, and then use the whip to hit all those switches on the other side of the mine field, and it's all yours."

◊ ◊ ◊ ◊ ◊

The Monkey King's rage is legendary, and he did not disappoint. The spider who was an old man leapt from tree to rock to earth and back as tree trunks and boulders flew. He laughed as he sprang over great fissures that opened under his feet, and as the Gold Monkey sank forever into the center of the earth.

Fortunately, this particular Gold Monkey was far enough away from human habitation that none were harmed. Even the animals had seen what was in store and had fled, as if from a forest fire or tsunami. The next time, we would not be so lucky.

When the Monkey King's rage was spent, the valley of the Gold Monkey glowed red with molten stone, bubbling from the depths. Sun Wukong waded from the lava and sat on a fallen tree trunk, which smoked under his buttocks.

The old man who was a spider sat down beside him.

"Is there a problem?" he asked.

"This is not the Gold Monkey I was looking for." Sun Wukong's voice hissed like steam escaping a smoldering tree.

"Oh, well, why didn't you tell me that before you dragged me halfway across Africa?"

"I? Dragged you?" The Monkey King's fingers dug into the bark, which burst into flames around his hands. He was dangerously close to flying into another rage.

The old man seemed oblivious. "You think I'd go tromping around and neglect my garden and my twenty-sixth wife if you hadn't insisted I bring you here? If this wasn't the Gold Monkey you wanted, you should have said so from the start."

Sun Wukong pulled the empty beer bottle from his robes, thrusting it in front of the old man's face. "This!" he said. "This is what I am looking for."

The old man pushed Sun Wukong's hand away, until it was an arm's length from his face, then adjusted the distance a bit more. "Old eyes," he explained. He studied the bottle carefully. "Well, I've never seen anything like it, and I know Africa like I know the back of my twenty-third wife's hand. She was Italian, you know."

"I must find it," Sun Wukong said. "I *must.*"

"Then," the old man said, "you must travel north. To Europe."

"Europe? What do *they* know of monkeys?" Sun Wukong's voice dripped with contempt.

"Not just any Europeans. You need to find the people who have traveled across the world in search of fame and fortune, raping and pillaging and crushing all those who stood in their path, taking what they want and leaving smoldering ruins behind."

"You want me to go to Britain?" Incredulous.

"Only if you want tea. No, if you want to find the best, most robust, most perfect beer in the world, who better to lead you to it than the Vikings?"

◊ ◊ ◊ ◊ ◊

The chill evening wind cut through Sun Wukong's tattered silk robes. Just half an hour prior he had been sweating in the Congo's rainforests, watching the lava cool and painfully extracting information from the old man on where to best find the Vikings who could help him find his Gold Monkey. It had been mid-afternoon in Africa half and hour ago. In Norway, it was getting dark—and cold—very fast.

He stumbled out of the woods, a dense forest of pine and fir with a small clearing of newly fallen trees where he had landed, and into the road. A car swerved and beeped frantically, narrowly missing Sun Wukong before skidding to a halt in a cloud of burning rubber. The driver leapt from the car.

"Oi, mate!" he called. "You awright?"

Sun Wukong frowned. Had he missed Norway and landed in Britain after all?

"I am looking for Vikings," he said. "And beer."

"Come t'the right place then, aye?" The driver walked up to Sun Wukong on unsteady legs and clapped him on the shoulder. His breath smelled strongly of spirits. "Lucky I come along today. Hop in, my friend, there's a bar just a bit up the street, where there's a friend you've just got to meet."

The man drove on the left side of the road, swerving into the right lane only long enough to avoid oncoming cars and trucks, and screaming "Arse!" and "Wanker!" as they passed. Yes, Sun Wukong decided, this was Norway, and he was in trapped in an automobile with an insane Englishman.

Against all odds, they arrived alive at the pub. It was an old, steep-roofed cabin, built of stones and logs. Though no name graced the establishment, smoke rose from a chimney, promising warmth, and neon signs flickered in the windows, promising drink. The Englishman squeezed his classic Aston Martin between a beat up Volvo and a rusted snow plow, slamming on the brakes and screeching to a halt a mere fingers-width from a stone restraining wall.

Sun Wukong fumbled with his seat belt and stumbled out of the car, still dizzy from the drive and sudden deceleration.

The Englishman cackled. "I barely hazard now to think how you'll be after a bit of drink!"

The bar was dark and smoky, crowded and loud. A group of boisterous Finns sang ribald sea shanties in one corner while the Germans at the next table corrected their grammar. The Englishman pulled Sun Wukong in and shut the door behind them, and then spoke, his voice cutting through the din.

"Greetings, once and future friends, for sins long past to make amends, my Asian pal what I just found grants one and all a free next round."

A cheer rose from the patrons of the nameless pub, and many stood to greet Sun Wukong with warm hugs and claps on the shoulder. When the hubbub settled, Sun Wukong saw his drunken English friend in the far corner, speaking to a tall, thin man with dark hair and pale skin who sat alone at a small table. Both of them looked in Sun Wukong's direction.

The bartender flagged him down as he walked to the table. "What'll you have, friend?"

"Gold Monkey," he said.

"Never heard of it. Does it have banana liquor in it?"

"No. It is a beer. If you don't have it, any beer will do."

The bartender handed Sun Wukong a glass mug filled with a thick, dark liquid that foamed and dribbled down the side. "You've got quite a tab. How did you want to cover that?"

This was how the Monkey King discovered that his purse, and all his gold, had been stolen. By now, he knew, the old man who was a spider would have already have spent half of it on his twenty-sixth wife, and the other half on the woman who would some day become his twenty-seventh wife. He was in a foul mood when he reached the table.

"I am..."

The pale dark man stood, towering over the Monkey King. "I know who you are. Do you know who *I* am?"

Sun Wukong studied him. Yes. He knew. Fledgling god of mischief and discord for an anemic-looking people whose eyes gave them a look of perpetual astonishment. Barely a few thousand years old, this godling sought to intimidate him, the Monkey King who had bested the great Dragon himself. Even with his fine robes in rags and the ridiculous hat atop his head, with his bramble-torn and insect-gnawed flesh, he had more divine majesty in the tip of his nose than this upstart could dream of.

Sun Wukong let that knowledge settle, unspoken but clear, around them.

Loki—for it *was* Loki—did not back down.

The bar cleared quickly, patrons shuffling nervously out the door, the bartender rousting those who had fallen asleep in their chairs. He closed the door quietly behind him as he followed the last customer out the door. All that remained was Sun Wukong, Loki, and the mad Englishman.

"You are in my realm," Loki said. He flexed his fingers like a gunfighter as a slow smile played across his lips.

"I am on a quest, and I will not allow some pathetic Western godling to stand in my way. Especially not one that's barely out of swaddling and already lost his worshipers. If you aid me in my quest, you'll be rewarded. If you hamper me, not even the vultures will find your remains."

Power crackled around Loki's fingers, spreading to engulf his body. He breathed menace.

"Friends!" interjected the Englishman. "Countrymen! And you two, too! There's enough power between you to turn this whole place to goo."

Both pairs of eyes flickered in his direction, and then back at each other.

"Look here, lads. Mebbe I can be of assistance. If I can help the Chinaman find what he's looking for, there's no need for all the blood and gore, and for all your precious honor, none will look askance." He waggled his eyebrows.

The Monkey King did not look away from Loki. "I seek the perfect beer. Help me find it, and you will earn my gratitude." He pulled the empty beer bottle from the remnants of his robes and handed it to the Englishman.

"Why, all the clues you need are here, on the label of your beer!"

"I do not know your barbaric script."

"Well, then, let's see. This says, 'Gold Monkey, Victorious Brewing Company, Triple Ale.'" He handed the bottle back to Sun Wukong. "Ale is the Yank's abbreviation for Alabama. That's where you'll find your perfect beer for sale."

"Good. Then it is to Alabama I must go." The Monkey King turned to the Englishman and bowed. "My thanks."

"Not so fast." Loki still glowered and glowed dangerously. "There is still the matter of your tab."

"I have no money."

"Then I'll take something in trade."

Sun Wukong spread his arms. He had nothing. His passport was gone. His purse was gone. He had even lost his bullwhip in the raging lava.

"I'll take the hat," Loki said.

When the Monkey King had gone, leaping high into the sky and somersaulting in the direction of Iceland, a fox slunk out from behind the bar, shifting as she walked.

"Well played," she said.

The Englishman bowed. "All the world's a stage," he said, "but this play's nearly ended. Shall we be off to America, to see a god offended?"

A fox's playful yips joined his puckish laughter, while Loki looked up cheap air fare on the Internet.

◊ ◊ ◊ ◊ ◊

Sun Wukong walked along a lonely country road. Dust covered his feet and ankles, and gravel from the road got into his sandals. The sun sat high in the sky, and though it was not yet noon, the heat rose in waves from the broken gravel roadway. On either side of the road were deep drainage ditches, whose muddy bottoms spawned tall reeds and insects, and beyond those lay endless fields of tobacco, alfalfa and corn. Mosquitoes swarmed around his head, and black flies clung to his arms and legs, even as he swatted them. He immediately regretted giving up his ridiculous hat.

Within an hour he was tired. Within two, he was parched. Within three, he had become woozy from the heat. He had seen not a single person in all that time.

And then, from up ahead on the road, he heard noises. He hurried up a long, low hill, and as he approached the top, the noises resolved into a voice.

"You turn me loose, y'hear? You turn me loose right now or I'll kick the stuffin' outta you."

The sounds of a scuffle increased, and Sun Wukong broke into a run, hoping to intervene. Perhaps, he reasoned, a grateful person might actually be of some assistance in his quest. But when he reached the top of the hill, he stopped and stared. It wasn't a person there at all, but a rabbit, who had managed to get both his front paws and one rear paw stuck in a large, vaguely human-shaped lump of tar with a straw hat stuck atop what might be a head. Still, the rabbit could speak, so it might be able to help.

"Hello," said the Monkey King, bowing to the trapped rabbit.

The rabbit nodded in Sun Wukong's general direction. "Howdy. Don't mean to be rude, but I can't shake hands right now. Or much of anything else."

"This is as regrettable as it is understandable. Perhaps we can be of mutual assistance to one another?"

"Yeah, that sounds great! Anything you need, I'll find a way to get it to you. Just help me get…" The rabbit gritted his teeth as he pulled, stretching the tar, but not managing to escape.

"Yes, of course." Sun Wukong looked around for something he could use to help pry the sticky tar off the rabbit, or the rabbit out of the tar.

"Hurry, hurry!" The rabbit struggled frantically, rolling around and kicking with his one free foot. "Fox'll be here soon, and if he find me like this…"

With a mighty kick, the rabbit launched both himself and the tar dummy into the air, and toward Sun Wukong. The Monkey King turned just in time to put up his hands, keeping the tar from slapping against his body.

"What have you done?" he roared.

The rabbit stretched his neck to look around the lump of tar at Sun Wukong. "You're not stuck, are you?" His eyes were wide. "Oh, no! Fox'll get me for sure!" He thrashed in panic, and soon both of Sun Wukong's feet were stuck as well.

Once the Monkey King was thoroughly trapped, the rabbit carefully extracted his limbs from the tar. The fur on the three paws was coated with Vaseline. He pulled a handkerchief out of his back pocket and cleaned off his fur, all the while ignoring the Monkey King's curses. Once his hands were clean, he reached into Sun Wukong's robes and extracted the beer bottle.

"Well, what do we got here? The perfect beer?" The rabbit poked at the label with one paw. "Victorious Brewery in Downingtown, Pennsylvania. Thank you."

He slid the beer bottle into his vest pocket, and bowed formally to Sun Wukong. Then he wheeled a motorcycle out of a nearby briar patch, kicked it into life, and within a few seconds was lost to sight.

Sun Wukong struggled with the tar dummy until he was exhausted. Hours passed. The sky began to dim—a blessed relief from the sun, but on the off chance that someone drove down this road, they were more likely to strike him than rescue him. Then, just as dusk set in, he heard the sound of tires on gravel. The oncoming car sped up the road, showing no sign of slowing until the very last moment. It pulled into a skid, spraying the Monkey King with hot gravel and coming to a stop a fingers-width from his face.

The door of the sports car opened and a man staggered drunkenly from within.

"Oi, mate," he said. "You awright?"

◊ ◊ ◊ ◊ ◊

Once again a reluctant passenger in the mad Englishman's Aston Martin, Sun Wukong rubbed and picked at the tar on his feet and hands. He flexed his toes and bemoaned the loss of his favorite sandals in the hungry maw of the tar dummy.

Downingtown, he learned, was not in Alabama. Nowhere near Alabama. The Aston Martin made good time, notwithstanding the driver's need for frequent rest room breaks and easy distraction with truck stop waitresses and truckers. Still, the rabbit had had a significant head start, and they were unable to catch up to him.

It was a cool Sunday evening when an Aston Martin pulled up next to me
at a red light. The driver hit the horn a couple times and rolled down his window.
My spousal unit lowered the window at her side. The driver was a merry looking
fellow. A crazed looking Asian man sat next to him.

"Hullo, luv," the driver said, "I fear I've gotten turned 'round. It's Victorious
Brew Pub where I'm bound."

I laughed. "Follow me."

My spousal unit gave me an odd look. It had been a strange day, and this was
not the first query I'd gotten about the brewery. Earlier in the day, a rabbity sort of
fellow on a motorcycle had stopped me outside the supermarket to ask. Not long
after, two people showed up on my doorstep, a beautiful Japanese woman with a
fox fur draped over her shoulder with a stunningly striking Scandinavian man on
her arm. I gave them directions.

"That writer's thing of yours is tonight," my spousal unit said, "isn't it? I want
to come."

So we arrived together, me and my spousal unit and the mad Englishman and
the Monkey King in his tattered silk robes. We climbed the steps to the front door.

"Finally!" Sun Wukong said. "Finally I have found the Gold Monkey!"

This was my first clue that this was the culmination of a course of events I
had set into action with a drunken statement months before.

Unexpectedly, the Englishman placed a hand on Sun Wukong's chest, barring
his entrance. "I've got bad news, but I must insist, I act now in loco parentis: the
sign here says, 'no shoes, no service.'"

The Monkey King ranted and raved, but his friend was adamant.

"There's some stores nearby," I said. "You can get shoes." I gave them
directions. "I'll save a couple seats for you."

◊ ◊ ◊ ◊ ◊

I was, as usual, running a bit late, and the rest of my writer's group was
already there. They'd gotten a big round table in the corner. As we walked toward
them, I got the uncomfortable feeling of being watched. I was not wrong. The
rabbity fellow was there, sitting at a table near the door. The Japanese woman was
with him, as was the pale Scandinavian guy. He scowled at me. Three others sat
with them: an old black man with laughter in his eyes, a raven-haired woman with
a beakish nose, and a man with greyish brown hair and a wolfish grin. He caught
my eye, and my tattoo itched. The coyote tat, not the other. Like it was alive under
my skin.

And I remembered the feather and the fur that I'd found in the back seat
of my car, along with the empty bottle of Gold Monkey, and started putting the
pieces together.

I needed a drink.

I introduced my spousal unit to the group, and we placed our order. She was drinking Hop Devil. I asked the waiter for good bourbon, and failing that, whatever was most similar to good bourbon. He gave me something called Old Horizontal. It would have to do.

I was finishing my second by the time Sun Wukong returned. He was wearing jeans and a kelly green Philadelphia Eagles t-shirt—the Eagles emblem centered over a football. The tattered silk looked better. I waved them over, and signaled the waiter.

"I'll have another of these," I said, "and I'll get these guys' first round."

Sun Wukong nodded at me, then turn his head with a certain majesty toward the waiter. He clasped his hands on the table in front of him, his fingers interlaced, and when he spoke, it was with calm anticipation. "I seek the Gold Monkey."

◊ ◊ ◊ ◊ ◊

Sun Wukong seemed gratified by the cheer raised by several of our number, and for a few moments, the fear that sat in the pit of my stomach eased. At least, it did until the waiter returned with pint glasses a-foaming. He set a glass in front of the Monkey King, who gazed at it with longing. He enclosed it in his wrinkled hands and held it up in front of it his face. He breathed in its scent. He raised it to his lips. He tilted the glass.

Gulp after gulp, the golden liquid disappeared between the Monkey King's lips.

I held my breath.

Nobody else at the table yet knew what was at stake. They did soon.

The Monkey King slammed the glass on the table. It shattered in his fist. Beer splashed out of the other glasses on the table and into the nachos. The table cracked.

"This," he said, "is crap. I was promised the perfect beer, and it is *crap!* I have traveled the world, fought my way through jungles and tar balls for the perfect beer, and it is *CRAP!*"

Behind the Monkey King's howl of rage, I could hear laughter, yipping and cawing and howling as the Monkey King rose to his feet with fists clenched and murder in his eyes.

◊ ◊ ◊ ◊ ◊

I could tell a tale of wisdom and bravery, where through sheer force of will and wit, I overcame the Monkey King's rage and saved the day. I could, but it would be lies, and my spousal unit has a mean back-of-the-hand. What can I say, I married an Italian. And she's the one who saved us. All I did sit there, frozen in terror, imagining all the grizzly ways my spousal unit and my friends and everyone else in the restaurant were going to die. And I've got a vivid imagination.

My spousal unit, who had been taking a sip of her beer at the time of the Monkey King's outburst, was the only one whose beer was still standing, as it were. She stood up, reached over and stuck it in front of the Monkey King's face.

"Try this one," she said.

He seized it angrily from her hand and chugged it.

"Not bad," he said. He shouted for the waiter.

"Yes, sir?"

"Bring more of this. Many more."

"What were you drinking?"

"Hop Devil," my spousal unit said. "I'll have another, too."

Many rounds later, the Monkey King stared into a fresh glass of Hop Devil Ale. "I do not understand. This is not the perfect beer. The balance is all wrong. It is a bit bitter, and far too hoppy. I can barely taste the malts. Why do I love it so?" He put his head in his hands. "And why is the Gold Monkey so bad? It was supposed to be perfect."

"It *is* perfect," I said, a half-dozen Old Horizontals under my belt. "That's the problem. It's like the Platonic Forms, the so-called Golden Mean—something that's so idealized that it ceases to be anything *but* an ideal. Beauty comes from deviation from the mean, and is far from universal."

"Ah." The Monkey King nodded sagely, and wandered off to find the vat. He would not rest, we understood, until he drank the vats dry. We ordered another round, while there was still beer to be had.

◊ ◊ ◊ ◊ ◊

We are a group of modest indulgence, but this was an unusual circumstance, and we'd all sworn to leave our keys untouched until the morning. We could hear from the frantic whispers of the staff that Sun Wukong had gotten into the vats, and bets were laid as to just how many he would drink dry.

"He will drink them all."

The speaker tossed a handful of beads on the pile. He grinned at me, and sat between me and my spousal unit.

"He will drink them all." A stack of krone fell to the table. A ten thousand yen note followed, and then some pound notes, and a wrinkled old one dollar silver certificate. The dark haired woman laid a single black feather on the stack before she sat with us, and finally, a dark, wizened hand produced an embroidered silk purse, heavy with gold coins.

We sat and drank and talked and laughed, this group of writers and ancient tricksters, long into the night, as, one variety after another, the Victorious Brewing Company ran out of beer. When the beer and the staff were exhausted, a well sated Sun Wukong joined our merry band. He burped loudly, then congratulated us all on a jest well played.

The mad Englishman bowed. "The pleasure's ours, my cheeky monkey, to synonymize you with a donkey."

Alison stared at him. "That has got to be…" She clapped her hands over her mouth, still too wise to risk angering a god.

"…the worst rhyme ever!" Paul finished, not nearly so wise.

"There's hardly a Shakespeare round these times from which this Puck might draw his rhymes." He glared at me. Pointedly.

"I'm sorry," I said, though I didn't quite understand how I could be responsible for Puck's poetic failures. Still, I blushed and looked away, and that's when I noticed it.

It sat, shining gold and beautiful, atop the stack of bar bets in the middle of the cracked table.

"What's that?"

It was a stupid question, and nobody bothered answering. It was an apple. A beautiful, perfect apple, made of solid gold. I wanted it. No, I needed it. More than anything I had ever seen, I *needed* it. And I was not alone in this.

Loki was the first to find his voice. "She found out."

"Yes, she did." The fox woman swallowed nervously. Her fingers twitched, reaching of their own volition toward the golden apple. She clasped her hands together and shoved them into her lap.

"Yes." Starkly beautiful and beautifully mad, Eris, Goddess of Discord and architect of the Trojan War, stepped from the shadows. "Yes, she did. It's okay, you're all forgiven for forgetting to invite me to the party. See? I've even brought a nice, shiny present. For whichever one of you that can keep it."

Ah, but that's a different story. For another time.

MONKEY BUSINESS

by Frank Roger

The bus creakingly ground to a halt and the driver said in a raspy voice, "Urumbatti." About a dozen passengers grabbed their bags and backpacks, and got off the bus, mostly tourists, young people clad in shorts and T-shirts and sporting trendy hairdos. Rutger Tarquini followed their example. He didn't wear the typical tourist "uniform", but he realised his white skin would mark him as a tourist anyway.

Urumbatti attracted its share of tourists, but it was too small to harbour any hotels or even guest houses, so most visitors stayed in one of the bigger towns in the area and took the bus when they wished to explore the village's unique sights and features. Urumbatti was still a traditional village, deservedly renowned for its artistic craftsmanship, especially its woodcutting. Moreover, the village's location at the rim of the tropical rainforest turned it into an ideal operating base for eco-freaks eager to get a taste of unspoiled nature. The romantic Makhaaba Falls were another hot tourist attraction.

But however breathtaking these falls and the village's other treats might be, they were not why Tarquini had come to Urumbatti, unlike the other tourists who had got off the bus along with him. His fellow passengers walked off in different directions, and behind him the bus disappeared in a cloud of black exhaust. Tarquini put on his cap, a welcome protection against the merciless sun, and started his exploration of the village, a collection of wooden houses and huts, with only a few brick buildings added, set against a stunning backdrop of lush foliage and a bright blue sky. The scene could have been taken from a postcard.

His sight-seeing tour was quickly completed, and he quickened his pace, despite the scorching heat, as he noticed a handful of shops at the outskirts of the village, his reason for venturing out there. They fit the description he remembered reading in the reports he had seen. He entered the biggest of the stores, greeted the man behind the counter, and bought a bottle of water, some fruit and a dog-eared copy of a map of the area.

As there were no other customers and the shopkeeper did not appear unwilling to engage in conversation, he said: "Do you mind if I ask you a few questions?"

The man shot him a quizzical look, but the smile did not leave his face and he nodded.

"Allow me to present myself. I'm Dr. Rutger Tarquini. I'd like to find out more about something unusual that happened here..."

"Oh," the shopkeeper interrupted him. "No doubt you're talking about my special customers. I'm afraid you've come too late. They no longer drop by here. I'm sorry."

"I know, but I'm investigating this matter for professional reasons. It won't take too much of your precious time..."

"Okay," the man said, clearly resigned. "You must have heard the stories. Well, they're not just stories. They're facts. It's all true. I sold stuff to apes. They had money to pay me, so I sold to them, as I do to any customer who has money. But I admit I had some doubts at the beginning."

"Wait. The beginning, maybe that's where we ought to start. Could you tell me how these apes discovered money and its use in shops in a village inhabited by human beings? I'm willing to believe all that truly happened, but I'd like to hear a detailed account from someone who was directly involved in it all. So please, tell me the story from its very beginning."

"I had noticed some older male apes keeping a watchful eye on my shop and everything that happened here. Now apes are notoriously curious, and they often leave the forest to take a look at us and our strange activities, so there was nothing that aroused my suspicion. But it became clear afterwards that they observed how I ran my business. When dogs or other animals entered my shop, attracted by the food, they were chased away. When beggars or other people without money entered, they were also told to leave empty-handed. But people with money could get whatever they wanted. So one day the apes tried it out for themselves. One of them, an older male, entered my shop, when no other customers were around, pointed at a wooden bowl and put a banknote on the counter. At first I thought it was a joke, that someone had perhaps trained the ape to do this and had given him money, but the creature insisted. It was for real."

"Do you have any idea where the ape got the money from?"

"I found out soon afterwards. The apes had noticed that musicians and jugglers did their thing wherever tourists were around, and collected money after each act, and so they imitated them. I heard stories of groups of apes performing crazy antics and all sorts of hilarious stunts for tourists, and then a cute young ape would go and ask for a little money from the small crowd of spectators, extending his hand just like his human counterparts. Apparently it worked. The apes had found a way to earn money. They didn't steal it, as some folks claim. They were honest. There's no law against apes performing an act in return for payment."

"So you sold to the apes?"

"Yes, as soon as I knew they were serious and had worked for their money, so to speak. I also found out the apes were aware of the difference between banknotes of various sizes, and that they were entitled to change. They actually waited for some coins before they left with their purchase. You couldn't fool them. Well, not much."

"And what did they buy?"

"Mostly books and newspapers," he said, chuckling. "No, seriously, they bought things they could use as tools in their everyday life. I sold them a lot of wooden spoons and forks, bowls, mugs and bags, stuff they couldn't make themselves or find in the forest. They never bought fruit or water. They clearly knew the value and usefulness of everything I sell. They're by no means dumb creatures. I wish I could say the same thing about all my human customers." He chuckled again.

"How did the villagers react to your selling stuff to apes?"

"Very badly. People frowned upon it, openly criticised me for selling stuff to animals. My argument that I sold to anyone who had the money to pay was dismissed. Selling to animals was simply not done. Even if these animals had earned their money in an honest way. It just isn't right, they said. Some poor guy who has no money comes in here, and he's sent away, but an ape who was clever enough to snatch some banknotes from those tourist morons is served. It just isn't right, they kept repeating."

"And do you see their point?"

"Yes, I do. But I run a shop, and it hurts to send a customer away who has the money to buy what he wants, even if that customer happens to be an ape. Some people just couldn't grasp that."

"What about the local authorities? Did they support you?"

The man shook his head vehemently. The smile had left his face; this was obviously an issue that had caused him some bitterness.

"The local authorities supported the majority who wanted to see my practice of selling to apes brought to an end. I kept saying that I broke no law and didn't harm anyone, but they remained deaf for my arguments. And when one day a dozen or so of the poorer guys chased away an ape customer of mine and threatened to burn down my place if I didn't mend my ways, the authorities didn't intervene. They let it happen. It was clear what side they were on. So I had no choice. I had to turn away my 'special' customers. I didn't see any of them back, as they were chased off whenever they ventured out of the forest. I'm sure they'll never return here. Who knows what they're doing with their money now. Maybe they've gone elsewhere to perform their act, collect their payment and go shopping, who knows. But Urumbatti doesn't do monkey business anymore, that's for sure."

A few other customers entered the shop, so Tarquini thanked the man for his time and left. He strolled around the village and had a cup of coffee until he could catch a bus back to Jalafreen, the town where he stayed in a hotel.

Later that night Tarquini had a beer in the hotel bar, and let his thoughts roam freely on what he had discovered. At one point another guest took a seat on the barstool next to him, ordered a beer, and placed a strange object in front of him. It was a sort of wooden sculpture, very crude, like a child's awkward attempt to cut a vaguely human figure from a piece of wood. The man studied it, turned it around and placed it carefully back. He noticed Tarquini's interested gaze and said:

"Do you know where I got this? You won't believe me, pal."

"Tell me anyway," he replied.

"This afternoon I did a boat trip on the river, and afterwards when our boat docked there was a bunch of apes on the jetty, selling these pieces of art. Honestly, they make these things themselves. They showed us a few apes who were busy hacking away at wood with makeshift tools. I don't know where they got the idea, or the idea to sell their productions. And, you won't believe this, but these apes had money. They had different currencies, even US dollars and euros. They refused a small banknote I offered them, and gave me change when I handed them a greater note. They clearly knew what they were doing. And these apes went after every tourist they spotted. Isn't that incredible? You don't believe me, right? Well, go and take a look for yourself, pal. And buy one of these pieces of ape art now that they're still cheap. This thing here may be a formidable investment, my friend." The man burst into laughter, and then shifted his attention to the game of pool some people were playing at his left.

"Incredible indeed," Tarquini whispered, staring at the crude work of "art." The apes must have seen the woodcutters at the villages here, he thought. And they must have concluded this was a money-making opportunity for them. They've discovered the notion of trade and quickly developed a working system. And maybe this is but the first step in an evolution that will take ape society in a new and unsuspected direction. Who knows where this will end? Will their concept of a trade-based economy and a monetary system take them along the same paths as it did human beings? Will there one day soon be rich and poor apes, will there be social classes, based on the amount of money they'll have amassed and the power they wield because of it? Will some apes steal money from others, will some go as far as to kill for money, will there be greedy apes and big spenders? Will money and everything it entails radically transform ape society and finally rip it apart, much as had happened with human society? Are we witnessing the onset of a stunning evolution here, or the harbinger of a vast tragedy?

Tarquini shook his head. The man next to him ordered another beer and handed the bartender a few banknotes, thereby inadvertently knocking down the wooden sculpture. Tarquini caught it before it could fall to the ground, and studied it. It was very crude indeed, and not beautiful in any sense of the word. It probably had been made without any artistic ambitions, merely as an object that could be offered for sale. But as the man had said, it might well be a formidable investment. Maybe I should buy it from him, he thought. See? He had been right. Its value was already rising...

Evolution Happens

by Rebecca McFarland Kyle

Evolution happens. Even the most devout creationists faced with an illness will choose antibiotics that fight evolved germs over out-of-date remedies. People make evolution happen. When the Victorian-era dog shows made canines popular pets, over 200 different breeds emerged through selective breeding.

Same with GMO foods, but the results weren't a lovable pup which fits in your purse. Few people heard when the third generation of animals fed GMO grains went sterile. When the news finally got out genetically-altered food was sterilizing humans, it was too late for everyone but two groups: the nature nerds like my partner and me and the ultra-rich.

Not to worry. The same folks who brought you corn crossed with frogs developed a way to live forever. And why shouldn't the general population trust them? There were plenty of reasons, but the general population isn't that bright, particularly when many of them were on one or more anti-cholinergic drugs. You know, statins, antihistamines, antidepressants, all of which caused serious mental impairment. Add to that, erectile dysfunction drugs were allowing men with mental and physical defects who probably shouldn't breed to add to the population for two generations. Viagra turns out to effect hormone levels in the next generation, too. If only they'd had a baculum like chimpanzees, they wouldn't have needed the drugs. Yes, there are many times I think that chimps are better than their human ancestors. Men often agree when they learn chimpanzees have a penis-bone.

Thanks to Bill Clinton's "Chimp Act," my partner Chantal and I run a chimp retirement home far from the midst of society. We have a mutual avoidance pact with our mostly redneck neighbors; and we live on what we can grow organically. Our payment is chump change; the Feds didn't notice us in the austerity frenzy.

Like a lot of scientific discoveries, our evolutionary experiment was accidental. We get chimps from labs, circuses, show business, and pet homes. Most are sterilized. When we got a load of pets from a hoarder late one night, we checked them in and set them in a cage with food and water.

I woke next morning hearing my partner calling, "Jeanine!"

I hurried outside to discover the new chimps were monkeying around. As soon as it was safe, we separated males from females and considered.

"You know, we've never had a baby," Chantal looked wistful. Considering our lifestyle and the growing sterility of the general population, we weren't likely to be *comadres*.

That settled it. We created a nursery for the expectant chimps and neutered the males. We had the mothers listening to Mozart, various language tapes, anything educational we could find.

We already had smart chimps. The show biz chimps could sign, drive, and act as human as your average redneck. So, when they were not watching videos of their own shows, we set them up as teachers for the children.

Those baby chimps learned quickly. Within months, they were doing everything the adults could and more. Chantal and I looked at each other one night after one glass of wine too many and agreed we'd try another generation. So, we matched up the smartest of the male and female children and bred them.

This time, we added electronics. The chimps were not just signing, they were pointing to words we'd programmed on older-model iPads. Soon, they could ask for a banana by tapping a screen. The brighter ones were forming sentences. I think if we gave twelve of them keyboards, they might come up with something better than the current slate of literature.

Chantal and I were hooked. We bred the smartest chimps again. The show-biz chimps could drive a car with a human commanding. The first litter could understand directions pre-programmed into the GPS well enough to drive the car. The second litter could program the GPS with the icons and get to their destinations with guidance. They formed complete sentences even earlier. The third generation became the leaders of the chimp colony, patiently teaching their elders new skills.

Ironically, the chimp population was getting smarter as the human population's abilities decreased. More than half the population was overweight and ill. Add to that, a whole pharmacopeia of "life-sustaining" chemicals which didn't guarantee quality of life. Or perhaps the hypnogogic state most folks experienced was what was actually intended by the ruling classes. They created a manageable and undemanding workforce. At that point, we turned off the news. If we'd been watching, we'd have gotten more ammo.

Throughout the breeding sessions, we'd taken pictures and videos. We were ready to publish a scientific paper or at least sell our films to *National Geographic* when we saw the line of people coming for the sanctuary. We're not really on the public radar. Other chimp retirement centers have had their day on the sun, but we've deliberately remained private. Homophobic rednecks are just one part of the issue. Now, we were breaking our government contract by making babies.

This was the most motley looking field trip I'd seen. The procession trudging toward us were shapeless with flesh the bluish white of a fish's belly. None spoke, save for grunts or coughs. I counted six, but there was no telling how many more followed.

"Get the shotgun," I turned to say to Chantal, but she was already running toward the gun-cabinet.

"What do you want?" I called out, once they were within hearing range. A fog of stench rolled in ahead of them. As a science major, I'd smelled decay. But this was different: rot and excreta mixed with malign neglect and some powerful chemistry.

They shambled forward, staggering into the electric fence. Sparks flew from their wires, but they pressed on, not feeling the pain even when their clothes caught on fire.

"Fence could short out."

Chantal brought the shotgun to her shoulder, ratcheted it and shot the forerunner full in the face. That brought him down, but it didn't stop his friends.

"Shit!"

We blew away all six. Once we were sure no more followed, we opened the gates and pulled the bodies as far down the road as we could from our land and burned them.

That night, we turned on the television only to find static.

Local radio was the same.

Online was better. Isolates and shut-ins were still on their computers—as long as that lasted.

Were they zombies?

The general conclusion was, not quite as the films depicted, but close as bad hygiene, pollution, and modern chemistry could create. No one found a way to reach anything but the animal portions of their brains. Two things they had in common. They were hungry and they felt no pain. If you didn't have something to feed them, your flesh was fine.

The only encouraging news was you didn't become one of them if they bit you. You just got an infection which wasn't treatable by any of the current antibiotics. If the bite was on a limb, you should amputate. If your head or torso was afflicted, pray you died fast or eat a bullet.

Shooting or beheading was method of choice for extermination. Even city dwellers were helpless. Visiting flesh-eaters were often EMTs or policeman.

We gathered all the ammunition we could find, including all the jars of coins we'd saved and gravel from the road. While we were isolated, we figured if the first group found us, others would follow.

One thing going for us was that our compound was off the grid save for the electric fence and freezers. We'd converted our home and the chimp houses to solar while there was grant money to do so. We still had food and seed enough to plant. Plus, we had a well and a rainwater system. Our generator would power the fence and freezers when the power quit, for awhile.

The next onslaught came at night. We woke to chimps screaming. The creatures were coming at the fence from several directions thrashing through the stickery underbrush despite tearing the clothing and skin.

"That's Mr. and Mrs. Claxton." When they found out about us, they'd brought pie and welcomed us because they were taught to love their neighbors no matter what.

I shot them through a blur of tears.

Same with the family who spat whenever we passed.

On and on through the night. By the light of day, I left Chantal to guard the perimeter and I scavenged every gun and bit of ammunition I could find from their homes. And I brought Lincoln, the Claxton's Golden Retriever, and from another neighbor two Collies and their flock of sheep.

Chantal shook her head. "All we need are more mouths to feed."

"I couldn't leave Lincoln," I said. "And the Collies never did us any harm. The sheep will feed the chimps…"

Chantal nodded.

"The zombies are not eating the animals," I realized.

Chantal raised one brow.

I didn't know what that meant and we didn't have anyone to ask. The net had only lasted a few hours.

Worse, we didn't have time to figure it out.

Lincoln's bark alerted us to visitors. He and the two Collies established routine patrol of the premises without any prodding. They needed a job to do and soon enough, the herding dogs would have no flock.

Nothing happened when the first one touched the fence. Chantal ran for the generator as I ratcheted the shotgun and fired.

The power wasn't coming on.

By the time I was done, I had a bruise on my shoulder from the back-lash and I could practically taste the stench. Bless the dogs, they'd taken down some of our attackers, because there would have been no way for both of us to have gotten them all.

"Good job," I said to Lincoln and his two pals, whom I'd dubbed Harriet Tubman and Rosa Parks. I checked them over and found no bites.

"We're down to coins and gravel," Chantal said.

"I could go further…"

She shook her head. "With this many here, you think you'd be safe?"

"I could drive the Range Rover and see if the Wal-Mart's still got stock."

"People closer to town have probably already looted the store," Chantal reminded me. "We have gas for one trip. We can't waste it."

We couldn't sleep. One of us watched for invaders while the other broke glassware and whatever else sharp was available to fit in the guns.

Chantal looked at me and after five years of being with her I knew what she was thinking. Time to end it. We euthanize the chimps and dogs and use whatever was left on ourselves.

I glanced up just in time to see a ragged man stagger through the gates. The shotgun was so heavy, I almost couldn't lift it, but I got him just before he reached Chantal.

"Rocks," I said, unable to give up on the life we'd made and the woman I loved. "We'll get rocks and sling them at them."

Who let the chimps out? I don't know the answer to that one. Was it one of the dogs, who were all a bit too clever with latches, or had the apes just pulled a Houdini? The next time we were attacked, the chimps set up a howl from the depths of Hell.

One of the show biz chimps was driving his little car full of baby chimps straight toward the creatures. They got out, swarmed the invaders and literally busted heads. The average male chimp is three to four times stronger than a man. The creatures were toast.

The chimps used rocks like their forebears did to crack nuts on the creature's heads. They'd leap from the trees onto the attacker's shoulders and simply pound their brains into pulp. Some tripped their prey and used heavy sticks to beat them.

I'd never been so proud—even if I was a peace-loving tree-hugging Mom.

Chantal and I embraced for the first time since the attacks, dancing around like a pair of drunk kids. The chimps joined us giving each other hugs and high fives.

"We did it! We did it!" I heard the mechanical voice from the iPad.

I don't think we would have heard the helicopter if the animals hadn't set up a fuss. I started to run for the shotgun and realized that no way could any of the zombies fly that kind of complicated apparatus.

Instead, I ran to a clearing, waving and screaming for help. I normally abhorred civilization, but I'd seriously give it a try if it meant safety for me and mine.

The chopper landed, sending dogs and chimps into a frenzy.

"We're here to scout out and see if there are any normals left," the female pilot said, once she'd landed and the blades of her craft stopped turning.

"We're not infected," I said. Chantal merely nodded, too exhausted to speak.

"I see your animals defended you," the pilot continued. "We've got some amazing footage from the air."

One of the babies with an iPad walked up to the pilot and busily typed. "Hello flying lady."

"Hello, fighting monkey," she replied back.

"Banana, please?" the chimp baby asked, making big eyes at the pilot.

"You certainly deserve one."

I glanced at Chantal. After all our work, what we'd probably get known for was the Zombie Fighting Chimps. On the other hand, we survived and there were too many others who didn't.

We have a new contract now with the US Army. Neither of us particularly like breeding chimp soldiers to work with their canine units, but the dogs and chimps are happy to have a job to do. Both species work together better than most humans. We've been promised they'll have Kevlar suits if they actually go into battle against armed opponents. They all seem to enjoy their work helping to fight off the creatures who've gathered in hard-to-reach places.

The wisest among them have said they want to save their "people." Who'd have thought our primitive forebears could possess such a lofty goal?

Monkey See, Monkey Do

by Frank R. Sjodin

[Personal Journal of Dr. Joyden standard date {classified}]

I'm made an emergency landing on a nature reserve, fourth planet from Interrdis, after surviving an attack from a bounty hunter. It may sound adventurous, but the event invoked more ire than excitement. Our limited communication has made it clear that his target is the Ice Princess.

Autopilot put us down gently on the Peacock continent, beneath a canopy of untouched rainforest. Reserve energy is insufficient to power any repair automatons if I want to keep our defenses running, and I can't rely heavily on solar or wind due to the massive local flora. Defense comes first. I plan to hide among the heavy foliage for as long as it takes to repair our engines and return to space. If we must remain for an extended period, the rainforest provides a suitable locale for my experiment. No equipment has been damaged, nor has my prize specimen. After all the professional and legal risks I took breaking her out of Orion's Zoo, I took every precaution to insure her safety.

I lost track of the renegade during atmospheric entry. After witnessing his performance firsthand and reading copious reports on his ship, I must assume he has survived his emergency landing and still poses a serious threat.

His ID was obscured from my scanners, but upon analysis of the combat data and running his vocal pattern through a database, I've made a strong hypothesis concerning his identity. I believe him to be one Nameless Shane, primary aliases Gunlock and Cocksure. His ship's performance matches documented reports of outlaw craft *Crimson Katana*, *Chisum Tail* and *Saint George*, all of which tag to his various alter-egos. He's known best for gun-slinging and unparalleled ship-to-ship combat, as I discovered firsthand.

Had I known what to expect, I would have concentrated my first volley to cripple his weaponry rather than sensors. Ace pilots aided by sensors can rarely hit a lone cloaked missile at close range, especially when surprised. He eliminated three, targeting with his naked eyes.

A bounty hunter of his reputation is doubtless equipped with probes and scan equipment independent of his ship, as well as alternate transportation.

To prepare for his imminent attacks, I amplified our force-field to handle gunship fire, and launched a perpetual rotation of sixteen security drones. Our remaining energy is consumed primarily by powering Anastasia's arctic chamber.

After assessing damage, I estimate that repairs may take several weeks. Considering that reserve energy can maintain our defenses for six months, I have decided to accelerating the experiment and proceed while here.

The rainforest provides sufficient contrast to Anastasia's natural habitat to provide the mental catalyst for the next phase. I've linked the security drones with the data gathering program running in her quarters, so nothing will be lost when she is moved outside. There will be an immense quantity of new variables to factor in, however, the most dangerous of which will be Nameless Shane.

◊ ◊ ◊ ◊ ◊

[Hunter's Log #4]

This's been the best hunt in years. Dr. Neuro-bio-loco's giving me a bigger challenge than the Boziori Bosses, but it's a game of wits and will, not sharpshooting and firepower. Been awhile since I kept a log, but I'll want to remember the details of this hunt later.

The wily bastard gave me a run in space! Only 'cuz I underestimated him. Put up surrender protocols, then hit me with shadow missiles while I came in for docking! I anticipated his second volley and shot 'em down between us, and we both took some of that blast. Then my engine caved. I scored a few hits on him, we both went down, and I lost him.

Probes ran wide recon on the upper atmosphere for three days before I made a guess to which land mass he put down on. I didn't put out too many ground probes, since I figured he'd be fuzzing and logging probe frequencies. I sent 'em where I didn't think he'd be, to throw him off if he picked 'em up on a wide scan. I went in myself to search where I guessed he'd most likely hid up.

The planet's gorgeous, but legwork here is rough. Humidity fucks with the hoverbike, cloud and tree cover cut out most solar power, and it rains every day. Hostile wildlife's everywhere, but my shootin' handles the predators. The bugs ain't as bad as on populated worlds, since they ain't mutated or adapted to humans, but the swarms are big as skyclouds. I only got a week's worth of immuno-amplifier, so I spend a lot of time on full-suit seal.

One good thing is I got no law, civvies, or urban trash to get in my way, and I must say I prefer the pains of nature to the shit of humanity. The animals aren't exactly peaceful, they treat me like any threat. But animals fight for survival, not for hate. Even if they survive on cunning instead of strength, there's no money or politics, just competition. When you kill an acid-spitting lizard you can eat him for lunch. I've brought in men who did worse to children, then watched judges and juries set 'em free. None of that shit out here in the wild.

Take for example the apes. I been watchin' 'em eat, fuck, and fight. They share food and mates sometimes willingly, sometimes by force, just like people. But when one starts taking too much, claiming all the best grub or pussy, the others club him to death. Sometimes the females even gang up against a male who takes too many by force. The biggest, meanest, smartest brutes raid other tribes, but only when they can get others to follow 'em. Apes got no real leaders, no long-term goals, don't build nothin'. The smart ones realize the leaders are temporary, and the dumb ones die young. But hell, they got plenty of different stuff to eat, horny females, and monkey whelps. They got a better life than most of civilized humanity!

One group has been tailin' me. First they tried scaring me off their turf, till I blasted a few. Then they let me pass with plenty space. They been following me about a day behind, unaware that I can see 'em with my binocs. Every couple days one of 'em approaches and tries to communicate. Some beat their chests or toss clubs at me, and I send 'em packing with live fire. Others leave fruit when they think I'm asleep, then hide and watch if I eat it. When I kill a big predator I leave a bit of cooked meat behind for 'em, just for fun. They throw these crazy monkey orgies when they find it. It's a hell of a show!

Anyways, I'd been doing legwork for six days when I found my prey. Doc was expecting probes, had no idea I'd hunt on foot. His security drones gave him away, just like I hoped, and I ran a basic snatch and hack job on one of 'em. I ripped his crash coordinates from it, stuffed it with eight grams of C-nite, and sent it home for suicide and sabotage. I never heard the explosion but I saw smoke the next day.

That didn't manage to take out the force-field, so I been camped outside the crash site for a week. Doc set up a few wind generators within his field, and comes out every day with his prize specimen to taunt me. He talks to her in sign language, but keeps a shock-collar on her. She stares through the field at the local apes, and they, well, go ape for her. I guess to an ape white fur and green eyes equates to sex goddess. They learned real fast about the force-field, but test it every day.

I tried negotiating with the doc, but he tends to unload bullets and grenades every time he has a guess at my location. Communicating tends to give me away. One day he gave me a speech about the strength of his force-field and caliber of his guns, but all the firepower in the galaxy won't make him a fighter. He knows it, too. He ain't hardly put a scratch on my suit. Course, I haven't done much more damage to his ship since he wised up about drones. They got complex self-destruct program traps now. His defensive programing is wicked. One blew after I was sure I'd bypassed counter-measures, and I damn near lost an arm. I dropped any hack plans after that.

So it's a siege. Least I got apes bringing me food. Wish I could train 'em and take 'em with me, they make good company. Now I get why so many hunters still use hounds.

They gimme ideas sometimes, like I tried using gifts to draw the Ice Princess out of the force-field, but her collar keeps her in. To try getting' some new ideas for a plan, I lit up a few spliffs of deep zen three and recorded this log. I'll get a new plan soon, meanwhile I'm harassing the doc enough to slow his repairs. If his engine gets running before my auto-repair bots patch up *Saint George*, I may loose him for good. Course, if I get my ship up first I can ground-pound his force-field, I'll just have to be ginger so I don't accidentally roast the Ice Princess. That'd piss me off almost as much as it would the apes.

[Personal Journal of Dr. Joyden standard date {classified}]

The experiment has become so enticing that I'm spending less time repairing the engines and more time observing Anastasia's interactions with indigenous primates. I'll spare you the scientific details, as they can be found in my daily reports.

Basically, Anastasia is changing the way she thinks about the world, herself, and others. The changes appear to be permanent, and only one dose has been administered. Unfortunately, this means that until further experiments are conducted, it cannot be assumed that the drugs are the predominant cause of change. Still, behavior and brainwave alterations are unmistakable. Her sign language skills have not improved notably, but her body language accent has altered significantly.

Her brainwave patterns no longer contain the unique similarities to brain patterns observed in both advanced simians and underdeveloped human children—the reason I specifically needed her for the experiment. However, her brainwaves are neither conforming to a human pattern nor one in sync with patterns recorded from the local apes she is so enamored with. She is producing completely new brainwaves, undecipherable without further research.

The indigenous primates obsess over her, and much like the bounty hunter besieging us, are constantly attempting to lure her away. The intentions and methods of the apes vary greatly from Shane's tactics, but both result in constant frustrations.

Our renegade friend has had little success since his drone attack, which heavily damaged our engine core. Whenever I take Anastasia outside the ship, he and I play a game of cat-and-mouse. At first, I became suspicious whenever he approached the force-field, fearing he was setting up field-disrupting devices. I doubt at this point he has any, however. I believe his only motive is bluffing to cause psychological distress and stall my repairs. Perhaps he has reinforcements on the way, or has put into motion some other plan requiring time. I've taken aggressive measures to ensure that he's under more stress than I am. One-way shielding allows me to fire on him without risking return fire, and ammunition remains plentiful.

The plans of the apes are much clearer and in fact more disruptive than Nameless Shane. The force-field is set to a frequency allowing most audible vibrations to cross it, so we hear the apes every morning. At sunrise, they launch stones, shouts, wood, and feces at the force-field for hours. During the afternoons, when I observe Anastasia's behavior in the jungle, several large males flock to the edge of the barrier to engage in courtship displays. She immediately developed an interest. Thankfully her shock-collar is set to keep her from exiting the force-field, and I carry a remote activator as well, should her frustrations turn aggressive. She often throws tantrums when I tell her she cannot cross the barrier to join her suitors.

Male apes have also been leaving her gifts of food and simple found tools. This has connected to some element of her native ape-society, and resulted in her preferring males who leave gifts over those with elaborate mating displays. Shane actually tried this tactic as well, though I responded to his offering of grilled meat with bullets. It is possible that the apes picked up the idea of offering food from him, though I have no evidence supporting this.

Anastasia has learned that while she cannot cross the barrier herself, she can toss food or stones in favor or insult towards her suitors. She is vexed that they do not comprehend sign language, but has no trouble communicating through provocative body displays aimed at her favorite males. Although appearing quite humorous to a human observer, these displays send the apes into such a frenzy of lust that some are not content to masturbate by hand and attempt to hump the force-field. Hilariously, one lost favor with the Ice Princess by attempting to impregnate a rotten melon he had brought as an offering after watching her pat her rump.

At the end of the day, when the apes have exhausted themselves, they return to the jungle and sing. Anastasia has tried several times to join in the cacophony, but I return her to the ship for sleep, forcefully if necessary. An erratic sleep pattern is another variable I am trying to eliminate.

I must return to my repairs soon. I work most efficiently while Anastasia sleeps. My estimates as to time required for repairs have been so inaccurate that I stopped bothering to calculate them. When Shane approaches at night, I prefer to let the auto-turrets deal with him, unless repairs have driven me to the dire stage of frustration in which hurling grenades into the darkness and screaming obscenities becomes a worthwhile emotional release.

I must again note that conjectures expressed concerning the experiment in my personal journal lack sufficient evidence to be considered accurate. All data-supported hypotheses and specific information remains in my official reports, as well as possible results of the research. Perhaps when I have escaped the threat of capture, I will return to this planet to collect specimens, and observe if Anastasia's visit has had any lasting effects on them.

◇ ◇ ◇ ◇ ◇

AUDIO RECORDING:
"Catazz" TAVERN: DSC Outpost 892; SSD 9.16.56
{irrelevant audio filtered}

"You won't collect on the doc if you left his body—"

"So? I got the snow monkey and she's worth tenfold."

"How'd you manage to get past that force-field to bag her?"

"Heh, good question. All I had to do was outsmart a scientist and some monkeys!

Doc was taking her into the jungle every day, still within the force-field, but outside his ship. The local apes thought she was some foreign sex princess or something, so they're bringing her monkey gifts and try to get at her every day. Anyways, this snow monkey's as randy as any ape, but doc's got her on a shock-collar to keep her from running. I guess he's gotta keep her virgin for his experiment, or himself, you know?"

"Hahahah!"

"The collar she's in's identical to what I use, just no manacles. I'm betting she's worn it her whole life in the zoo, and thinks her shocks are coming from the force-field.

So one day, I toss one of my cheap shock-collars and a clicker to the wild apes. Then I set up in a treetop blind with max distortion, then set my binocs to record the show.

At daybreak, two huge fucking apes try to offer the collar and clicker to her. After fighting, the meaner one claims the collar and the smaller the remote. Now about this time, both apes notice their white princess is wearing a collar, and the doc notices they've got one, too. He knows they got if from me, so he starts scanning for me instead of watching the apes.

This is when it gets good.

Alpha male puts on the collar, emulating the Ice Princess, while his bruised buddy starts poking buttons on the clicker. Soon enough, the big guy gets zapped and realizes he can't take the collar off. A few jolts later, his pal recognizes the power of the red button. Now Beta male is out for revenge, showing off his dominance to the female. And she's riveted, but not cuz he's impressing her. I can read her simple mug like a flash ad, she keeps looking from the males to the doc, figuring out how her shock-collar works. Beta boy is gettin' a bit too cocky, goading Alpha into attacking, then zapping him when he charges. Then Alpha nabs a stick and smacks the remote out of his hand, smashing it. Beta picks up the red button and tries to zap him back into submission, but no dice. Alpha trades the stick for a rock and caves in Beta's skull.

Meanwhile, doc's been scoping for me and missing the show. When his prize specimen starts signing to him, he has no idea what he's in for. He lowers his eyes from the scan scope, and starts to sign back. With one hand signing and the other on his gun, he's left the remote on his belt.

She grabs his gun with one hand and the clicker with her other, then tosses the clicker. She rips the rifle from him and bashes his head till he stops moving! I got the whole thing on video, and the look on his face is worth more than the bounty on him! He's crying, screaming her name while she pounds him to death.

Satisfied, she wiggles her ass at Alpha who's starting to get hard, then picks up the clicker and eventually finds the collar release. She locks eyes with Alpha, and lets out a howl that seems to call every ape in the jungle. Slowly crossing the force-field, she picks Alpha as her first prize.

I could nab her whenever at that point, but I kinda felt like I owed them apes, so I gave 'em a day to celebrate and fuck the Ice Princess. I think she appreciated it even more than they did."

"If she's still on your ship you better have more'n a shock-collar keeping her put!"

"You think I'm as stupid as that scientist? I kept her drugged and in stasis the whole trip here. I warned zoo personnel to keep her out until they get her home, but they didn't listen. Shit, I already got paid, let them deal with her."

"What'd she do when she woke?"

"I didn't stick around to find out! Imagine how pissed off she must be! Shit, she's probably pregnant, and was just forcibly torn away from a planet of sexual paradise."

"Only thing worse than an ugly pissed-off whore is one stronger than you who thinks she's a princess!"

◊ ◊ ◊ ◊ ◊

Galactic Gossip Gazette - Flash!
GREAT ESCAPING APE!

Anastasia the Ice Princess, famed "Galaxy's Smartest Ape" and genetically re-created "Missing Link" has made another escape from Orion's Historical Super Zoo! But don't get your hopes up, bounty hunters! Besides her abduction by Dr. Joyden two years ago, this is her third break-out, and Orion's is confident they can retrieve her unaided, according to this public statement from President Torn:

"We found her ourselves last time, and there's little doubt where she's headed. We have no idea where she learned to fly a ship, but I for one am interested to see if she'll manage to land this time, or if we'll have to pay another fee for her crash disturbing a nature preserve."

It seems you just can't keep a royal ape down!

by Jessica McHugh

To go straight from the academy to the field meant one of two things. One: you had impressed your superiors so much that they believed you absolutely vital to the mission. Or two: they were trying to get rid of you, whether it meant forcing you into AWOL or into a pine box accompanied by a sad letter home. To this day, I don't know which fate they had in mind for me, but I can't imagine they sent me to Nigeria because I was head of my class; I was more like the torso. I knew nothing about Nigeria or the Yoruba people. I didn't know anything about the snakes or gorillas, except to ask before I got close to either, and I certainly didn't know anything about Vodun (or "voodoo" as I said only once before being strictly corrected). Even after we were on our way to Nigeria, my superior officers didn't tell me anything. They wanted ignorance. Ignorance encouraged silence, and even if I did have the courage to speak about what I'd seen during our mission, I wouldn't be able to do so with hard facts. Dr. Jacob Knight was the only man to offer up a bit of truth, and he only did so in a death rattle. At the time, I didn't know how much truth was in the words that bubbled out of his mouth, but I quickly learned just how much my superiors, especially Sergeant Moore, kept secret from us all.

He called me Brandon—not my name. It wasn't until long after that I learned his son's name was Brandon. Because he thought he was speaking to his son, it made the last words he said even sadder. But the sadness swiftly fled when fear returned. It always returns, no matter how much I plead or bargain. Fear wins and there's plenty of it, but I should back up. I'm getting ahead of myself...

The journey was smooth sailing at first. Even with my ignorance and the bullish arrogance of Sergeant Moore, I actually thought I was about to take part in a grand adventure. I didn't realize then how naïve a notion that was. Nor did I realize that my superiors were so..."Evil" doesn't seem like the right word, but it's the only one that leaps to mind, so it has to be somewhat fitting. It's no wonder they kept the true objective of the mission a secret.

We touched down without incident and started toward the Yoruba homestead. It wasn't until the houses dwindled and gave rise to clustered jungle that the fear started to set in. There was a clear division between military and anthropology in our small company. Obviously, I was more soldier than anthropologist, but I didn't feel qualified enough to interject into either side of the debate. For that reason, I kept my head down and mouth shut. I simply nodded as the doctors briefed me on the regional wildlife and Yoruba customs. I continued my obedient, if not robotic, nod to Sergeant Moore's instructions of "If I say 'shoot', you shoot."

We were nearing the Yoruba homestead when Dr. Jacob Knight spotted something of interest through his binoculars. A few exclamations were all he gave us and leapt out of the jeep with the words "Cross River Gorilla" on his lips and a glazy excitement in his eyes. It was abrupt to say the least and I hadn't the foggiest idea what to do until Sergeant Moore shot me a look that seemed to say, "What are you still doing here, fool? Go after him!"

My M16 was primed before I hit the ground, but even with trusty Lulu aching for action, there was no part of me that wanted to dive into the knotted jungle as enthusiastically as Dr. Knight had. I called his name a few times, hoping to coax him out, but it was for naught, and when I looked back at the car, I was promptly pushed into the bush by Moore's forceful glare. Once inside the jungle, I felt as tiny as the tiniest boll weevil; albeit, a weevil with a rifle. The sound of a nearby gasp pulled me to the right and there I saw Dr. Knight standing frozen behind a tree with only his head curled around the trunk.

"Sir?" I asked and he hushed me harshly. "Sir, we should get back to the jeep. Lord knows when we'll reach the Yoruba."

"The Yoruba are not far off. Neither is she," he replied.

Before I could push for elaboration, a mammoth tree straight ahead shook madly. My jaw dropped as I watched a massive gorilla dive out of the branches and land on the ground with an earth-shaking thud. Her face was black, wreathed with reddish brown fur and she snorted madly as if our scent irritated her nostrils. Her colossal body was oddly shaped. It appeared as though her bones were about to break through the skin, and there were large patches of matted gray gunk scattered through her fur.

"I've been waiting all of my life to see a Cross River Gorilla," Dr. Knight whispered. "I've traveled farther and deeper than anyone and never caught a glimpse. But here she is. I wasn't even looking for her, and here she is."

"Yes, she's lovely. Let's go," I said and tugged on his arm.

He growled as he shook me away and the beast added a growl of her own, far more ferocious than the doctor's. I pointed my rifle at her and she huffed: grunting and sighing as if to say "Oh, you stupid, stupid man-child."

"She's bigger than I thought. Much bigger. My God, she's enormous."

"Yes, she is," I said as the rifle began to shake in my arms.

The gorilla started towards us, looking less and less like a gentle giant with each stomping step. Her gait was strange. I couldn't recognize a gorilla's normal gait, but it couldn't have been as jerky or as stiffly lumbering as the one advancing upon us. As she grew closer, other odd attributes also became clear: gaping wounds dripping gray ooze, broken fangs, and a sickening stench that distance had been kind enough to keep away until then. Backing away only made her move quicker, and before long, she was a mere ten feet in front of us. It was then that I noticed how much Knight's fear had increased.

"What do we do?" I asked him and he shook his head frightfully. "Come on, you know all about these river monkeys, right?"

"I do, but…"

"But what?" I snapped and the gorilla roared so forcefully that the howl blasted several branches bare. "Is it not what you thought it was?" I asked and he shook his head again.

"It's definitely a Cross River Gorilla, but something's wrong with it. The wounds on its chest: they're infected. Worse than that. They're rotting. No, they're…"

The beast drew closer and I saw what the doctor saw and more. The gorilla's wounds weren't just rotting. Writhing in the gray fluid pouring from the gorilla's wounds were hundreds of maggots. I nearly lost my stomach right there, but I feared the sudden upheaval would draw the animal faster. I focused on keeping the sickness down while the doctor stepped out from behind the tree, drawing a syringe from his pocket.

"Are you crazy? What are you doing?"

"I need a sample. Just a small sample."

"You need to get your ass back here, Doc," I said, but he ignored me; no surprise there.

All I could do was lock the gorilla in my crosshairs and pray. I can't know if it was my prayers or simple nature, but the ape's eyes were drawn away from us. The beast, in all of it's viciously corroded glory, became enraptured by a passing butterfly. It would have made me chuckle if not for the acidic fear gnawing my tongue into immobility. While the gorilla was distracted by shimmering iridescent wings, Dr. Knight advanced. She made small yipping sounds at the butterfly and dug at the dirt anxiously, but when Knight buried his needle in her immense thigh, her eyes shot to him.

"Easy, girl. That's it. That's my girl," he sang softly as he drew back the plunger and filled the syringe.

The gorilla's body shook with building rage as it raised paw much larger than the doctor's head, even with its missing digits.

"Maybe you should move, Doc."

"I'm just about finished," he said and capped the vial of thick, gray fluid.

"Is that how it's supposed to look?" I asked, but he didn't answer.

The gorilla clamped its paw around his arm, and her nose twitched madly as she pulled him closer and closer. My fear for Knight increased, but he was too entranced by his wonder to worry. Even as the beast's mouth became an unnaturally wide cavern of broken stalactites into which his arm disappeared, Dr. Knight could not pull away from the creature he'd been craving to see for so long, no matter how grotesque.

My scream came first. It was more of a warning to Dr. Knight that if he didn't move, his scream was sure to follow. He did not heed my warning, but my scream was powerful enough to pluck the others from the jeep. The initial bite was slow. The gorilla closed her mammoth mouth around the doctor's arm, almost daring him to pull back, but he didn't. After a life's search, he couldn't turn away. He needed to see the Cross River Gorilla up close. He needed to feel it, even if it meant—well, he couldn't have known what would happen any more than I could know why he stood there and took it. Her fangs tore straight through his arm as if it was paper, and the doctor finally screamed. At last, the enchantment was severed, and as he pulled himself out of the gorilla's clenched jaws, so was his arm. He was on the ground by the time the others arrived, shrieking and clutching what was left of his limb. As the gorilla loomed over him, dripping gray fluid onto his face, the maggots fell as well and started burrowing into his shredded forearm.

"Shoot, you idiot!" Sergeant Moore screamed; I had a feeling that while the "shoot" was for everyone, the "idiot" was for me.

I emptied my magazine into the gorilla's chest, sending chunks of rotten flesh flying through the air until there was a spacious hole in which I could see her broken ribcage, as well as a gray lump of flesh that looked like it may have, at one time, been her heart. A few soldiers nabbed head shots, but it only gave the gorilla pause and she glared at those shooters as if memorizing who to take down next. She grasped Dr. Knight by his stump of an arm and hoisted him into the air.

"Hold your fire!" the sergeant shouted, but Knight begged for more.

"Kill her!" he screamed.

That was all Dr. Knight was able to get out before the beast dug her fangs into his forehead and tore away his face. It was still hanging from her teeth when she growled and threw him aside like a rag doll. She lunged at me, and more nimbly than I thought myself capable, I flipped my rifle around and whipped it across her face. She roared and I bashed the butt against her teeth, shattering two of the remaining fangs and knocking Knight's face free. I hurled Lulu at the gorilla and dashed for the doctor while the others unloaded their magazines into the beast. Jacob Knight lay broken several yards away with every inch covered in sloppy scarlet. His teeth were horrifyingly exposed and his remaining hand was bent backwards so far that his fingers were touching his wrist, but the worst part was that Dr. Knight was still very much alive.

"Brandon," he squeaked, barely moving his lipless mouth. "I'm sorry, Brandon. I wanted to see it. I wanted to see it."

"Just take it easy, Dr. Knight. Don't try to talk."

"You shouldn't be here, Brandon. This isn't appropriate for children. I'm not sure it's appropriate for me."

"What isn't appropriate, Doc?"

"Trying the save the soldiers with Vodun. The Yoruba don't like it."

"Save what soldiers?"

"The dead ones. On the battlefield," he groaned.

He was sweating blood. That's when I noticed he wasn't as scarlet as before. He was now oozing gray fluid, and dots of gray pus were starting to bubble out of his face.

"Doc?" I whispered, but he was deathly silent and still—until he wasn't.

His body twitched with a wet crack. Then, he twitched again with a series of pops and squelchy snaps. His arms bent unnaturally and abruptly lengthened, stretching his skin to its limits and beyond. A guttural howl was trapped in his throat as he awkwardly got to his feet and gnashed his teeth hungrily. I held up my hands as if that would do something. I tried to reason with him as if *that* would do something. Thankfully, the rifle Sergeant Moore aimed over my shoulder actually did something. The shots blasted Knight backwards, far enough for us to retreat, but for a dead man, he caught up quickly. His gait was as rigid as the gorilla's, but he was extremely fast. When he reached out desperately, his bones burst through his fingertips, but before he could reach us, something intercepted him and knocked him off the path. The Sergeant and I turned to see Dr. Knight and the Cross River Gorilla standing opposite each other, panting ferociously. With his new elongated limbs, the doctor resembled an insect and stood clumsily as he hissed at the ape.

"I thought that bastard was dead. You were supposed to shoot it in the head!" Moore shouted at the remnants of the company.

"We did, Sir. Fifteen times. It won't go down, Sir."

The gorilla's roar shook the jungle, and when we heard a sloppy snap-crackle-pop, the company turned to see the beast holding Dr. Knight's head in one hand and his deformed body in the other. Dr. Knight was dead…for good this time. It hurled the head at us, but it hit several branches before it rolled to our feet, and the gorilla dropped his protracted body to the ground like a useless lollipop stick.

"Alright," Sergeant Moore said and cracked his neck with a grunt. "Cut that fucker's head off."

"If you do that, you won't get your serum, Sergeant Moore," a nearby voice declared.

The man looking down on us from the cliff was US Military for sure, but he was wearing tribal trappings and flanked by what I could only assume were Yoruba soldiers. There was also a man dressed in a striped robe with a red cloth draped around his neck, holding strange wooden rods that he shook every so often. I felt safe to assume he was some sort of priest. He gestured to the Yoruba soldiers and they immediately fired several darts at the gorilla. Before Moore could scoff at their idiocy for thinking darts could take it down when bullets couldn't, the beast collapsed, unconscious.

"It's a special sedative. Nothing else seems to work," said the military man on the cliff.

"I know something that will," Moore said and withdrew a machete. "That animal killed my men, Sergeant McNab."

"Then by all means, cut off her head, but you will have come all this way for nothing. Your coveted serum comes from this creature's flowing blood, and I'm afraid the original host is long dead," McNab replied.

A shudder traveled through the Yoruba as if the same memory had suddenly laid siege to them all. With a grunt, Moore signaled for everyone to lower their weapons.

"So you do care about the soldiers after all. How touching," McNab continued. "Shall we proceed with the transaction?"

He nodded at the priest, but the priest didn't move.

"What's the problem, Sergeant McNab: don't have your dogs as well trained as you thought?" Moore snickered.

"We are not dogs," the priest said sternly, but McNab viciously yanked him close.

"Look, you said this gorilla's blood would bring dead people back to life. You swore it."

"Yes, it will, but why would you ever wish such a thing? Especially after what I told you about my son?" the priest asked with his voice sticking in his throat on the word "son".

"Your son wasn't a US soldier. We're built of tougher stuff than him."

"It is easy to declare so when the devil isn't in your reflection. I can admit now that my reasons for resurrecting my son were selfish. What about yours? Why do you wish to raise the dead?"

"So that soldiers who fall can stand back up," Sergeant Moore replied. "The dead can keep fighting and be stronger than they ever were in life."

"At what cost?!" I blurted. "You saw what happened to Dr. Knight!"

Sergeant Moore spun around and growled at me through clenched teeth, "Go deaf, kid."

"We can't use it as is, of course," McNab said. "It will require tweaking. And plenty of testing."

"Of course. Riley, Martin: come with me. The rest of you: get your asses back to the jeep," Moore commanded, but I couldn't will my feet to move. "Did you hear what I said, Private?"

"No, Sir. I'm deaf, Sir," he replied and his lip began to curl cruelly, but before it became a full-blown sneer, I turned on my heel and headed back with the others.

Was the derisive reply necessary? Absolutely not. But how much worse could it get? They wanted me ignorant from the beginning, but I and the rest of the company definitely weren't ignorant in the end. Maybe the details were lacking, but we knew enough. Vodun and zombie soldiers. That was all we needed to know to earn that pine box and a sad letter—not right away though. They made us wait.

Still, I wait. While they do their tinkering and testing, I wait. All I can hope is that they've gotten it right by the time they reach me, that they've perfected the serum taken from the gorilla's blood. But since they're quickly approaching Test 17, I tend to doubt it. That's why I'm writing this now, in the vain hope that someone will read it, that someone will kill that beast and stop the cycle. As long as that monster is alive, they'll keep trying to raise the dead. And it won't stop with them. The infection will spread beyond the Yoruba and then, no one will be safe. The world will be doomed. As long as that gorilla is out there, the dead will rise.

As long as she's alive…

God willing, I won't be.

by Kristen McHenry

They said these gibbons were special, just for the girls, and to Sweeny this made sense. Girls and monkeys went natural together. The gibbons were going help them feel better about the war, the teacher said.

"They are called 'therapy monkeys' and they are very costly to train," Sweeny explained to her mother, who was having her day in bed. Sweeny had rehearsed this on her way home. It made her feel knowledgeable.

"Monkeys have diseases in their spit," her mother said. "Stay back from the cages." She signed the permission slip, turned to the wall, and covered her head with the quilt. "Now be an angel and bring mommy an egg-and-toast."

It was hard for Sweeny to sleep, thinking about the gibbons. The encyclopedias had almost all been used for fire, but they still had F-G. She read that gibbons are *frugivorous, diurnal* and *arboreal.* She repeated these words in a whisper: *frugivorous, diurnal and arboreal.* A mystery. The libraries were long-gone and now Sweeny had to find mysteries wherever they presented themselves: A glass vanilla lip gloss skittering down an alley, two long wrinkled hands cupping a lighter, a blue foam roller stuck in a raspberry bush. But the monkeys would have real mysteries; eye mysteries. Gibbons, she read, went together each morning to the edge of the woods and sang to let everyone know which part of it was theirs.

Sweeny put the book down and pulled the rags out of the hole in the floor to see if it had gotten black-dark outside yet. The hole was left over from the war, but Sweeny couldn't remember if had been there years or only months. It *was* black-dark, and Sweeny smelled the comforting burn of pesticide. Through the hole, she sang a high, meek song about their frailty, about her mother's days in bed and how little they could ask for nowadays. She crammed the rags back in and fell asleep with F-G open on her stomach, the gibbons hugging her ribs.

They were taken to the monkeys in a dirty mint-green bus with ripped-up seats. Sweeny sat next to Fionna, who wore boy's plaid shirts and used to chew gum all of the time back when you could get it anywhere. Sweeny had always admired Fionna's easy-going ways. "What if a gibbon tried to kiss you?" Sweeny asked Fionna. "If he took you in his big fat arms and pushed you against the cage bars and tried to kiss you?" Fionna yawned.

"I'd scream," she said.

They all had to get out of the bus and be counted and put T-shirts on over their clothes before going into the low hut that held the monkeys. The T-shirts were green and yellow and read "Go, Go Gibbons! Experience for Youth." Sweeny was proud of hers. A full-hipped young woman in glasses and a baseball hat came out from the hut and waved at them. "Welcome!" she shouted. She said her name was Patty! She told them not to strike the monkeys, throw things at them, make noises, or mock them in any way. She told them to keep their hands to themselves and be respectful of the monkeys because they were shy, just as shy as people could sometimes be. She told them that these monkeys were specially trained to be loving towards children, but even they had their limits. She told them that they were not to wander off on their own and they were to do what their guides told them at all times. Sweeny listened impatiently to the woman's preamble about their cutting-edge monkey therapy program, and finally found herself heading into the odoriferous hut. She looked around for the gibbons but at first there was just museum stuff, a boring man talking when you pushed a button, and a life-sized diorama of monkeys in a rain forest.

But they kept heading down some straw-covered stairs and Sweeny felt dizzy when she could actually hear the snorts and grunts of the gibbons. "Your gibbons," said Patty, "have been hand-selected for you based on your personality type." Sweeny didn't recall telling anyone about her personality, but she figured maybe they watched of that sort of thing now because of the war. "We would like you to interact lovingly with your gibbon. To trust him or her. To explore the joy of sharing with them."

Sweeny was assigned to Apartment 18, "Roland." They unlatched the door to his pod and let her walk right in. Two smiling young people in polo shirts, a man and a woman, stood outside, clutching clipboards. The room was empty, but she could sense a lurking, musty presence nearby. She sat down in the thin straw on the floor and ducked her head demurely. Then she began to sing again, her weak, high song. She felt a brightness upon her; a rustle from above the platform, two black eyes. Then, a thick rubbery hand, pressing into her tiny bones. Sweeny was crying from fear now, but the hand stayed. She opened her eyes and looked at Roland. He pulled his lips back and patted her hand. He released her and ran to a wooden box in the center of the room, where he pulled out a blue spinning top and pushed it at her. Sweeny took the top and spun it hard. Roland shook and made hooting sounds as the top hummed and blurred across the floorboards. There was a clatter as the top sputtered to a stop on a soft spot in the wooden floor. Roland clapped and screeched.

Sweeny crawled over to the top, curled her fingers around the rotted wood, and pried it loose. A cold green rush of air filled her mouth. She glanced at the clipboard people, but they were looking down and writing something. She yanked again, and again, and peered down into a windy vacuum through a hole about the size of her nine-year-old head. She quickly grabbed some straw and the old wood and shoved it all back into place, then made the "come here" gesture to Roland, all while watching the clipboard people closely. Roland lumbered over to her and hunkered down. Sweeny pointed to the hole and put her finger over her lips in a "shhh". Roland hugged himself tightly and sucked on his lips. Sweeny whispered to him and moved back to the center of the room.

"What else do you have to play with, Roland?" she asked loudly. The clipboard people smiled and made a notation. After they had played with a beach ball, an abacus, and a pop-up book, the clipboard people blew a whistle and Roland began dragging all of the toys back into the chest. Sweeny winked at him when she shook his hand goodbye. Afterwards the girls got rice cream and a free book mark at the gift shop.

That night, after her mother had fallen asleep to the radio, Sweeny took the rags out of the hole in the floor and leaned in. This time she sang of Roland the Guardian, the great monkey protector and God of all Guardians. She sang of his devotion and his suffering. She sang of his courage and selflessness. She sang of his cleverness with counting and his gracefulness with beach balls. She stuck her head far down the windy hole and howled for Roland, guiding him with her voice. She shone her penlight into the hole and winked it on and off. But Roland didn't come, and her mother slept all of the next day, even when Sweeny got back from school.

Sweeny went out to the stoop and sat in the cold, sour air, watching for a mint-green bus to take her back to the monkeys. But very few vehicles came down the street since the war, and Sweeny got hungry. She went inside and made egg sandwiches, but when she went to wake her mother, her mother didn't move or open her eyes. Sweeny covered her back up and went to the living room and sat her on bedroll. She ate both of the sandwiches and fed the crumbs to a trio of ants.

The next morning Sweeny stayed home in bed with her mother, waiting for her to open her eyes. But throughout the day, her mother's skin grew cooler and her eyes never opened. Sweeny knew that this was death, that this is what it did to a body. She took a clean rag from the basin in the bathroom and carefully washed her mother's face with it. She brushed out her hair and covered her up to her chest with the quilt. They didn't have a phone, so she wouldn't be able to call anyone until she went to school. She would have to tell the teacher. Sweeny made a glass of powdered milk and sat next to the hole in the floor. She wanted to sing but she couldn't open her throat even to drink the milk. She only wanted to sit as still and rigid as she could. She would not move again. No matter what, she would not sing, just sit. She would take only the number of breaths needed for bare survival. She would not allow thirst or hunger to sway her. She would let the mice scramble over her legs and wouldn't move a muscle on her own behalf.

Sweeny woke up in the night, cold and uncovered. Her hair was wet and matted, and her eyes were crusty. She decided to try to scream. She sat up and opened her mouth, but she could not make noise. If she could not sing again, Roland would never come. She put her head into the hole in the floor and managed a weak whistle. The whistle gave her strength and she found herself able to make a small grunt, then another, then, finally, a long, resonant bellow. She screamed and screamed into the hole, until she began to frighten herself and stopped.

In the morning, she got on the bus for school. She had not taken her sink-bath or combed her hair or changed out of her clothes. She sat in the back alone and turned her head away from Fionna when she tried to sit next to her. At lunch, she told Mrs. Morgan about her mother. Mrs. Morgan took Sweeny to the sick room and there were phone calls. The other kids got to go to the gym to play for the afternoon. Someone brought Sweeny a cheese sandwich and a sliced tomato and hot chocolate. Mrs. Morgan was crying. When the hallways were clear, Sweeny opened the door to the sickroom and left the school. She left her book bag and ran and ran and ran, stopping only to vomit up the tomato and chocolate.

When she unlocked her apartment, her mother's bed was empty. Sweeny made up the bed and went back to sit on her bedroll. She imagined Mrs. Morgan opening the door to the sickroom and gasping. Everyone asking *where is Sweeny where is Sweeny oh where did Sweeny go*. Sweeny thought it would be a good song: *Oh where oh where did Sweeny go, well a-hunting with her monkey-oh, heydy-hiedy-hiedy-ho. Where oh where did Sweeny go, well she went a-swimming with her gibbon-oh*. Sweeny began to sing. She felt gut-punched with a wild joy. She spun and cackled and did her mad-woman dance, a dance she only did alone in the night when they had a fire and there was thunder. When she began to cramp, she stopped and laid down, her ear on top of the rags on top of the hole in the floor. The sun moved across the ceiling then across the back wall, going sticky and thick then vanishing altogether. No one came for her, but they would. She would be adopted, or go to a Home. There would be no gibbons because of their diseased spit. They wouldn't have a hole in the floor or any mysteries.

In the night, her heart began to thud so heavily that it hurt her ears. Her heart tripped like heavy feet on a bad floor. Thunder sounded in her head but it was not weather-thunder, it was monkey-thunder, blood thunder, it was the song of the gibbons claiming their stake in the world, massing in hordes to sing their song of boundaries, of home. She thrust her hand into the hole in the floor and waited for Roland. When finally his clumsy, dry, familiar hand found hers, she held on.

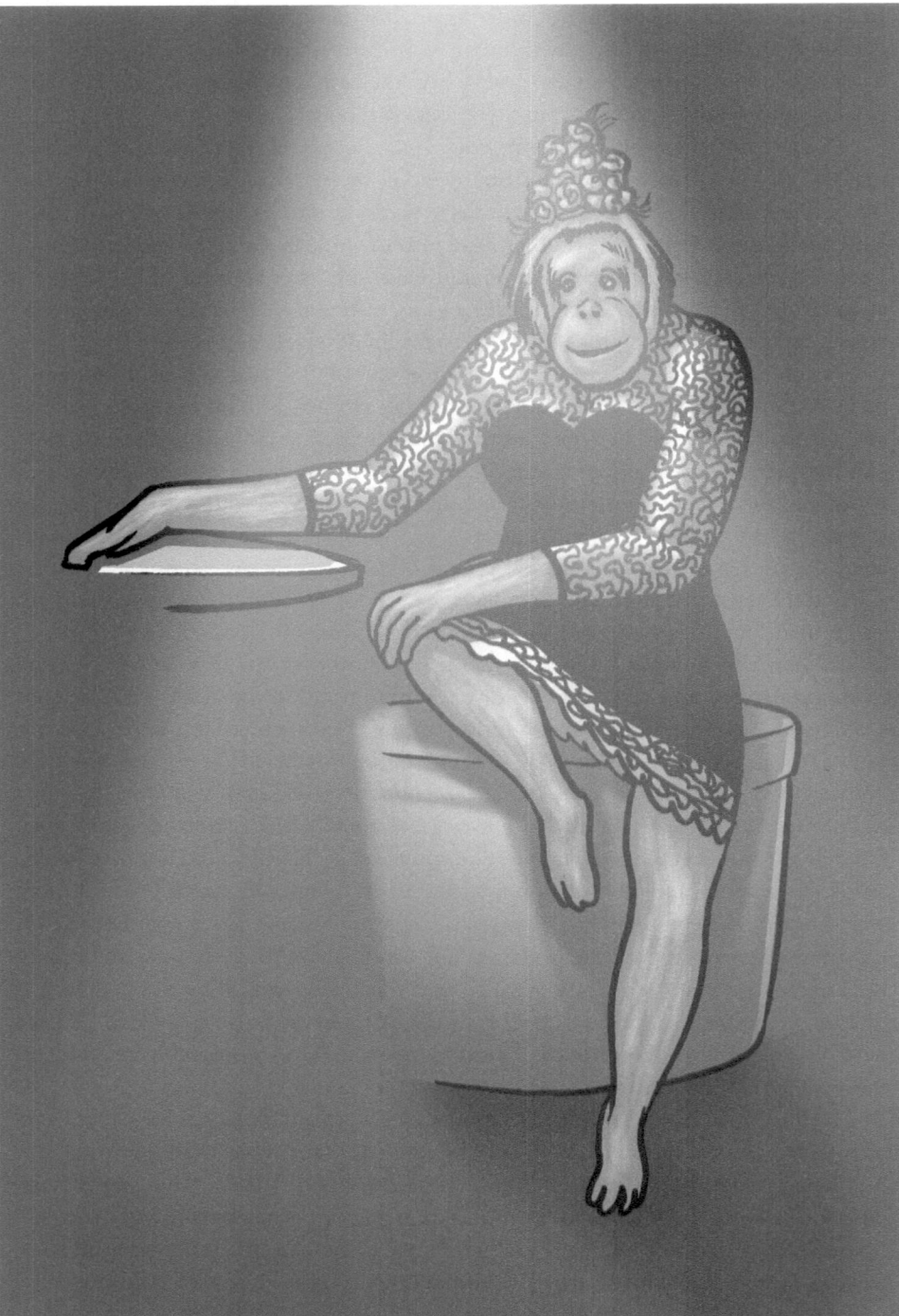

NO MONKEYS IN MONKEYTOWN

by DeAnna Knippling

1. No Monkeys in Monkeytown

The bartender at The Monkeytown Arms rubbed a shot glass over and over in his towel. Neither towel nor glass were clean. "We don't serve your kind here."

Orion stood straighter, stretching his vest tighter across his broad chest. The only thing keeping him out of the Fort Sill Nature Preserve for Greater Apes was this job, and he had to bring back his target this time, or he'd be locked up and sent back. "I'm looking for a chimp."

"We don't serve your kind here."

Orion peered into the dark until his eyes adjusted, revealing an empty bar except for an orang female in the corner. "What about her?"

"Peaches?" the bartender asked. "She ain't no monkey. She works here."

Orion snorted. "I need to talk to her."

"We don't serve your kind here."

"Don't worry about it, Dave," the orang purred. Her fur was shaved off except on her head, where it was piled high and decorated with silk flowers. She wore a scarlet and black lace dress that had been stuffed in the front to display what looked like human teats. She slid something from her table into a velvet bag and tied it tight. "It's a monkey thing."

"You be all right?" The bartender looked at Orion and didn't see a runt, a *hathscha* who would never have his own troop. He saw a three-hundred-pound gorilla. Yet he reached under the bar regardless.

The orang tapped her fingers along her cheeks, then crossed her hands past each other. "You'll know if I have trouble."

The bartender looked away as the orang dragged her nails over the cloth of Orion's shirt, digging them in lightly before removing her hand, a grooming gesture. "You have to pay."

Her touch made his skin crawl, and he bared his teeth at her. "I don't want your filthy body. I only have questions."

She clutched the bag, flaring her nostrils. "I may have answers." She swept past him, into a shadowed hallway and up the stairs. She smelled of fruit and flowers. "For a price."

Something up in the rafters followed them.

◊ ◊ ◊ ◊ ◊

Mi Tao led the pretend-human up to her room and let Absalom, her marmoset protector, slip inside the room before she closed the door. A small table on a single turned-wood pedestal sat in one corner. "Do you know the monkey cards?"

"I didn't come here to have my fortune told," he said. "I'm in a hurry."

"They all say that."

"I just want to find a chimp. General Regis. I know he's here. He's wanted for counterfeiting."

"Who do you work for, the Army?"

"The Pinks."

She raised an eyebrow. "Not much difference, anymore. Tell me, do you believe in magic?"

"Just tell me where he is."

"Hell's Canyon."

"Where is that?"

She wagged a finger at him. "Come with me, and I will show you. But I warn you, you will see forbidden things. The government doesn't want him because he's counterfeiting. They want him because he can control the dead."

"Don't be ridiculous."

She fluttered her hands toward her chest. "As you say." She looked up at Absalom and whistled through her teeth. He dropped onto her shoulder, chittering at the *hathscha*, who stepped backward. She laughed. "You're afraid of a little marmoset, are you? And you think capturing that chimp will be an easy matter."

"What's that he's carrying?" The *hathscha* pointed at Absalom's wrists, which were tied with small, thin leather packets.

"Poison needles," Mi Tao said. "I always make sure assistance is near when I bring callers to my rooms. Are you certain you don't want your fortunes read?"

He pinched his fingers together twice.

She stripped off her dress by pulling a leather tie down one side; it fell apart in two halves that opened like a clamshell. She scratched her fingernails into her sides, then hung the dress on a hook on the wall. Absalom climbed into her hair and started untangling the loops and throwing the flowers on the floor.

"Do you know why it's called Monkeytown? Because only a few years ago, it was filled with all kinds of apes. *Hathscha*. They were here to make better lives for themselves, working at the silver mine. To live free of both the laws of men and the laws of apes. It was a kind of paradise, as long as you were willing to work. The mines were owned by a chimp named General Maxim, and everything in Monkeytown belonged to the apes.

"And then he died and left the mines to his so-called son, General Regis. Or so they say. Then the apes disappeared and disappeared, until there were no more monkeys in Monkeytown."

"What about you?"

She didn't answer him. "The wagons still roll up the trail, heavy with ore, and the few humans who live here grow rich. No one will speak of what happens in the mine."

"I don't *care*," he said. "I don't give a damn about those *hathscha*. We all have to prove ourselves. Justice is not my problem. Bringing back General Regis alive is my problem."

"And when you work for the humans, you have to prove and prove and prove, and you will never have any troop to show for it."

He bared his teeth at her.

From inside a wardrobe, she removed a leather jacket covered in long, orange orang hair and put it on. It would have been better if he had let her read the cards. She would have hinted at the truth, then. She closed a series of hooks and tied the laces at the top and bottom, and then she looked like an orang again. She hated playing the whore. But she had no room for pride, in serving the *ronnok*.

"Take them off," she said.

"What?"

"Where we are going, you cannot wear clothes. You would be killed in a heartbeat. But the humans cannot tell us apart, when we do not play dress-up for them."

"No," he said.

She waved her hands toward her chest and led him down the back stairs, Absalom peering at him through her loosened hair

2. Hell's Canyon

Just past the gravel trail, rocks rose in painted, jagged teeth, row after row of them, like those of a shark. On the other side of the trail, a small creek ricocheted down a narrow crack to join a larger stream that smelled of cattle. The trail wound downward among the rock teeth, and pebbles skittled off the path to ricochet downstream.

"What is this place?"

"Hell's Canyon," the orang muttered.

His horse's ears twitched as a larger piece of rock bounced down at them, hit the path, and clattered away. A cave gaped a few hundred feet up in the rock above them.

"What's that?"

Her weight shifted behind him as she looked up at it. "Their Hill of Bones is past a dropoff at the back of the cave. It hasn't been used for years."

Orion shivered. Apes who lived in the traditional way piled their bones all together, the dead on top of the dead on top of the dead, until you couldn't tell them apart. "Some of the human ways are better. To be buried separately, not all jumbled together."

She fluttered her hands on his back, snorting. "You'll never get a troop, thinking like that. Who wants to be alone, in death?"

The steep path followed the creek downward until they forded another small stream, the water only going up to the horse's fetlocks.

Just past the water, the orang murmured, "Stop."

Orion reined in, and she dangled off the horse's side, dropped, and waved at him to stay. She knuckled quickly to the next turn in the path, hesitated, then went around a large rock. Orion shifted, patting the big horse, not quite ready to dismount.

She backed into view until she was past the rock, then softly knuckled back to him. "Tie the horse here, by the water. But don't tie him too tight. If the dead ones find him, he should be able to run. And take off your clothes and walk normally, for *ronnok*'s sake."

He shook his head and followed her along the trail. But he walked gently, making little sound, and took off his hat before he peered around the corner.

Around the turn, the landscape opened onto a hill made of gravel, topped with long, low wooden buildings made of weathered gray wood. Daylight shone through gaps in the walls, and some of the boards had fallen. The windows were open frames into darkness, the shutters fallen off on most of them. The creek poured loudly though a narrow pinch in the rock at the bottom of the hill, where a wood trough leading from a small gray building added what looked like a steady stream of blood to the water.

On the far side of the hill, gorillas stood motionless, watching a couple of wagons come down a gully. He would have thought them statues, but he could see flies buzzing around them. One of the apes turned from the far side of the hill and circled back toward them. The orang tugged at his arm, but he couldn't move: the front of the *hathscha*'s face had been torn away, leaving pale muscle. As it came closer he could see red tears running from where the *hathscha*'s eyes had been, now black holes tinted with red. It reached the other side of the hill and circled away.

"Monkeytown Silver Mine," the orang whispered. "Please. You have to stop acting human here. It will only get us killed."

"It was dead," he said.

She grunted. "Are you going or not?"

He watched the gorillas until the wagons had reached the stream and forded it, then took off his clothes, folded them, and put them in the horse's saddlebags. He tried to buckle his gunbelt back on.

"That won't do a thing to them," she said. "You could burn them and scatter the ashes, and they would still have no rest. You will only reveal yourself if you wear those."

Hands shaking, he put the guns in the bags with his clothing.

Damn this place. And damn that orang. She ran on all fours, her knuckles digging into the sharp gravel of the hill, toward a pile of rubble. He followed her, one eye on the gorillas helping unload the wagons, which looked to be full of rotten meat, trying to keep himself perfectly upright.

◇ ◇ ◇ ◇ ◇

Mi Tao passed the dormitory quickly, hoping that any of the foremen who saw Orion would overlook him. But the low-lying areas of Hell's Canyon turned quickly to dusk, even in the early afternoon, and they crossed the yard and reached the collar of the sump shaft without incident. She climbed the pile of rubble on the lee side, took one last look toward the dormitory—she felt eyes on her—and started climbing into the foul air of the mine.

Some of the cracks in the shaft were natural; some had been augmented with railroad spikes. She climbed past the first level to the fourth and stopped at the drift, then climbed further down, just far enough that Orion could feel the dark hole of the drift opposite them. Air blew the hair from her vest into her mouth and she spat it out as she gripped three spikes and scratched the edge of her vest with her other leg.

"Where are we?"

"General Regis is that way," she said. "You'll come to another downward tunnel. Go around it and over an old fall. It's tight, but you can make it. Go to what looks like the end of the tunnel. Search the back of the tunnel until you find a couple of wood supports that are loose. Push them out of the way. Behind it is another tunnel, very thin. If you can make it through the old fall, you can make it through the tunnel. It splits to the left and to the right; take the left-hand tunnel only. General Regis's offices are down there. Take him if you can, but watch out for more of those guards. If I'm not back by full dark, leave me."

One hand moved toward his hip, then away. "What about you?"

"I'm not here to collect your bounty for you, *hathscha*."

"Good." Orion gathered himself and jumped overhead through the thin light of the tunnel, into the darkness. She heard a grunt and his paws scrabbling along the loose rock of the tunnel floor, then the padding of feet. She paused to listen: but no sounds of a fight followed.

She climbed downwards. Absalom shivered in her hair, and she tucked him inside the top of her vest. The walls went from dry to damp in only a few feet, and soon enough her foot broke through a layer of dead leaves, shit, and other garbage floating on the surface of the sump water. She jerked her foot back and tried to shake the wet, clinging things off her, but the more she shook, the more the garbage intertwined around her feet.

She reached—she had *very* long arms, even for an orang—until she found the next handhold, then let her lower body dangle as she tried to remember where the handhold after that would be. Something metal pinged against the shaft where she'd been a second ago. She groaned and dropped into the sump, then went limp, moving only enough to shift Absalom to her back and keep one ear free of the filth.

Above her, something chuckled, then scrabbled and slid on the gravel of the drift, where Orion had gone.

◊ ◊ ◊ ◊ ◊

The tunnel was too short to walk upright in, yet when Orion settled onto his knuckles, he felt taller. The orang groaned and fell, splashed; he backed into the tunnel and waited. Someone chuckled, then gathered, inhaled, and leapt across the sump shaft. He waited. Its silhouette against the dim light of the shaft was small, agile, and the size and shape of a chimp as it slid across the look rock toward him.

He grabbed it, spun it against the wall, and clutched it by the throat. "Move and I kill you."

"Orion?" the shaking voice asked. "That *is* you."

He leaned forward and sniffed. "Sirena." Then dropped her and stepped back. He knew her too well to think of her as *safe*. But she only sank down to her haunches and coughed.

"Why are you here?"

"I work for the owner."

He smelled the lie more than heard it, but it wasn't unexpected. "I'm here to bring him in."

"Bring him in? Bring him in?" She slapped her hand on the wall and stood. "Never mind about that. Just you and me, let's get out of here while we still can. I want to find a place without humans or apes. Without any lies."

"What do you mean?"

"Less talk. More climb." She stumbled toward the entrance of the shaft, and he grabbed her arm. "Leggo. You aren't mad about that monkey I killed down there, are you?"

He bussed his lips. "No. I'm angry about Fort Sill. You betrayed me."

"Let's not talk about Fort Sill."

"Why did you do it? I could have defended you from Merrill."

"It's not important."

"I thought he killed you."

She tried to pull away again, and he dragged her further down the tunnel while her legs scrabbled against the tunnel floor. "Don't, Orion. Can't you smell it?"

All he could smell was the foul water of the sump. He dragged her past the tunnel in the floor, which sucked down air with a low whistle, and to the rockfall. "You go first."

She snapped her teeth at him, and he snapped back. "I won't go back down there for you. I don't belong to you, Orion. I'm not in your troop."

He lowered her until he was breathing into her face, inhaling her breath. "Then it won't matter what I do to you," he said.

She slapped him, just like a human girl. A real chimp would have bitten him.

He grunted a laugh at her. "Merrill didn't kill you and destroy your body. You left with him. You whore."

"It was for love." She wrenched away from him, climbed the pile of rubble quickly, and disappeared into a crevice.

"If you're a female, either you're part of the troop, or you're a whore. Like that orang. It's not love."

Her voice echoed back at him: "You don't know anything about it."

He pulled himself into the rockfall with his hands. His head fit easily, but the rocks dragged against his shoulders, and he had to shove one ahead of the other in order to fit. He felt one sharp rock cut him open all down his side. The other end of the crevice was tighter, and he pushed against the sharp rock with all his might. He came free unexpectedly and rolled down the other side.

When he had looked into the darkness of the sump shaft, he had thought it absolute blackness. And then in the tunnel, he had known that the sump shaft was brighter, and the tunnel contained the real darkness. Now he looked for the glint of Sirena's eyes and wondered if he'd ever see light again.

But even more than the darkness, it was the smell that made him hesitate. The sump and tunnel had smelled foul…but the smell on the other side of the rocks burned his lungs and made him sway on his feet.

He had smelled death before, at the Hill of Bones on the Preserve, back when he was trying to live two lives. At the human school, the boys had laughed at him when he had asked what a mother was and admitted that his sire didn't play catch with him. So he had stolen a ball from one of the boys and asked his *nukka* to play with him. She'd chewed the ball to bits, but they'd played with rocks after he'd made her understand. She had lost her voice in an accident with their silverback, and could only sign *sorry, sorry*. He'd brought her a yellow dress with shell buttons from the trash pits, and she'd worn it every day while they'd played.

She had practiced with him for months, then thrown a rock at the silverback's head, trying to kill him. He'd mauled her and left her for dead. When Orion had tried to drag her inside their hut, the *ronnok* had blocked his way, baring their teeth at him like animals.

And so he had dragged his *nukka* to the Hill of Bones, stopping at the bottom to roll her on her belly, raise a rock over her head, and smash it into her skull. He'd thrown her on top of the pile. The flies rose off the bodies but quickly landed again, covering them in shimmering blackness. He'd howled at her: *Go away, then. You aren't my mother.*

But he'd buried her dress. Away from the silverback, away from the *ronnok.* Alone, in death.

That was the smell of this place.

Sirena hissed, "What are you doing? Aren't you coming?"

Orion followed Sirena down the tunnel.

She grunted, and he heard wood shift. "Help me."

He reached forward until his fingernails touched wood, which shifted as Sirena tugged on it. He found the edges of it—it was a full railroad tie, and he was surprised Sirena could move it at all—and pulled it away. The smell that came up made his arms go weak, and the tie tipped forward, thumping heavily against another heavy piece of wood.

"Orion!" Sirena gasped. "You almost hit me."

"Sorry." He picked up the tie again and leaned it back toward him. It stuck against the roof for a moment, but he tugged on it, and it fell toward him. He dragged it to the opposite wall and left it there. The foul smell continued to rise up. He took a deep breath of it. Another. Another.

"Does that make it smell better?" she asked incredulously.

"He's dead down there, isn't he? You left him for dead, like you did me. That's why you want to get out of here."

"You want to find out, start walking. He's to the right." Her voice came from behind and above him, as though she had climbed back into the crevice.

Orion moved two more railroad ties, one to the left and one to the right. The orang had been right: the tunnel was narrow, but not as tight as the hole through the rockfall. Ironically, he had to stand like a man (albeit with his head sunk down onto his shoulders as far as it would go) in order to fit into the right-hand tunnel, edging downward sideways with one hand searching the walls ahead of him and bracing his chest and buttocks against the rock. A rumbling sound came from the tunnel, but it was so quiet that he wasn't sure whether he was hearing it or feeling it through the stone. After what might have been a few hundred feet or a mile of tightly-spiraled, downward tunnel, that he could see light, a kind of red mist that floated near the ceiling and cast shadows from his hand when he held it in front of him.

As he walked, the red mist filled more of the tunnel until his head was in it; it might have been smoke for all that he could smell with his deadened nostrils. The mist blinded him, but there was nothing to do but push forward until his knuckles knocked into wood. He grabbed for the board before it could fall and was lucky enough to catch the edge of it.

He edged closer. The end of the tunnel was a little wider, and he was able to squat under the mist, peering out the crack in the board.

In front of him was a kind of chapel, only without benches. A large cave had been carved out of the rock, and rows and rows of mixed apes sat under a deep cloud of red mist and waited. The apes had been dead a long time; he could see the white of bone under their hanging flesh.

They all faced one side of the room, where a pedestal had been placed to lift something red above the heads of the apes. It was too small, and surrounded by too much red mist, and his eyes smarted too much, for him to make out what it was, but it seemed to be waving at him. His ears rang, and he could almost hear voices.

His *nukka* chattered on in grunts and sign language about hot tea. Sirena told him to be quiet, or Merrill would find her and kill her. His own voice, telling her that he would protect her, no matter what anyone thought of it. Sirena saying— she had never admitted it, in life—that she wanted a lover, a human kind of lover, someone who would love her and her alone. He told her he loved her, would always love her. She answered that she belonged to Merrill now, and that she could not speak to him again. It was what she should have said, instead of faking her own death rather than tell the truth.

In the ringing of his ears, she screeched at him. *I thought you'd understand, that of anyone, you'd understand. To be able to take a lover before you'd killed a hundred* hathscha. *To live without such murder on your hands. To be able to live and breathe and love without the weight of the* ronnok *at your throat. Freedom.*

The ringing changed. *The power to never have to obey the humans again, or the apes. The power to live freely. The power to become one who is served, rather than one who serves.*

The board fell from his fingers, but the apes didn't notice. He took another step forward. Another. The mist surrounded him, soothed him. Freedom

3. The Red Monkey

After she climbed from the sump water, Mi Tao stroked the top of Absalom's head. His breath whistled in and out of his mouth in tiny, quick gasps. She breathed onto him, and his chest fluttered, then returned to panting. The smell coming from the tunnel was less, even though its floor was only inches from the level of the water in the sump. Shit and garbage curled in dried lumps on the floor, which shook slightly underfoot.

She brought him to her lips and kissed him, then tucked him into the top of her vest again. She walked forward through the dark, the tunnel narrowing around her, until she reached a blank wall. She stopped to sign a spell, and it surrounded her and Absalom. The red mist would do nothing to them for a long while, although the sooner they were out of it, the better. Luckily the *hathscha* would be walking tunnels that would take him nowhere near it.

She said another spell, and light shimmered underfoot. She walked toward the rock wall, and it slumped before her, rolling off the sides of the spell, solidifying in drips. When she was through, she released the spell and was bathed in the red glow of the mist. The tunnels rumbled so loudly that her ears ached almost immediately.

Some of the red mist poured out of the hole and up the tunnel, but not too much. She crouched low under the mist and looked from left to right. The tunnel sloped downward to the right, so she turned that direction, the red mist filling the tunnel until she could see nothing. But the dreadful rumbling that filled the tunnel suddenly became louder, and she reached out until she found the opening in the tunnel wall, the one that led downward into the pit.

She had never been this far before. She'd never dared. She paused a moment in honor of the *hathscha*, who must have drawn the guards upwards to him, for there were none to be heard in the tunnel now. Then she slid over the edge of the opening and dangled down to what must be there: the handholds for going downward into the pit.

She climbed down until she was past the mist and could see the pit fully. It stretched downward for another thousand feet, and she swayed. The bottom of the tunnel was filled with a red haze of stone chips as the machine at the bottom ground downward imperceptibly but inexorably. Pipes led down to the machine, or perhaps led upward. The great machine itself was colored red with dust and so loud that she couldn't hear it any more, only feel it. She stuffed some of her hair into her ears, and more of it into Absalom's, then continued to descend slowly from handhold to handhold.

The *hathscha* under General Maxim had built it, engineers who had fled service at mines to the East. Far better than anything a human could have made. Had General Maxim known what he would find when he started digging here? Probably he had believed nothing of the legends, only in the silver.

The handholds ran out before she reached the machine; she could easily take the fall, but she couldn't see how she could get back up again. She would have to find a different way. She watched the machine for a time, then dangled off the last spike and dropped.

At the top of the machine was a door that opened by means of a metal wheel. She sealed it behind her as tightly as she could, then pulled the hair out of her ears with relief. She waited until her ears stopped ringing, then pressed her head against the bare metal of the next door. She heard nothing, and loosened the door.

As soon as she had opened the door a crack, Absalom slipped through. She waited a few moments, and then his tiny head reappeared as he chittered at her.

The other side of the door held no threats she could see, but contrasted with the bare metal of her entrance: red velvet carpet covered the floor and the bottom halves of the walls, and golden wallpaper the rest of the way up and across the ceiling. Crystals connected with gold wire shivered under gas lights turned so low as to be nothing but a shimmer—but after the tunnels, a shimmer was all Mi Tao needed. Red velvet chairs and couches filled the narrow lounge, with a gold-colored runner down the middle, leading to the next dogged door.

The machine shuddered, and glass clinked from a small cabinet along the wall, behind a short table. Behind the first two cabinet doors were decanters of liquor in a divided tray, each bottled separated from the next by a velvet box. One of the bottles had broken, and the bits of glass— dry but still aromatic— jostled against each other. It was only then that she noticed the room did not smell of death.

Behind the third door was a safe. Her hairs stood on end, and she hissed between her teeth. Absalom ran up to look, but she held him back with her hand. The door of the safe was loose on its hinges and groaned when she opened it.

The top shelf of the safe held a stack of stiff envelopes full of paper, and she was sure that if she opened them, she would find all kinds of treasures from the human world; humans were fond of putting their treasures to paper, as though to write a thing down was to give one power over it.

But she was more interested in the gold collar in the larger, bottom part of the safe. It was made of fine, small links that her nail couldn't scratch, and was sized to leash a marmoset. She took the collar out and wrapped it around one wrist.

The machine shuddered, and the door of the safe moaned as it swung on its hinges. She pushed it closed, but it was locked open. She heard another moan, this time from the other end of the room: the other door was opening. She backed behind one of the chairs, but not soon enough.

General Regis screeched, "You!"

"General. If that's your name." She moved to the center of the carpets to give herself more room for her spells and raised her arms to sign. He was close enough to smell, and that meant he was close enough to attack. She signed the spell even as he leapt at her, and the rustle and glint of magic rushed at him.

It should have pushed him back, but instead burst like a bubble. He landed on her and went straight for her throat. She pulled her feet up under her, braced them on his chest, and shoved, whipping his head back before his teeth could close, but she still felt the hair on her neck rip away. The chimp's face was ugly with scars, and he wore a red-coated uniform, like a member of royalty rather than a military general.

They circled each other around a short table. He swung at her, she dodged back.

"You're no whore," he spat. "You're here to steal the Red Monkey for the *ronnok*. But why now? Did Sirena tell you?"

She dodged another of his grabs. She was big for a female orang, but his arms were still longer. "I'm sure she didn't mean to. But she can't resist her little hints. She talks almost as much as a male with a whore."

He bared his teeth at her.

"She didn't tell me you could resist magic, though," she said.

His hand reached across his chest for a moment, and she saw that his breast pocket bulged. A protection charm of some kind that would likely protect him from physical as well as magical harm. She backed away from the table toward the cabinet, and he followed her, hoping to back her in the corner, rip out her throat, and piss on her corpse, no doubt. But over the cabinet was a crystal chandelier, and it shivered with more than just the shuddering of the machine as Absalom hid in it.

"A particular talent of mine," he said. They could both smell the lies on each others' fur; it was just a matter of finding out *how much* was a lie. He swiped at her, and she stumbled over one of the chair legs, and he caught her vest, which was as well built as a second skin. He pulled her closer as she dug her nails into the chair, her arms stretching wide.

He yanked her away from the chair and she went flying toward him. She clawed the pocket open, and whatever had been in his pocket went flying, even as he clutched her close to bite: "Now, Absalom, now!"

General Regis shook his head and stepped backward. She didn't know whether the poison would be strong enough…or weak enough. She supposed she owed the gorilla a chance to satisfy his idiot dreams of somehow becoming the equal of the humans by bringing General Regis to "justice." As the chimp stumbled and went down, she grabbed one of the full bottles of liquor from the cabinet, and hit him across the back of his head. He slumped forward over his legs, then leaned to the side, drooling blood onto his carpet.

Mi Tao raised her arms, and Absalom jumped into them. "You precious thing," she cooed at him, scratching him delicately. After a few seconds, he jumped down to the floor, an pointed excitedly at something small and red lay smashed into the carpet. When she examined it, it was a tiny red paw no bigger than Absalom's.

4. The Price of Freedom

Metal pinged off the wallpaper, and Mi Tao dropped to her belly beside the table. A shadow lingered on the other side of the far door.

"He called you a whore," the shadow called.

Absalom crawled up on her shoulder, and another dart pinged, this time against glass. No telling where it had bounced off to.

"You're here to steal it, aren't you?" The shadow moved, shifting her weight. "Trust me. You don't want it. You don't know what it does to you. If you want to keep the power, you have to keep killing. Otherwise they turn on you."

Mi Tao stroked Absalom on the head to keep him calm, but he jerked away from her hand and ran under a chair. She sent him a silent wish for good fortune, then started to crawl toward the opposite chair, trying to get closer to the door. A needle buried itself in the carpet just past her side.

"The digging," the shadow continued, as though she hadn't just tried to kill her, "he keeps digging because he's greedy. I left Orion in the chapel with it. He's dead already. He attacked me. He deserved it. He's just a stupid *hathscha*."

Suddenly the assassin scrabbled away from the door, screeching in fear. "Don't hurt me! Don't hurt me! Save Orion! We have to save Orion! I can lead you to him."

Absalom trotted back to Mi Tao across the carpet, looking smug. "I think you scared her, love." He ran under her hair, chittering contentedly. To the assassin, she called, "Lead the way, traitor."

"I'm not a traitor!"

"And I'm not a whore." Mi Tao bent over and picked up the red paw from where it had fallen; she tucked it into her vest and ducked through the other door, half-expecting to be poisoned or hit over the head as she came through. But the chimp only led her out of the ship and over a series of pipes that carried cold water to the machine and hot water away.

"It's magic, the way this machine works," she said, jumping across pipes.

Mi Tao hissed as her feet hit the hot pipe. "No. Just engineering. General Maxim's apes did this, you know, before Regis came here and killed him and ruined everything."

"I didn't know."

"You knew."

They reached the top of the pit, then crept along the hallway until they reached an arched doorway. Inside, hundreds of apes swayed back and forth as they watched something small and red on a pedestal on the other side of the room.

"There," Sirena said, pointing into the crowd. "He's there." Mi Tao couldn't see him. Suddenly, the chimp shoved her into the room and screeched. The great dead apes turned, and Sirena backed away from the room. Mi Tao signed a curse, and flung the power at the chimp, who screeched and ran for all she was worth.

At least that was done. She signed a spell of protection, and light flashed under her feet in a dappled pattern, like shifting sunlight through branches. The dead ones pushed toward her, their eyes covered with a red film that dripped like tears and crusted on their faces and fur, but the spell turned them away, and Absalom hid inside her vest, shivering. He had never trusted her talents, preferring to rely on quickness and sharp needles. Sparks rose from the rock where her spell touched it, and the apes' fur smoked where they tried to touch her.

She pushed forward. She was a quarter of the way through the apes. Halfway. Three quarters. The spell began to dim beneath her as ape after ape threw himself at her, trying to wrestle her to the ground. Her years of training would come to nothing: she might be able to reach the Red Monkey, but she could not return with it.

She could destroy it—it was only a statuette, after all, and could be broken— or she could make a life sacrifice and take on its power for a time. But as the assassin had said, it was a kind of power that continuously needed to be fed, and she wished to leave the burden and wisdom of using it with the new, united *ronnok*, the convocation of female elders who would bring the mixed races and overthrow the humans. It had been her *nukka*'s dream, and it kept her power focused when she should have been broken and shivering with exhaustion.

She reached the Red Monkey. She couldn't think. The only other living thing inside this horrible chamber was Absalom. To destroy the idol was to damn her people to slavery. To sacrifice Absalom was unthinkable.

She reached up and grabbed the idol with her long arms, pulled it down, and flung it on the floor. It smashed with the sound of any piece of stoneware hurled in anger. One moment it had embodied power over death; the next, it was shards of red on the floor. Within a breath, the mist disappeared.

The apes collapsed. She had failed. She had worked for years to obtain this power for the *ronnok*, and then she had destroyed it over a stupid monkey. She scratched Absalom on the head, kissed him, and promised him fresh fruit. They would travel to Spanish Mexico and disappear in the jungle. They would be gone for months before the *ronnok* knew what she had done.

She picked up the pieces and wrapped them in the cloth covering the pedestal, then tied them into a bundle. She would find a way for the pieces to be given to the *ronnok* somehow. A way that didn't involve facing their wrath. Even carrying the bundle, she felt lighter. She felt like laughing.

She picked her way through the rotting dead until she found the *hathscha* and nudged him with her foot. "Wake up, you. I know you're only sleeping."

He opened his eyes. "What happened?"

"You were turned to one of the dead by the statue. I smashed it."

"What happened to Sirena?"

She had sent him into the caverns to die. She owed him many things. "She came back to save you...she was lost in the fighting." He might not smell the lie in that.

"The General?"

"In a mining machine below."

His upper lip shuddered as he waited for the worst. "Dead?"

"Knocked out. I knew you wanted him."

The *hathscha* rolled onto his side, then pushed himself up on his knees. "Show me." He wiped his face, smearing the trails of red tears across his cheeks.

◊ ◊ ◊ ◊ ◊

The orang carried a small, rattling bag with her. "What is that?"

"A souvenir." She led him without further comment as the rumbling grew louder, until his ears felt as though they would bleed, until they stood at a narrow window looking over a vast pit. She tied the bag around her, then started descending on a series of pegs, then jumping lightly onto a sturdy metal pipe.

They worked their way downward. The pipes held, although some of them leaked after he had passed.

The machine ground on, kicking up red dust that looked like blood. She brushed away a layer of dust and rock chips from a small hatch, opened it, and went inside. He could barely follow her. She stood before a second door. "I left him in there."

He pushed open the door, then leaped through it. Before he knew what he was doing, he swept Sirena into his arms and buried his head in her neck. After a few seconds, he noticed her struggling and let her go.

He let his eyes fill up with the sight of her, his nose with the scent of her. She screeched and hurled herself at him, attacking. He stepped back from her. "Sirena...Sirena...it's me. Orion."

He stumbled over something and looked down. Shock almost knocked him from his feet. "Merrill," he said. The chimp was dressed in a silly uniform of some kind, with a red coat and gold braid. His face was covered with scars that reminded him of the wanted posted the Pinks had given him of General Regis. But surely it was not him. Sirena bent over him, cooing at him, poking him, trying to get him to wake up.

"What did you do to her?" he asked.

Mi Tao, still on the other side of the door, turned and started to climb up the ladder to the door outside. In a second, he pinned her face against the wall of the machine. "What did you do?"

The orang gasped, and he dropped her. She pulled open the top of her vest. Her chest was covered in blood; her little pet marmoset had been crushed between her and the wall.

"Absalom," she whispered.

"What did you do to her?" He grabbed her head and made her look at him.

Her eyes were filled with tears. "She tried to kill me."

"What did you do?" he roared.

"I took away her mind."

He backhanded her, and she landed against the ladder and fell down. He picked her up again; she was murmuring something as he hit her again.

Suddenly, something horrible grabbed him from behind and wrapped fire around his throat. He couldn't breathe. He raised his hands to try to tear the thing away, but it scrambled through his fingers and pulled harder. Blackness surrounded the outside of his vision, and he sank to his knees, then rolled onto his side.

"That's enough," the orang said, and it let go of him, scampering toward her, crawling up her shoulder, and hiding in her hair. Something red, trailing something long and gold.

She reached into her vest and handed it something small and red— the same color, actually— and it chittered in approval.

"Don't touch me again," she told Orion. "I owe you nothing."

He tried to croak out that she owed him for Sirena, but nothing would come out, and he couldn't force himself to move. She climbed out of the hatch in the roof and was gone.

He lost consciousness for a time. When he awakened, he picked up the General and a bundle of manila envelopes from a safe hidden inside the liquor cabinet and carried him upward inch by slow inch, trying to keep Sirena from hitting him with rocks as she tried to defend her mate.

He had to get the General back to the Pinkertons.

He knew no other way to the surface, so when he reached the strange temple, he walked through it to the tunnel entrance, trying not to step on too many of the dead apes around him. All males. All *hathscha* of every species. They had searched for a better life, away from the humans and the *ronnok* and from murdering each other to earn their troops. Apes caught between the human and the ape worlds, accepted by neither, looking for purpose and work and peace.

He brought the General out to the last of the twilight and laid him neatly on the ground, straightening his clothing. Sirena helped him, cooing and patting his fur. For this, she had betrayed him. And Merrill, in turn, had betrayed this little paradise and taken it over for greed. Not for *her*.

He found a rock the size of his head and smashed it into the General's face until it was gone, despite Sirena's screeches.

He dressed, put his guns on, and tried to get her to come back with him to the horse, but she ran away into the shadows.

It would be a long ride to Fort Sill. But he thought he might be able to make a caravan of it on the way back, if he sold some of the stock certificates in those envelopes. He'd come back with an army and some lawyers showing that he owned the place from top to bottom. General Orion.

And then they'd take down that damned sign.

AUTHOR BIOGRAPHIES

Terry Alexander (*Mac and Steve*) lives in Oklahoma. His work has appeared in anthologies from Living Dead Press, Open Casket Press, Static Movement, May December Publications, Rainstorm Press, and Pro Se Press.

Mike Berger (*Fascination*) is an MFA, PhD, and now writes poetry and short stories full time. His work appears in seventy-one journals, and he has published two books of short stories and eight poetry chapbooks. He is a member of The Academy of American Poets.

Mike Bogart (*Monkey House*) is an MFA candidate and Follett Fellow at Columbia College Chicago. His work has appeared in *Connu*.

David S. Briggs (*Empire Statement*) has previously been published in the *Paterson Literary Review* and *U.S. 1 Worksheets*.

Cecelia Chapman (*Monkey Business*) is an artist working in film, writing and mixed-media. Visit her online at ceceliachapman.com.

Julie Mark Cohen, PhD, PE, SECB, (*Unabashedly, Eduardo.*) is a consulting structural and forensic engineer. She has selectively published four dozen flash fiction and short stories. "Unabashedly, Eduardo." is one of 85 stories in her recently-completed SciFi novel, *Asymmetrically, Seyfert*. Two flash fiction pieces, "A Temblor of a Different Magnitude" and "Manmade Hazards," were published online and in print by the *Grey Sparrow Journal*, the former nominated for the 2010 PEN/O. Henry prize. She is the author of two dramatic, suspenseful, nearly-completed novels, *Shear Folly* and *The Fourth Alarm*, each with unusual, engaging protagonists: structural engineers. Julie is seeking a literary agent and can be reached at jmcohen1028@gmail.com.

Caroline Cormack (*The Great Gertie*) lives in London, UK, a city she loves. She has been writing fiction since childhood, although these days her stories feature more dead bodies and fewer ponies than they did back then. Her work has also been published in *Bete Noire* magazine and in the anthology *Ain't No Sanity Clause*. Caroline can be found on Twitter, usually procrastinating when she should be writing, as @bookclubdropout.

John Grey (*Meanwhile, Back at the Lab; Ham's Poem*) has been published recently in the *Echolocation*, *Santa Fe Poetry Review*, *Caveat Lector*, *Clark Street Review*, *GW Review* and the *Potomac Review*.

Jimmy Grist (*Kong, Still Conscious, Reflects on His Visit to New York*) draws comics and writes stories. You can read *Dinosaur Kid*, a webcomic in watercolors, online at www.jimmygrist.net.

Christine Hamm (*Gorilla; My Darling, the Gorilla; Gorilla Girl*) is a PhD candidate in English Literature at Drew University. She won the MiPoesias First Annual Chapbook Competition with her manuscript, *Children Having Trouble with Meat*. Her poetry has been published in *Orbis*, *Women's Studies Quarterly*, *The Adirondack Review*, *Pebble Lake Review*, *Poetry Midwest*, *Rattle*, and many others. She has been nominated four times for a Pushcart Prize, and she teaches English at CUNY. She has published three books of poetry; Blazevox released her third book, *Echo Park*. Christine was a runner-up to the Poet Laureate of Queens.

Sarah Hilary (*Wonderland by Night*) lives in the Southwest of England, where she writes quirky copy for a well-loved travel publisher. She's also worked as a bookseller, and with the Royal Navy. An award-winning short story writer, Sarah won the Cheshire Prize for Literature in 2012. Her debut novel, *Someone Else's Skin*, will be published in February 2014 by Headline in the UK and Penguin in the US.

DeAnna Knippling (*No Monkeys in Monkeytown*) is a freelance writer and editor in Colorado Springs, Colorado. Her first book, *Choose Your Doom: Zombie Apocalypse* was released in November 2010 (www.doompress.com). She was recently published in *Three-Lobed Burning Eye*, *Silverthought Online*, *Crossed Genres*, and *Nil Desperandum*. She received an honorable mention in Best Horror of the Year, Vol. 3, and has been published in **Big Pulp** multiple times.

Viktor Kowalski (*The Lost Apes*) is a pen name for two young pulp loving authors hailing from Croatia, Europe. So far, Viktor's fiction has appeared in Pulp Empire's *Pirates and Swashbucklers* and *Heroes & Heretics* anthologies, with several other pulp titles slated for publication in 2012.

Born on Friday 13, **Rebecca McFarland Kyle** (*Evolution Happens*) developed an early love for the unusual and black cats. She currently lives between the Smoky and Cumberland mountains with her husband and four cats. She has three young adult novels and a Weird West novel currently in the works.

Pete McArdle (*If an Infinite Number of Monkeys…*) is an occasionally sentient carbon-based life form who's getting perilously close to his expiration date. He likes to think this adds a certain urgency to his writing. Before he croaks, he'd like to purchase a big black Charger with the vanity plate "A NUN'S TALE." One never knows, do one?

Kristen McHenry (*The Gibbon Remedy*) is a resident of Seattle, WA, where she is a poet by night, manager of hospital volunteers by day. She has her bachelor's degree in theatre arts and filmmaking from The Evergreen State College. Among other publications, her work has been seen in *Bare Root Review*, *Numinous Magazine*, *Tiferet Journal*, *Sybil's Garage*, **Big Pulp**, and the anthology, *Many Trails to the Summit*, published by Rose Alley Press. Her chapbook *The Goatfish Alphabet* was runner-up in qarrtsiluni's 2009 chapbook contest, and was published by Naissance Press (April 2010). Her most recent chapbook, *Triplicity: Poems In Threes*, was published by Indigo Ink Press in September 2011. Kristen serves on the editorial staff for Literary Bohemian, and teaches creativity workshops in her "spare" time.

Jessica McHugh (*Test 17*) is an author of speculative fiction that spans the genre from horror and alternate history to epic fantasy. A member of the Horror Writers Association and a 2013 Pulp Ark nominee, she has devoted herself to novels, short stories, poetry, and playwriting. Jessica has had twelve books published in four years, including the bestselling *Rabbits in the Garden*, *The Sky: The World*, and the gritty coming-of-age thriller, *PINS*. More info on her speculations and publications can be found at JessicaMcHughBooks.com.

Much to his embarrassment, **Bernie Mojzes** (*The Taste of Gold*) has outlived Lord Byron, Percy Shelley, Janice Joplin and the Red Baron, without even once having been shot down over Morlancourt Ridge. Having failed to achieve a glorious martyrdom, he has instead turned his hand to the penning of paltry prose in the pathetic hope that he shall here find the notoriety that has thus far proven elusive. In his copious free time, he co-edits an online magazine known variously and non-exhaustively as *Unlikely Story*, *The Journal of Unlikely Entomology*, and *The Journal of Unlikely Cryptography*. Should Pity or perhaps a Perverse Curiosity move you to seek him out, he can be found at http://www.kappamaki.com, wherein one might find a list of other titles to avoid.

Lon Prater (*The Hound Dogs in the Bougainvillea*) has worked in the Reactor Compartments of USS Enterprise, edited the military's textbook on arms deals, and kept things safe in the produce and laundry industries. He lives, writes, and games in Pensacola, Florida. Visit www.LonPrater.com to find out more.

Frank Roger (*Monkey Business*) was born in 1957 in Ghent, Belgium. His first story appeared in 1975, and since then he's added hundreds of story credits in more than 35 languages in all sorts of magazines and anthologies, including several collections of his fiction. Frank also produces collages and graphic work in a surrealist and satirical tradition, which have appeared in various magazines and books. His work is a blend of genres and styles that can best be described as "frankrogerism", an approach of which he is the main representative. In 2012, a story collection in English, *The Burning Woman and Other Stories*, was published by Evertype (www.evertype.com). Find out more at www.frankroger.be.

James Frederick William Rowe (*Superior/Inferior; An Ode to Ham*) is a young poet and author out of Brooklyn, New York, with works appearing in *Heroic Fantasy Quarterly*, *Andromeda Spaceways*, *Tales of the Talisman*, and most notably **Big Pulp**. When not writing fantasy, science fiction, and horror fiction and poetry, he is pursuing a Ph.D. in philosophy, is an adjunct professor, and works in a variety of freelance positions. The poems featured in this issue are no doubt much to the horror of the poet's late grandmother, Elizabeth Sundberg (1918-2011) who would be daily tormented by her grandson's insistence on speaking about disgusting monkeys to get a rise out of her. James' website can be found at http://jamesfwrowe.wordpress.com.

Carrie Ryman (*Strange Companions at London Zoo*) lives in Mukwonago, Wisconsin. She attended Kent State University and has had her work published in *The Binnacle*, *Inwood Indiana Press*, **Big Pulp**, *Quail Bell*, *The Awakenings Review*, *Loco-thology: Tales of Fantasy & Science Fiction* (Loconeal Publishing), *Erotique*, *Traveling Poet Society*, *bestnewpoems.com* and *baseballbard.com*. Carrie has participated in CVNRA's Nature Writers' Workshop and AllWriters' Workshop, as well as community events to promote literature. She has provided poetry and fiction reviews for the *Sotto Voce* magazine and has read her poetry at Martha Merrill's Books, Brady's Café and Arabica Coffeehouse.

Henry Sane (*The Man Who Brought the Monkeys*) is an avid enthusiast of literature with a degree in English from Columbus State University. His fiction has recently been featured in *The Medulla Review*, *Jersey Devil Press*, *Subtle Fiction*, and *Stanley the Whale*, to name a few. He currently manages the online publication *Swamp Biscuits and Tea*.

Timothy Sayell (*Case of the Accursed Amulet*) has been published in magazines such as **Big Pulp**, *Flashing Swords*, *Ray Gun Revival*, and *Abandoned Towers*, where he also has a monthly serial and a review column.

Frank R. Sjodin (*Monkey See, Monkey Do*) has been published by TWIT publishing and in a local hippie Chicago magazine. He's a professional actor, clown, and theatre artist, and writes on the side.

Beth Ann Spencer (*Back Story; Bigfoot Takes a Lover; Singing in Place*) edits poetry and short fiction for Bear Star Press (www.bearstarpress.com). She lives in Cohasset, California, with husband Antoine Baptiste and Ivan, their sled dog.

Michael D. Turner (*The Last Winged Monkey*) is a writer from Colorado Springs, Colorado. His writing has appeared multiple times in **Big Pulp**, and in *Aberrant Dreams, AlienSkin, Between Kisses, Flashing Swords, Every Day Fiction*, and *Tales of the Talisman*.

Ian Welke (*The Coaling Station*) is a genre writer living in Long Beach, California. An affiliate member of the HWA, his short stories have appeared in **Big Pulp: Interrogate My Heart Instead**, *KZine*, and the Alt-Hist anthology *Zombie Jesus and Other True Stories*. His first novella, *The Whisperer in Dissonance*, is coming soon from Omnium Gatherum Media.

Cheryl Elaine Williams (*Dilemma*) resides in Pittsburgh PA and has been published by tabloids *The Sun* and *The Weekly World News, Chicken Soup* anthologies, Hellfire Publishing, Dorchester media, and through Smashwords and Amazon online publishing. She's currently working on a 90K Young Adult angel romance.

ARTIST BIOGRAPHIES

Ken Knudtsen (*cover illustration*) is a writer, artist and loyal drinking buddy. He has been fortunate to have worked on projects ranging from David Geffen ("Inventing David Geffen" - PBS), Wolverine (Marvel Comics), and, of course, the adventures of a little girl and a crazy monkey ("My Monkey's Name is Jennifer" - SLG Publishing). It is never a bad idea to surprise Ken with a bacon snack.

Gregory Woronchak (*interior illustrations*) is a freelance artist and designer from Montreal, Quebec. His artistic career began in traditional animation productions with local studios. He's created storyboards for several animated shows and storyboards for RPGs and video games. Over the last few years he's focused on independent comics; he has created artwork for a variety of small press publishers and is currently working on a new project. He also is available for commissions, including pin-ups, sketch cards, caricatures, and comic cover recreations.

CLONES, FAIRIES, &MONSTERS IN THE CLOSET

Edited by Bill Olver

gay warlocks, lesbian warriors, transgender femmes fatale, bi-curious neighbors,
dyke drug addicts, super-queeroes, fag freedom fighters, boys in uniform, doctors,
astronauts, murderers, prison bitches, drag queens &

Clones, Fairies & Monsters in the Closet

Order online at exterpress.com/catalog/monstersinthecloset

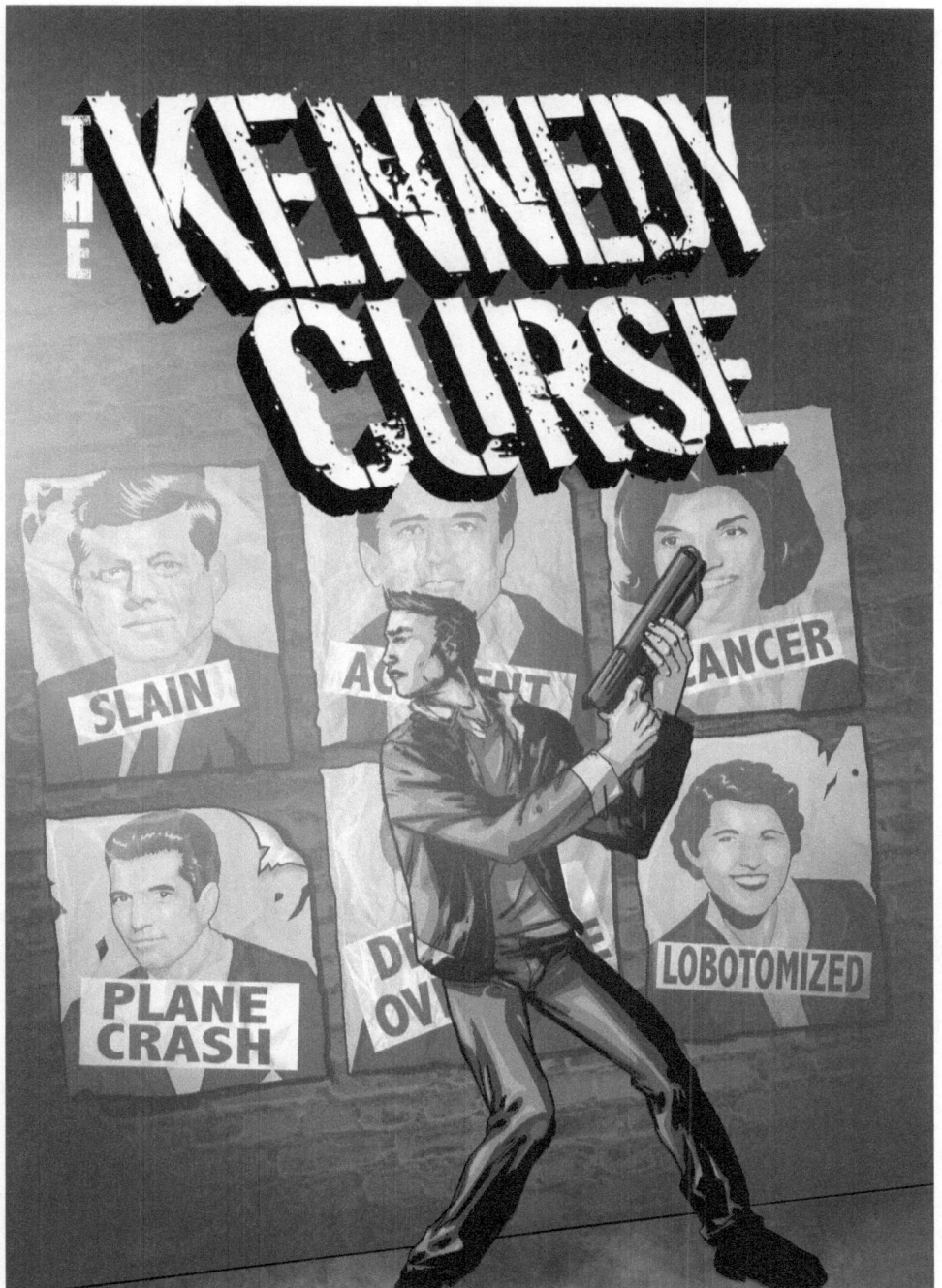

Tales of angry goddesses, child sacrifice, lobotomies, time travel, assassinations, prep school experiments, war, unrequited love, right-wing conspiracies, drowned girls, and the search for God.

Coming in October 2013!
Details at *exterpress.com/kennedycurse*.

BIG PULP

summer 2013 $12.00

"Catskin"
by
Arley Sorg

...and other stories

The son of a smalltown sheriff takes crime prevention into his own hands, but curiosity may kill the cat in Arley Sorg's "Catskin," (illustration by Phil Good). This issue
also features 20+ more horror, SF, fantasy, mystery, and romance stories & poems!

For contents and ordering details, visit:
exterpress.com/bigpulp/summer2013

BIG PULP

spring 2013 — $12.00

"A Question of Storage"

by John Bowker

A massive collection of porn inspires a brilliant MIT student to explore the limits of the human mind in John Bowker's "A Question of Storage," (illustration by Phil Good). This issue features 25 more horror, SF, fantasy & mystery stories & poems!

For contents and ordering details, visit:
exterpress.com/bigpulp/spring2013

BIG PULP

Winter 2012   An Exter Press publication

A string of grisly murders and missing persons cases puts a young police officer at risk of becoming food for worms in Joel V. Kela's "Lot's Crawlers" (cover illustration by Ken Knudtsen). This issue also features 25 more horror, SF, fantasy, mystery, and romance stories and poems!

For contents and ordering details, visit:
exterpress.com/bigpulp/winter2012

BIG PULP

We Honor Those Who Serve
by
Steve
Singleman

Fall 2012
$12.00
Exter Press

KNUDTSEN

A military archivist documents the memorial tattoos adorning the war heroes of a dystopian future, in Steve Singleman's "We Honor Those Who Serve," the featured story in the Fall 2012 issue of Big Pulp (cover by Ken Knudtsen). This issue also features 25 more horror, SF, fantasy, mystery, and romance stories and poems!

For contents and ordering details, visit:
exterpress.com/bigpulp/fall2012

BIG PULP

Summer 2012

THE PURLOINED PEARL
An Indonesian folk tale
by JAMES PENHA

an Exter Press publication

An Indonesian fisherman steals a dragon's pearl for his lover, but his avarice takes a grievous toll, in James Penha's "The Purloined Pearl," the featured story in the Summer 2012 issue of Big Pulp (cover art by Pete Schmitt). This issue also features more than 25 SF, fantasy, mystery and horror stories and poems.

For contents and ordering details, visit:
www.exterpress.com/bigpulp/summer2012

A British detective with a keen sense of ratiocination tackles one of his strangest cases in Adrian Ludens' steampunk mystery "The Biggin Hill Duel," the cover feature to the Spring 2012 issue of **Big Pulp** (art by Ken Knudtsen). In all, this issue features 25 SF, fantasy, mystery, romance and horror stories and poems.

For contents and ordering details, visit:
www.exterpress.com/bigpulp/spring2012

An Iranian dissident confronts his torturer and former lover in Elaheh Steinke's "Interrogate My Heart Instead," the featured story in the Winter 2011 issue of **Big Pulp** (cover by Ken Knudtsen). This issue also features more than 25 SF, fantasy, mystery, romance, and horror stories and poems.

For contents and ordering details, visit:
www.exterpress.com/bigpulp/winter2011

A scientist travels back in time to rid history of one of its greatest evils, but when the time comes, will she be able pull the trigger? Find out in James R. Stratton's "On the Road from Galilee" (art by Robert Hand, color by Phil Good). This issue features more than 20 SF, fantasy, mystery and horror stories and poems.

For contents and ordering details, visit:
www.exterpress.com/bigpulp/fall2011